Over an Ageless Yesterday

strange tales by

David Powers

Graveworm Press

Cleveland, Ohio

Over an Ageless Yesterday

Copyright © 2011 by David Powers

For more information contact:
    Graveworm Press
    the_worm@graveworm.com

ISBN: 1-929309-09-0
ISBN-13: 978-1-929309-09-2

Cover photograph by Ken Powers

201109P

Table of Contents

Author's Note

My short stories are always first posted free at **graveworm.com**. My collections are designed to create a "final edition" of the stories—let's call them "corrected versions," because by all accounts they are, the typos and inconsistencies that made it to the Web hopefully all removed. I hope it is also a more convenient way for readers to experience them.

However, some of the stories included in this collection were originally published in the following magazines, not on my website:

- "Oizus", *The Inflated Graveworm*, number 1 (December 1996)
- "The Cottage of Misplaced Time", *Lost Worlds*, volume 9, numbers 8 and 9 (July and November 1997)
- "The Dog and the Red Room", *The MacGuffin*, volume XV, number III (Fall 1998)
- "The Ghost at the Gatehouse", *Enigmatic Tales*, number 3 (December 1998)
- "F", *The Inflated Graveworm*, numbers 21 and 22 (November 2002 and January 2003)

Thank you for helping support my work by purchasing this collection. I sincerely hope you enjoy it.

David Powers

Over an Ageless Yesterday

And the moisture fades;
my brow softens as my shoes
turn for home.

I have forgotten the sound
of the delicate footsteps
which carried me here in the first place.
Through the saplings and the vines,
over rough bridges and trees,
through leaves silently rustling
in the shimmer of a moonless night.

I pull my hat down over my heart and wait,
watching for the sun to slowly rise and glimmer
beneath the tears on my face.

The Wind

"My daughter," the man said. "My little girl." His voice no more than a whisper as a slow curl of breathy vapor drifted from between his lips and dissipated.

Milo Jackson let the man's head down gently, resting it in the snow. His own breath was heavy; voluminous thunderheads that shrouded his face. He shook his head once, trying to clear the dream, but the body wouldn't go away. He wiped apple-size tears from his cheeks and looked up into the dark night. The wind had cleared away the clouds and the stars winked like tiny, studded eyes waiting for him to move.

Milo dragged in a deep breath and scooped up the body. With an unlikely finesse, he managed to open the door to the back seat of his car and slide the man in. He hesitated half a second, then went around to the trunk and opened it, digging around for every blanket he could find. These he methodically placed over and around the body, telling himself over and over that he was a first-string running back for the Cleveland Browns, not a doctor, and he wouldn't know a dead body if it—

"If it ran out of the woods and collapsed in front of me," he mumbled aloud. He slammed the car door and walked off a few paces, pulling his phone out of his pants pocket as he did so. He glanced over his shoulder at the car, then turned back to the woods and dialed the police. He told them all he knew: How the man had stumbled out of the woods and collapsed, and how he'd mentioned a cabin and his little girl. Milo told them the body was in the car, wrapped in blankets, and that he was going to follow the man's tracks back to the cabin.

"No, sir, stay with your car until we—"

"There's no time," Milo had said simply. "Get a medic out here, too—he might be alive for all I know. I'm going to find that little girl."

"We have your cell phone number, sir," the dispatcher said evenly.

"Good," Milo agreed. "Then you'll know where to find me."

Milo Jackson flipped the phone shut and slid it back into his pocket. He moved over to the man's tracks and followed their line with his gaze, off into the darkness of the woods.

"I never should have gone to see what it was," the man had said. "Don't let them get my little girl. My daughter. My little girl."

Milo tried not to think too much about it. Like Coach said: "Keep your head in the game, Milo. The action's in front of you— just keep moving forward." Milo put his head down and trotted into the woods.

* * *

Milo didn't like the woods much in daylight, but the crisp darkness around him now seemed edged like a knife and full of the sounds of things that meant him harm. He was breathing heavily from the exertion, but he wasn't cold. He looked around himself as he walked, the moon and the snow lighting the woods in relief: Dark, leafless shapes like the bones of supernal beasts littering an ancient giant's graveyard. He could see his tracks snaking away behind him, and the fuzzy outlines of the indentations he was following ahead.

A noise suddenly cut through the stillness: A knocking sound, like a rock flung into the trees, bouncing off branches as it fell back to the ground. Milo stopped, his eyes wide and his condensed breath puffing in front of him like a storm front. He heard it again, then a sharp electronic tune drowned it out; Milo jumped and snatched at his pocket to find his phone. He didn't recognize the number, but he answered anyway.

"This is the police, Mr. Jackson. Where are you?"

"Just follow my tracks—I'm in the woods, heading for the cabin, like I said. Are you at my car?"

"Yes, sir."

Milo stopped short of asking another question and rubbed his jaw with his massive hand. He was dimly aware of the knocking sound again and half turned in the direction it had come from—ahead and just to the right—then the cop was talking again.

"He's alright, Mr. Jackson."

"What?"

"The man in your car—he's fine. A little hypothermic, but they just took him to the hospital."

Milo let out a huge sigh. "Thank God."

"We've got a K9 unit with us, Mr. Jackson. Why don't you wait for us to catch up?"

"No way," he decided adamantly. "That man, he was crazy with fear—I could tell. He was afraid for his little girl out here alone." Milo glanced around himself again, at the black trees against the white snow; at the black span of sky cut across the horizon. "He must've run for miles. I've been walking ever since I called you."

"It's only been about 10 minutes," the cop said with a touch of humor. "We aren't *that* slow. Look, we're starting off now: Why not head back toward us? You'll only lose about five minutes—"

Milo turned and looked around, back the way he'd come. He saw dark, fuzzy bumps against the snow not too far away; dog-sized bumps he knew he should remember passing, but didn't. Five of them, loosely grouped, as if someone had tossed a handful of them down and walked off. The one nearest to him moved: Slowly—inconsequentially—like an animal getting used to moving in the snow. Milo let out a short yelp, snapped his phone shut, and took off running in the other direction, deeper into the woods.

* * *

Jiffy sat in the kitchen sink staring out the window into the woods. Her dad had gone out by the front door, but the furballs seemed to have moved to back of the house and she wanted to keep her eye on them. She'd seen what they could do and it didn't seem wise to leave them unobserved.

For one thing, they'd chased her dad away. The last she'd seen of him, he was running and screaming into the woods, three furballs giving chase with uncanny speed, pulled forward by a single, pink, fleshy arm and a three-fingered hand that shot out of the hump and recoiled like a frog's tongue, the fingers grasping the ground before it and pulling... pulling... pulling...

She shuddered and looked way from the window for a moment, at her feet in the sink, then back again. It was full dark now, but she'd turned on the yard lights. The furballs—maybe 15 of them—were milling slowly around the trees, their single, fleshy hands shooting evenly in and out as they moved. It looked like they were trying to climb, but with only one hand, it wasn't possible.

Another movement caught her eye and she saw a raccoon shuffle into the light. In a moment, they were on it: The sinewy pink hand of the closest one grabbed the hapless animal around the middle and crushed it. She saw just a flash of realization on the raccoon's face, that it was in danger. Its eyes widened and its mouth opened to yelp a warning cry, then the hand closed like a vice and the animal simply split in two. A few other furballs hurried over, and before Jiffy

11

gasped the raccoon had been torn apart as if five men had grabbed and pulled the same piece of tissue paper simultaneously.

And what if one of them had managed to grab her dad's ankle as he ran away...?

She looked away again as a tear slid down her cheek, but any tears that might have followed were stemmed immediately by a loud thud on the front porch. Her eyes widened wildly and she stared at the front door—had one of them finally figured out how to clamber up the porch steps with one hand?

The door rattled as something slammed against it. Jiffy screamed and leaped from the sink, heading for the loft. This had always been her plan if they made it to the porch: Climb up to the loft and kick the ladder away. She'd already loosened the bolts.

The door rattled again just as her foot hit the bottom rung. She heard a grunt, maybe even a strangled cry.

"Dad?" she screamed. "Dad!" She froze, halfway up the steps.

The door was solid. She heard another muffled cry, but it didn't sound like anyone saying her name. She started back down the ladder, but froze again when the door weathered another hinge-rattling blow. Why would her dad be pounding like that? Wouldn't he call out her name? Wouldn't he go to the window so she could see him?

Jiffy moaned with indecision and bounced lightly on the ladder. It could be a neighbor or a hiker or a hunter—or her dad, half mad with running for so long.

The door shuddered and the lock splintered. Jiffy squeaked and ran up the ladder to the loft, but she didn't kick away the ladder. Not yet.

"Dad!" she screamed again, crying now and slipping into hysterics. Why wouldn't he answer her?

"Lemme in!" she finally heard a voice bellow through the wood. It was a man's voice, but it was not her father's, and by the continued blows, he wasn't waiting for her to reply.

That door could keep a bear out, she dimly recalled her dad saying, once upon time—then the door cracked with a piercing groan and burst open, showered splinters into the room. A massive figure fell into the cabin and lay motionless.

Jiffy pulled her legs into the loft and tried not to cry. She could see the furballs beyond the door, beyond the porch—they hadn't figured out the stairs, then.

The figure moaned and started to get up.

"Shut the door, mister," Jiffy squeaked.

"Huh?" the man said.

"Shut the door."

Jiffy kicked the ladder away and scooted into the back of the loft.

* * *

Officer Tom Scott glanced over at his partner and let out a long breath, only then realizing he'd been holding it. Just ahead of them stood a third officer who was barely able to hold back a wildly barking police dog.

"What is it?" Officer Scott called out.

"No clue," the K9 officer called back. "It just moved again, and I think there's another one off in the woods. Heel, Jessie!" he added in a growl to the dog, to no avail.

"It's a raccoon," the other officer said quietly, but he wasn't sure he even believed himself.

"Jesus," Officer Scott sighed, letting out another long breath. "I hate the fucking woods. Let her at it!" he called out to the dog handler. "We can't stand her all fucking night cuz of a coupla damn raccoons!"

"I don't think—" the cop replied, but Officer Scott cut him off.

"Release the damn dog, Al! Christ!"

What happened next was later expunged from the official police report for fears of generating the "widespread panic" that officials always seem to think will be ignited if the truth is made public. Officer Al Chiffon dropped the leash and drew his gun in one well-practiced move as Jessie darted forward with a vicious snarl. The dog headed directly for the nearest animal in the path, but instead of turning and scampering off, it stayed put. In fact, the other critter they'd seen came bolting out of the woods toward the charging dog and its counterpart in the path.

The three police officers barely had time to register the fleshy, pink hand the critter used to pull itself along with before the other critter's hand shot out of the furball and caught Jessie squarely around the neck. The dog didn't so much as yelp before an ugly crunching preceded its body slumping heavily to the ground, independent of its head, which rolled off the fleshy fist and thudded to the ground itself. Then the second critter was on it, and the dog's body was deftly relieved of a back leg in one squeeze of the inhuman hand.

Al Chiffon screamed and opened fire. He squeezed off eight rounds, but the first two hit their marks: The creatures stopped moving with just one bullet each, parts of the dismembered Jessie falling loosely from three-fingered hands.

Al screamed again—a potent voice of rage, fear, and confusion—but didn't fire his last round. "What the *fuck*!" he managed to bellow. Behind him the other two officers stood motionless and pale, gaping judiciously. Officer Scott had his hand on the butt of his gun, but that was as far as his reflexes had got him before it was all over.
"What the hell was that, Phil?" Al asked, turning and looking at them. "You're the wildlife expert."

"There may be more," Officer Scott replied cautiously for his partner, pulling out his gun. "Keep your eyes peeled."

Al turned back to the trailhead. The only part of the carnage that still looked like Jessie was a large mass of meat that contained her tail. "Jessie," he whispered, sucking in a ragged breath.

Officer Scott moved forward a few steps, his gun trained on the nearest furry bump. "I better call that Milo guy," he said distantly. "Make sure he's... okay." He slowly holstered his gun.

"Cover me, Phil," he said over his shoulder as he pulled out his cellphone and dialed Milo's number.

* * *

Milo pushed against the door to test its resistance. He'd shut it and moved the couch over to hold it shut and it seemed like it would hold.

"It's okay," he said, more to himself than the girl who was still huddled in the loft. "What *are* those things out there?"

Jiffy didn't respond so he turned and looked up at her. Milo guessed her to be about eight or nine, her young face writ with defiance and resolve fueled by fear.

"Your daddy's okay," Milo said kindly, smiling. "He asked me to come and get you, make sure you—"

Jiffy started to cry, though she was trying to hold in the tears, her face still rigid with that defiance. She was not only rightly afraid of this stranger who had burst into her cabin, Milo could tell there was no way she was going anywhere without a fight.

"Hey, I know how that sounds. My name's—"

"Why isn't he with you?" Jiffy cut in curtly, the sound of her own voice boosting her confidence. She sat up straight and sniffed back the tears that had never fully emerged.

"Pardon me?"

"If my dad's okay, why isn't he with you?"

"He fainted," Milo replied. "He was exhausted and he was too cold. He had to go to the hospital..." Milo trailed off as Jiffy's tears finally spilled onto her cheeks.

"I don't believe you," she managed to sputter.

"I know, honey," Milo replied, trying to sound as kind as possible. *Maybe I sound too kind*, he considered. *So kind, it sounds fake.* Milo had heard from his father the same stories about strangers and their lies that Jiffy had undoubtedly heard from hers.

"Look," he added with a sudden realization. He dug in his pocket and pulled out his cell phone. "Call the police—they know I'm here and they're already on their way. Ask them about me. My name's Milo Jackson."

"Like the football player?" Jiffy asked incredulously, her small brow wrinkling.

"That's right, honey. I *am* the football player."

She eyed him curiously, looking him up and down and sniffing in a few ragged breaths. The tears had stopped again. Milo figured any girl who spent time on winter camp-outs with her dad probably regained her composure pretty quickly.

"I know, I look different than on TV. No helmet, no pads."

She still didn't respond, but she visibly relaxed, uncurling her legs and sitting up straight.

"I'm going to throw you my phone, honey," he said. As an afterthought, he pulled his wallet out of his pocket, too. "And my wallet. Call the police—really. And check my ID. I don't want to frighten you. I just want to get you out of here."

He glanced at the door, but kept the smile on his face and offered the girl a small, encouraging nod. She didn't nod back, but some subtle shift in her posture said she was ready to catch. He pitched the phone up to her and she caught it, then he flung his wallet, which opened in the air and flapped down closed beside her.

Jiffy grabbed the wallet and opened it, focusing immediately on Milo's driver's license. She tilted the wallet just right to catch the light and cut off the glare from the plastic sleeve that held the license, and her heart fluttered a little. He was Milo Jackson alright. She was in the same room as Milo Jackson!

Well, he's a Milo Jackson, she added to herself, hoping her brief excitement hadn't been obvious.

"Behind my license is my team ID," he said, as if reading her mind. "You know, to get in the weight room and stuff." He pantomimed the motion required to find the team ID and she mimicked him, slipping her finger behind the license. She pulled out the card behind the license and gasped, forgetting for the moment that she was trying to play it cool.

There it was: A very official-looking Cleveland Browns ID card, with hologram logos and everything, and Milo's picture with his name, number, and position under it. Jiffy glanced over at a crumpled pile of clothes in the corner of the loft—her team jersey with Milo Jackson's name and number on it was in that pile. If it wasn't dirty, she was wearing it.

Jiffy snapped back to the moment and looked down at Milo, her eyes narrowing suspiciously. It would be hard to fake that team ID, but she still had to be cautious. *Focus on the moment*, her dad's voice echoed in her head. *If you're ever stuck, just focus on the moment and take it bit by bit.*

"This still doesn't mean you're not going to hurt me," she pointed out.

"I know, honey. Lots of famous people are screw-ups—so call the police. Please. We have to get—"

At which moment Milo's cell phone rang. She looked down at the phone's display, which read "incomplete data," so she threw it back down to him without a word, a stern look of something close to anger on her face. He managed to catch it—*Like a pro football play-*

er, Jiffy thought—and flip it open. He eyed her warily, well aware that the wrong caller at the wrong time could blow whatever tentative ground he'd gained.

"Hello?" His face washed with relief. "Yes, officer—I'm at the cabin." He smiled at Jiffy and gave her a thumbs-up. "Yes, she's fine." His face darkened and he unconsciously turned aside as if to hide the conversation from the girl. "Yeah, I saw them. They chased me." Milo slowly took the phone from his ear, looking at it with wide eyes. Jiffy could just hear the tinny scream coming out of the earpiece—a small voice, out there in the woods, yelling "Shoot it! Shoot it! Shoot it!" over and over, the pitch rising with hysteria as the sound dimmed to a small buzz.

Milo glanced up at Jiffy and saw the panic on her face. He snapped the phone closed and tossed it back to her.

"Call 9-1-1," he said urgently. "Tell them to send more help. And don't forget to ask about me."

Jiffy nodded and swallowed slowly. Her hands were shaking but she held back the tears—*Cry later, Jiffy-bear*, she heard her dad telling her—and opened the phone. She pressed the 9. In response something thudded against the barricaded door. Milo moved over to the window and looked out. There was one of the furballs on the porch trying, it appeared, to grasp the flat of the door with its fleshy protuberance. Behind it another one was just gaining the top of the porch steps.

"Jesus," Milo breathed, glancing at the door knob as the thing thudded harmlessly against the flat of the door again. "They figured out the steps."

When he turned back to Jiffy she was crying, but softly, holding her breath to hold back tears, the phone pressed to her ear. In a dreamlike state Milo heard her trying to explain what was going on while the thing on the porch continued to pound at the door. The thuds seemed louder than anything, like the slow beating heart of a massive creature that may or may not be sleeping. All Milo could imagine was one of those tendril-thin fingers hooking the knob...

"She says to stay on the line," Jiffy's voice finally quivered, managing to break through the pounding.

"Good," Milo agreed, glad to have that obstacle out of the way. He glanced around the room, truly taking it all in for the first time.

"Do you have a back door?"

"She also said you recently reported that my dad was hurt," Jiffy intoned slowly.

"That's right, honey," Milo agreed, not too concerned with his alibi any more. "Did she tell you he's okay?"

Jiffy shook her head. Milo caught the movement out of the corner of his eye as he scanned the room and he sighed heavily, looking her in the eyes and holding her gaze.

"Well he is, I promise. That man who called... you know, before? He told me the ambulance has taken your dad—"

"You told me that," Jiffy whispered, but he could tell by her tone that she believed him now. On top of that, her eyes begged him to help her, to save her, to get out of this cabin alive. To be more than a man or a sports hero. The door thudded again and Milo peeked out the window.

"Christ," he gasped. "There must be fifteen of them—is there a back door, honey?" he asked with more urgency. He glanced up at her, but she was shaking her head again.

"She says to stay put," the girl replied distantly, emitting a small squeak as the door thudded again. She looked confused and so, so small. She knew the person on the phone was a cop, and cops always knew how to keep people safe, but in her heart of hearts, in the place her daddy said she should always trust, she knew they couldn't stay put. Not a chance.

"I don't think we can stay here," Milo said evenly, holding up his massive hands to her in a posture of surrender. "I think we're going to have to make a run for it."

"Well, I'm not going to jump down," she replied curtly, drying up her tears with a sense of purpose now that her mind was made up and this man—*Milo Jackson, the football star!*—appeared to be in agreement.

Milo dropped his hands and allowed himself a slight smile, then slowly bent down and picked up the ladder, standing it back in place against the loft.

"Why don't you come up here?" she wondered, just so she could hear again how they really only had one choice.

"They figured out the stairs, honey," Milo said. "And there's... so *many* of them. If we stay here, I don't think it will take them long to—"

Jiffy slid the phone from her ear and snapped it shut, then grabbed Milo's wallet and climbed down the ladder to the cabin floor.

* * *

Officer Scott hit the last of the fuzzballs with the first shot, and he was quite proud of that statistic. Not that he'd been keeping a careful tally, but of the 20 or so fuzzballs they'd just wiped out, he was pretty sure he'd landed the only first-shot killshot on a moving target. And move they did, at first in a one-mind pack like a school of fish that bows and twirls at the same moment, then after they'd started to pick them off (while he shrieked, "Shoot it! Shoot it! Shoot it"), they broke into small clumps of hunters trying to surround their prey.

Trying to surround them.

After the low fear returned and left the hysterical rage as nothing but a few shakes and a sweaty brow, Officer Scott looked sheepishly at the other two.

"Five in a row," he whispered, a proud curl running along his lips. "Three more shots, then we'll see how you do, Phil."

"Shit, Tom, I won't waste a single bullet."

It was small talk designed to keep their minds off whatever the hell was happening. They'd been moving forward picking them off as they saw them, trying to clear a path back to the cabin in Milo Jackson's footprints, when the pack had come out of nowhere in front of them.

"Maybe I should call Milo again," Tom said. "Let him know we're okay."

"No," Al Chiffon stated simply. He'd been walking in between the other two, picking off fuzzballs left and right without a single word. He hadn't spoken since they'd set off again, after the fuzzballs had got to his dog. Phil glanced at Tom across Al's back and shrugged.

"We keep moving," Al concluded. "We get the girl and we go home."

* * *

"I've been watching them," Jiffy said as Milo leaned a bookcase against the door then shoved the couch back up against it to hold it in place.

"Yeah?" he prompted. Jiffy nodded vigorously.

"They seem to form little herds or packs—whatever—but eventually they break up again and spread out. But if something moves— like a rabbit?—then they all run back together into a big clump and..."

21

She trailed off and Milo raised his eyebrows questioningly. This girl was sharp. Now that she was talking to him, he actually felt a certain relief. He knew he wouldn't have to get them out of this alone.

"And?" Milo prodded.

"They tear it apart," she finished simply.

"You said they weren't on the porch until I got here, right?" Milo checked.

Jiffy nodded. "So they aren't too smart," she concluded. "They just followed you up the steps. Lucky for us, that took them a while."

Milo stepped swiftly across the cabin and looked out the little window above the kitchen sink. He scanned the area illuminated by the outdoor lighting.

"I think you're right—there aren't any back there now. They all went around to the front. *Is* there a back door?" he asked, his mind blurring as he considered all their options. This was just like reading a blitz on the offensive line: The pieces may all have minds of their own, but they moved in a predictable fashion, if you could read them right.

"There's just the front door," she said softly. As if sensing what this meant, the creatures redoubled their efforts, pounding again and shuddering the wood. Ten minutes earlier Milo was sure she would have broken into tears again, but now her face was set. She was much more determined since talking to the police. Now she just wanted this to be over, to be back with her dad, and it showed in the dark set of her eyes and her grim expression.

Milo scanned the cabin and his gaze came to rest on the books he'd tossed off the bookcase before he'd moved it. "I'll throw a book out the kitchen window," he decided as he moved over and picked one up. "You watch and see if they move around to see what the noise is."

Jiffy nodded and stepped toward the front window. She suddenly looked so very small again—just a little girl out for a night or two in the woods with her old man. Brave beyond her years—and wily—but still so small, so easily broken.

"Wait!" Milo cried out, envisioning the creatures popping through the window in a spray of shattered glass. She wouldn't stand a chance. "Don't get too close! Don't let them see you move."

Jiffy froze, took a deep breath, then crept up to the window by the door and peeked out. There they were: Three on the porch—now just scratching at the door, after realizing their attacks were useless—two on the steps, and at least ten still out in the yard, milling around within the arc of light from the porch. And God knew how many more there were, off in the darkness.

Jiffy glanced back at Milo as he opened the kitchen window. The scratching at the door stopped almost instantly—they'd heard even so slight a noise as that. Milo snapped the window closed and turned to Jiffy.

"Where are they?" he whispered.

"Moving back off the porch," she whispered back. "Some of them should be back there by now."

Milo looked out his window and saw that a handful had indeed already come around to investigate. That worried Milo. They'd sent a scouting party to see what was going on, and if these creatures out-foxed him, it wasn't the quarterback who'd get sacked, it was a little girl who'd be torn limb-from-limb.

"They've stopped," Jiffy whispered so quietly Milo almost didn't hear her. "If we make any noise, they'll come back."

Milo didn't think. He did what the coach always said he should do: He turned on his game-brain and used muscle memory. His eyes narrowed as he flung the kitchen window open again and hurled a book out into the circle of light at the edge of the darkness. The handful of creatures pounced over to it with terrifying speed, pulled along by that vaguely human appendage. Milo slammed the window, then open it and slammed it again.

"They're all going back there!" Jiffy whispered excitedly. "And Jesus, mister Jackson, they can *move*!"

"Sh!" Milo hissed curtly, dashing over and pulling the couch away from the bookcase across the door. "Next time I move the bookcase and we run." He said it quietly, but sternly, and Jiffy recognized the focused look in his eyes. It was the same look that came through the face guard of his helmet when they did close-ups on TV. It was what her daddy called a game face, and she knew he couldn't see anything but the plan he had in mind.

"I'm going to carry you," he continued in the same low, stern voice. "I'm going to grab you like a 40-pound football and run, okay?"

Jiffy nodded slowly, the tears welling up in her eyes again. Before, when they'd just been thinking about it, it hadn't seemed so bad, but now that Milo was serious—now that she knew the danger was so very, very real—she was scared all over again.

"Turn on your game-brain," he intoned, his eyes flickering across her face for barely an instant.

"Maybe we should wait?" she squeaked. Milo glanced past her out the front window: Shapes were beginning to mill around out there again. They'd either got bored or had come back because of the sound of the couch being moved. Either way, they'd only gain a few seconds' head start. He turned and looked back at the loft again and considered it—but no. Even with the ladder removed the rustic walls left far too many footholds—or handholds, as the case may be.

"We can't risk it," he said. "If we run, we'll be heading toward the police—"

"But the police man was screaming," Jiffy reminded him weakly.

"He was also shooting his gun," Milo said. "It's our best hope." He turned his gaze back to her and his face softened. "And your daddy out ran them, Jiffy, so I'm pretty sure I can, too."

"Put on my game face," Jiffy said breathlessly, sponging tears from her eyes with her palms. Milo actually smiled, then nodded dourly.

"Use your muscle memory," he agreed.

* * *

They moved on in silence, slowly inching forward as they kept a careful watch for any movement that even hinted at one of the fuzzballs. Al's gaze wandered up as they walked, taking in all the angles that could contain a threat—and Christ Almighty, in the woods there were a shit-ton of them. He watched the leafless treetops scratching the starlit sky and considered the squirrel nests dotted here and there in the limbs—then he stopped cold.

"Shit," he breathed, bringing the other two officers to a stand-still. They both turned and looked at him to see where he was look-ing.

"What?' Tom asked nervously, afraid to look up.

"That squirrel nest up there just moved." All pulled out his flash-light and trained its beam on the nest. From their distance it was just a dark bump near the top of a tree.

"Christ, is that one of those things?" Tom wondered, finally looking up to see what Al meant. He hadn't seen it move, but it looked to be about the size of one of the fuzzballs. He shuddered to think of the strange, fleshy hand grasping the branch it was perched on.

Al moved his light around the dark canopy, outlining several more of the clumps in the trees. "They're just nests, right?" he asked in a panicked tone. "That's what my dad always said."

25

Tom looked around the woods again. It seemed pretty quiet all of sudden; Phil shrugged when he caught his eye. There certainly seemed to be a lot more of those things up there than he figured there were squirrels that would need them.

"What if the wind brought some of them down last night?" Al wondered out loud. "What if they live up there and they don't normally ever come down?"

"It was quite a windstorm," Phil agreed, trying to be helpful. Al snapped off his light and looked at him. "But what if they do come down, to feed?" Phil asked.

"Then we're surrounded," Tom stated simply, sharing a wide-eyed realization with the others.

Then they heard the sticks and branches start breaking, off in the distance, but getting closer. All three of them smoothly drew their guns and stood facing the noise.

* * *

"Shall we practice?" Milo asked her. Jiffy nodded, trying her best to keep her game face on. The massive man reached out tentatively and scooped her up like a large rag doll. He grabbed her around the waist with his left hand and tucked her in to his hip, then slid his right hand under her arm, her head tucked in the crook of his right elbow. He squeezed her tightly against himself and jogged in place a few paces.

"Then I'll run," he said out loud to himself and put her back down. "Was I hurting you?" She shook her head slowly. "Okay. Then go back to your window and tell me—quietly—when they're all gone. Okay?"

He moved over and grabbed a stack of books then went back to the kitchen window. One of the creatures was still milling around expectantly, waiting for another noise. He looked over at Jiffy and mouthed "O-K?" She nodded slowly, dreamily, and turned resolutely to her window. Milo threw his window open and tossed out the first book. The thing pounced on it faster than Milo had expected, then like a shot another one scuttled around the cabin and tore into it. Together, they tore the book in half. Milo considered that for a second—what it meant about not only their strength, but their grip—then tossed out another book. Now the creatures were herding, as Jiffy had put it, three of them pouncing on the second book while the first two continued to shred and assess their prize.

Milo tossed out another and another, trying to get them further and further away from the cabin and hoping they wouldn't figure out that books weren't good food. The back yard was quickly teeming with them, but the books seemed to be keeping them busy—they either didn't notice him in the window or didn't care. He tossed the last book out the window and dashed over to Jiffy.

"I haven't seen anything move since you tossed the second book," she whispered. Milo nodded curtly. His eyes had that distant behind-the-faceguard look again. He picked up the end of the book-case and carefully moved it aside.

"Anything?" he asked as he put it down.

"Nothing."

"No movement?" He glanced out the window himself for a few seconds, well aware of how slim their head start would be already. Milo saw for himself the expanse of unblemished snow fading into the moonlit blue of the woods.

"Ready?" he growled, turning her to him.

"My coat!" she gasped, but Milo didn't hesitate a second and picked her up, just like they'd practiced.

"We won't be in the woods long enough to need one," he said evenly, tucking her in as he opened the door. The air was crisp and there was a strange sound echoing off the trees—the sound of books being shredded, he realized, and loud enough to cover the sound of them leaving. He stepped onto the porch and took in a deep breath, jostling Jiffy once to make sure she was wedged in well. Then Milo hopped off the porch and ran, ran like he'd never run before, only vaguely aware that this football was so much heavier than all the others and that it was gripping his shirt with tight little fists.

* * *

"It's too late it's too late it's too late..." Al Chiffon repeated like a mantra as the noise crashed toward them. It sounded like it must be at least a hundred of the fuzzballs, pounding along on their fleshy hands and tearing apart whatever got in their way.

"Put your gun away," Tom suddenly said softly, but sternly.

"It's too late..."

The sound grew louder and louder.

"It's too late..."

"Al!" Tom cried. "You're in shock! Let me and Phil—"

"Holy Christ!" Phil shrieked as a massive shape faded out of the darkness between the trees, heading straight toward them. "It's huge!" He leveled his gun, his finger tightening on the trigger.

"No!" Tom yelled. In one fluid motion, the likes of which would not need to be exaggerated when he told of the miracle at parties thereafter, he knocked Al's gun out of his hand as Al squeezed off a round, and kicked Phil in the shin before he could pull his trigger.

The form kept coming, then Phil heard it, too: A voice as big as the form yelling, "Run!"

"It's *Milo*!" Tom cried. He looked at Al and saw panic-stricken eyes that were wide and unseeing. He didn't wait for confirmation. Defenseless and afraid, Al Chiffon turned and bolted away from whatever or whoever it was coming toward him.

"*Run!*" Milo shouted more clearly, barreling headlong toward them. Phil and Tom turned in tandem and sprinted after Al, Milo bearing down on them in a mist of kicked-up snow.

* * *

"Daddy! It's on!" Jiffy called into the kitchen. Her dad straightened up with a beer in his hand and closed the fridge door.

"Coming!" he called back, popping the top and tossing the bottle cap onto the kitchen table. He slumped down on the couch and put his arm around his daughter as she snuggled up to him.

"Where's mom?"

"Still at the store."

They watched the TV as the camera panned over the faces of the starting lineup, and whether or not it paused longer on Milo Jackson,

Jiffy couldn't say for sure, but she thought it did.

"That's his game face, Daddy," she said. "He looks mean, doesn't he? But it's just his game-brain working—that's what he called it. He said it uses muscle memory."

Her dad chuckled lightly and sighed, hoping his daughter wouldn't see the tears of relief as he tried to wipe them from his eyes without putting down his beer.

* * *

"Did we get 'em all?" the game warden asked the hunting party. He looked down at the hump of fuzzy balls in the clearing they'd made, the strange pink hands and arms lolling at lifeless angles.

"All the ones down here, yeah," one of the hunters replied. "We've been through this stretch of woods twice, front to back."

The warden looked up into the treetops and watched the branches swaying under the weight of the dark clumps in the uppermost branches. "How many are up there, though?" he thought out loud.

"God knows," was the terse reply.

F

It was just a painting, after all.

Henry Edgewater purchased it because he enjoyed the crisp lines of the barren room it depicted, the jagged edges of the uneven wood used for the makeshift table and chairs, and the detail in the shadows and grain of the walls.

Just the walls, that's all it showed. Two rough wood walls, coarse enough to create a handful of splinters, if you tripped on the uneven floor and put out a hand to stop from falling. Two walls, one on the left and the other behind a table—possibly a kitchen table, with two ramshackle chairs. Or, quite viably, this was the single abandoned room in a shack off in the woods somewhere.

Two walls, one table, two chairs, and a window. One window in the back wall, behind the table. Through the nine-paned glass you could see leafless trees, a section of lifeless lawn, a wedge of blue autumnal sky, and the careful brick side of a chimney.

That's why Henry had bought the painting, because of the evident life outside the apparently dead room that served as subject. He liked the juxtaposition. He liked that the placement of the chimney bespoke another room beyond an unseen door in the left wall.

Henry was thrilled with the possibilities the work left to the imagination, so he bought it and he put it on his bedroom wall across from his own window, and he smiled every time he looked at it, like a schoolboy first witnessing something beautiful before he understands that magic is not real.

Henry would smile, and a subtle change in the angle of the shadows would lead him to believe that the painting had smiled back.

* * *

Henry Edgewater felt a certain debt to the artist who had produced his new joy and attempted to delve into the history of his acquisition. The signature said, plainly enough, "Reginald Arburton," but Henry knew nothing of art history and went to the library to thank the man by reading up on his biography.

Marginalized, it turned out, had been the career of Reginald Arburton, who had operated out of his mountaintop cabin in Virginia in the late nineteenth century. Not only had he been American, but it was also pointed out that he had effected his only known work with the help of a *camera obscura* projected onto the back wall of his shack.

With no family to vouch for him, his biography was little more than a blurb in book of art history, a blurb that pit his brief career as somewhere between a fraud of art and the shadowy beginnings of modern photography.

Marginalized. One of a kind. It only made Henry love his painting even more.

* * *

After Henry first glimpsed the girl dash past the window in his painting, he took to eating dinner in his bed so as to watch the action on the canvas as most people watch a TV. Henry would methodically cut his steak and potatoes and carrots into manageable cubes such that he could, without taking his eyes from the image of the room, eat by simply stabbing at the plate with his fork, then chewing up whatever the utensil delivered. While the preparation made his meals more efficient, it actually began to take him longer and longer to eat.

Staring at the image, his mind naturally began to wander, and his eyes would follow. Invariably, it was at these moments, when his gaze was not fully on the image's window, that he glimpsed between the trees a splash of color that had not been there previously.

Sometimes, when he snapped his attention back to the autumnal, wooded lawn, Henry would catch the foot of a girl—white sock and black sandals—frozen for a second at the bottom left corner of the window frame, dodging behind the chimney, as if Reginald Arburton had painted it there to begin with.

Or rather, his *camera obscura* had captured the light of an image of fleeting life and had burned it onto the canvas, and the artist had painted over it. But upon closer inspection—Henry's knife and fork abandoned on a plate of half-eaten dinner—the sandaled foot would be gone, the yard beyond the window empty, and the trees not even swaying under the forceful push of an October wind.

Sometimes, as he returned to his meal, Henry would glimpse movement again just as he brought his head back up to concentrate. Sometimes he even caught the foot again, and would put his knife and fork back down and rise, only to discover he had been right the first time, and that no such foot existed in the yard glimpsed through the painted glass. Sometimes Henry Edgewater would yo-yo up and down like this five, six, seven times in a row.

Finally, he caught sight of her leg from the knee down and saw that the foot was not clad in a white sock, but in the white, knee-high hose of a young girl dressed up for church. Yet when he would examine the painting more closely, his nose millimeters from the surface of the canvas, he would find no appendage and no evidence of a girl having dashed past the window.

Once, he was sure, as he pressed his nose against the oil-made window to find her leg, he saw a slight blurring of the image as if his hot breath had condensed ever so slightly on a cool pane of glass.

* * *

At one point, Henry's eyes managed to capture the girl's back as she disappeared behind the chimney. Mid-run, her leg stuck out behind her, bent at the knee, beneath a fine white dress with blue frills. Her left elbow, too, was caught for a second as she brought it back to keep her balance, the skin of her arm pale and radiant in the autumn sun. At the top of the back of her dress, above the powder-blue frill of a collar, Henry saw the very back of her head where her blond hair was tied in a ponytail held with a shiny blue ribbon. The blond hair floated above the blue-frill collar without so much as a wedge of neck connecting the two, though surely the young girl had such a natural alignment of anatomy—but that's just how thin a sliver of her body had appeared in the empty yard beyond the glass.

Pleased with himself, despite the frustration of not having seen her in full as more than a blur through the window, Henry would sit back down and return to stabbing the food on his plate with his fork. Soon, he didn't even bother to get up, letting the sight of her leg and elbow and her back and her disembodied hair disappear back into the canvas in its own time, like the slow fade of an after image burned temporarily onto the retina. He just smiled—fork poised and frozen midway to his mouth—and blessed his good fortune for even a passing glimpse at the life beyond the barren room.

And, as usual, he was sure Reginald Arburton smiled back with a subtle shift of the shadows in the painting that didn't last long enough for Henry to even consider whether or not he had seen it.

* * *

It was two weeks later, to the day, when Henry managed to watch the entire event of the girl's progress across the yard. He watched as just one white dot that was the tip of her nose first broke past the right window frame, then sat in gape-mouthed joy as the girl dashed past the window, her foot disappearing behind the chimney after her bobbing blond ponytail with the blue ribbon and the bent left elbow with the powder-blue trim.

At first, Henry couldn't elucidate what he had seen. He set his knife and fork down slowly without taking his eyes off the painting, hoping it would play through the scene again, because what he had witnessed made no sense.

Little girls with ponytails and blue-trimmed dresses ran past windows giggling, after all, not grimacing intently and carrying a shotgun.

In fact, little girls didn't carry guns at all. The joy of finally seeing the blond-haired girl had been in the belief that she would be smiling and free and dewy eyed—the perfect juxtaposition to the resolute lifelessness of the subject room, which had first drawn Henry to the painting and the window. In his imagination, her elbow disappearing behind the chimney had been pert and soft and alive, not weighted at the wrist by the shank of a longarm. The black sandal had been clean, not the footwear of a gun wielder.

It made no sense and Henry sat and stared in stunned disbelief at the solitary work of Reginald Arburton, crafted in 1883 on a mountaintop in Virginia with the aid of a *camera obscura*. It made little sense that the virginal life glimpsed outside the nine-pained window would have appeared so dire and intent.

He did finally see the girl's brief passage played out again, several hours later, his meat and vegetables stone cold and his knees cramped: The slight backward curl of lips in profile beneath an open, staring eye, not looking for the next frolic across the way, but concentrating on some purpose that, for the time being, only played out in her mind, beneath a bobbing blond ponytail tied back with a blue ribbon.

Only this time, the girl hadn't been carrying a shotgun at all. A glint of light or a certain stretch of shadow had surely created the illusion before of a young girl running with a cargo she certainly could not heft, and this time Henry concentrated and felt certain her load had been a stout walking stick instead.

Rubbing his tired eyes, Henry finally stood and cleaned away his uneaten dinner, all the while replaying the image in his mind.

Definitely not a gun. Girls don't run with shotguns. So it had to have been a stout walking stick with which she had been entrusted until it was properly delivered, causing her the consternated look. By the time he had finished the dishes, Henry was quite pleased with this assessment. A young girl on some Sunday afternoon chore, delivering a new walking stick, carved by her father, to her neighbor, after church.

It wasn't quite the freedom and whimsy Henry had envisioned beyond the window when he had first purchased Reginald Arburton's only work, but it made much more sense than the deception his eyes had perceived when he first saw the little girl dash past that window.

It made sense in a realistic way that said the world had no time for the whimsy of little girls.

And with that, Henry was able to get some sleep.

* * *

Henry awoke with a start at first light and looked straight at the painting. The little girl with the blond hair and the problematic expression was there now, in the room, blocking Henry's view of the window. She stood in the foreground, her form cut off by the picture frame at the hemline of her dress. Her blue eyes were steely and cold, the stare causing eerie shadows to have formed above her cheeks and around her curled lips. She was not at all happy. In her young, frail arms she cradled a shotgun, the double barrels pointed to the ceiling, her small right forefinger resting neatly on the trigger.

She didn't move. She didn't dash back out of the room or hand the gun over or turn to the window. She stood motionless and stared, the trim collar of her dress now seeming neat and blue in a military fashion.

Henry rose nervously from his bed and moved over to the picture, glancing away to see if the image would change, if the walking stick would reappear in her clutches, or if the girl would vanish as before and leave the peaceful yard beyond the window untouched. But this time she held her ground. No fading afterglow image. No rubbing the eyes and making it go away.

The girl stayed and stared out at Henry, cradling her shotgun, until Henry was forced by a greater will to leave his own bedroom. And though he could feel her eyes following him as he turned his back and walked through the door, Henry did not glance over his shoulder to see if it was true; to watch her eyes actually moving.

When he did glance in again, some hours later, on his way out of the bathroom, the girl was still there. She hadn't moved an inch. But her eyes had met and held his own.

* * *

Henry found the art history book again and looked up the plate of Reginald Arburton's untitled defacto masterpiece. There was the rough-hewn furniture in the ramshackle cabin, and there was the nine-paned window and the quiet, autumnal yard beyond. There was no little girl with a shotgun to break the scene. Henry stared at the black and white plate for a good hour and caught no glimpse of anything beyond the window—no foot, no stocking, no blue-ribboned ponytail. All he surmised was that a black and white reproduction did no justice to the delicate balance of color and shadow and light in the original. The plate was not alive. It just didn't have the same vivid consequence as the original, which had captured the light of that moment in some combination of oils and photographic reality.

Henry finally looked away from the image on plate F, closed the book, and went home.

The little girl, of course, had been anticipating his return and looked over when he poked his head into his bedroom.

Henry retreated and spent the night on the couch.

* * *

Henry stayed away from his bedroom with the same vigilance he had first displayed upon catching a glimpse of the girl's movement. He no longer cut his food neatly into cubes, nor did he stare longingly at one spot on the wall waiting for something to happen. Instead, he sat quietly at the kitchen table and ate slowly, with great precision, hoping above all that nothing would happen. His ears were tensed to *not* hear the soft shimmer of a dress ruffling as a little girl stepped over a picture frame and entered Henry's bedroom.

There were lots of things Henry didn't want to hear, and for this reason he took to completely silent meals, with plastic utensils on plastic plates to help deaden the noise, all the while listening to make sure he couldn't hear the sounds he did not want to hear.

Then, one night, he heard voices. The high tinkling lilt of a young girl, answered by the large rolling thunder of a grown man. The sounds were too indistinct for him to make out words, and since they weren't the sounds he hadn't wanted to hear, Henry put down his plastic knife and plastic fork and crept over to the door of his bedroom.

The voices stopped. Henry slumped down and sat with his back against the wall, his head tilted to capture the slightest vibration of air that could be deciphered as language.

Surely, if the girl was speaking, she meant him no harm? Henry sat wide-eyed and listened, his ears almost aching from the lack of noise, just as his eyes in the encroaching darkness began to ache at the lack of light. He listened for one word to rise above the dark folds of air in his home and give his thoughts some direction. He needed only to hear a brief salutation—or even a threat.

Finally, frustrated at the lack of sound from within, Henry reached up and slowly turned the cold metal knob, pushing the door open far enough for him to stick his head in. He could see his bed, bathed in moonlight, left as unkempt as when he had last set foot in the room. Dirty socks still littered the carpet and a stray pair of pants decorated the bed's footboard.

Henry poked his head in and held his breath, allowing his eyes to adjust to the pale blue light from the moon. His bed took on more shape, less form; he could pick out pillows over cushions, bedspread over sheets.

With only half a thought, he glanced up at the painting of the coarse room, fully expecting the scene to be back to the way he had bought it. But, of course, she was there. At first, she didn't seem to notice he was spying on her, then suddenly her eyes flicked down and met his—still the only part of her brushed-in body Henry had seen move for days.

He withdrew his head evenly and shut the door firmly behind it.

* * *

Henry's couch became his bed, so much so that he almost wondered why he had bought a bed in the first place. Sometimes, when he was outside watering the flowers, he would glance in through his bedroom windows, not so much to check on her—for he knew she would be there, shotgun in immovable arms, below the same immovable expression that should never have been on the face of a pretty, young girl—but to remind himself what a bed looked like. The pillows began to look alien, the sheets unreal, and the mattress a waste of space.

Then his eyes would drift again to hers, and he would move on, hoping that she would speak again soon so he could hear what she had to say.

And at the moment when Henry wondered why his bedroom was still off-limits, he heard the voice of a young girl within say very clearly, "My daddy said you needed this." He had been on his way to the bathroom when the words were spoken, but he stopped in his tracks, half-turned to the bathroom, and concentrated for more words to follow.

But there were no more sounds. No rustle of a dress or spoken reply. No twitch of a trigger finger or the click of a cocking gun.

Afraid he would miss something, Henry sat down outside the bedroom door, but after a few minutes the call of nature became too great and he quickly went about his business. Afterward, he even prepared himself a quick meal. Then, with his back against the wall between bedroom and bathroom, Henry sat cross-legged with his dinner, his plastic utensils making a dull tap his ears managed to avoid in favor of hearing a voice.

"My daddy said you needed this," he heard again not too long after, ending all semblance of a meal. He tried to interpret the voice, the stretch of syllables and curl of vowels valuable clues to what had been intended between the twinkling of words.

"My daddy said you needed this."

Then, before Henry could fully consider the tone, a man replied:

"You're blocking my light, Fiona. The window—you're blocking the window." It was the hollow sound of a man in a small room not paying any attention to the one with whom he was speaking.

Then silence. The few seconds of non-sound left Henry afraid to breathe, afraid of missing the next words.

"Fiona? Shall we do another picture of you now?"

It was a question laden with irregular sympathies.

"You *never* paint my picture."

The single shotgun blast roused Henry from whatever daydream he had envisioned. The pastoral scene he'd imagined unfolding within the abandoned room was suddenly a mute and naive testament in the face of stinking reality.

The silence which followed became too much for him to bear, so Henry scurried back to his couch and tried to get some sleep.

* * *

When next Henry watered his flowers he felt his eyes drawn to his bedroom window and to the room beyond that contained a picture of a room with two walls and a nine-paned window, much like his own. At first, placing the painting opposite his bedroom window had seemed natural—somehow extending his room and turning the rest of his house into that quiet autumnal yard beyond—but now he wasn't so sure.

It meant Henry could, if he wanted to, peek in at any moment and see what was there. He had done a fine job of continuing to ignore his bedroom and the secret world it now contained, but still his eyes were drawn to the window above his flowerbed like a moth caught in prismatic triangles of light.

Carefully, he crept closer, telling himself he was not going to look for the little girl with the white dress and powder-blue lace trim. He was not going to see if she still clutched her shotgun. He was just going to see what his bedroom looked like—remind himself of its presence.

He put down his watering can and grasped the edge of the window sill, peering surreptitiously into the room. His eyes adjusted slowly to the light and he glanced at the wall.

The little girl was gone.

Henry Edgewater shifted his weight to see better, looked away briefly, then back at the image. It was just a painting of a rough, ramshackle room, empty except for a woodsman's table and two chairs. On the back wall he could just make out a nine-pained window that gave onto a sunny, autumnal yard beyond.

No little girl. No blue ribbons or blur of movement or black-sandaled foot disappearing behind the chimney.

The yard beyond was empty, save for a few trees, and Henry had no idea how to feel about that.

He backed thoughtfully away from the window and thought of nothing at all.

* * *

Henry assumed the thing had run its course, but soon he found himself again taking dinner in his bedroom, his meat cut into neat cubes he could easily stab without having to take his eyes from the window.

Only this time, it was not the painted window of Reginald Arburton that kept him entranced, it was his own nine-pained window, which looked out upon his own pristine garden and airy spring yard, because one afternoon, not long after reclaiming his bedroom, Henry had seen a little girl run across his property. A little girl in a white dress with powder-blue trim and black sandals, carrying something that could have been a walking stick—or a shotgun.

He hadn't seen her clearly. He had been changing the sheets on his bed, his clothes already picked up and put away, when he noticed the lingering scent—very soft and mostly imperceptible—of spent gunpowder. When he moved to his window to open it, he had seen a blur move across the frame—a blur he had registered as a form he thought he recognized.

A quick look at the painting had revealed no such anomaly in the yard depicted there. No rush of movement or glimpse of a ponytail held fast by a blue ribbon. No stockinged leg or black-sandaled foot disappearing behind the chimney. But when Henry turned back and considered his own yard, he saw it again: A girlish blur of white with blue trim, with a bobbing blond ponytail, set face, and strange cargo.

Henry dashed into his yard and scoured the ground where the girl had passed. There was no sign of her having come or gone. No careless footprint or flattened grass. No broken twigs or torn leaves. And definitely no dislodged blue ribbon.

So Henry watched the window and waited, to no avail. His cubes of meat, potato, and carrots were eaten soundlessly, his concentration on his garden and the yard beyond, but the little girl from the painting did not run past again.

When the sun finally set, Henry gave up and took his dinnerware into the kitchen. As he left his bedroom he glanced once more at the image of the rough-hewn room and spectral nine-pained window.

No blur of motion. No shoe. No ponytail. No girl.

* * *

At three in the morning, Henry Edgewater awoke to the sensation of eyes watching, though not watching him. He sat up in bed to clear the dream, but when he surfaced, the feeling was still there.

Then he saw, back-lit by silvery blue moonlight, a little girl standing sideways at the foot of his bed, staring at the painting by

Reginald Arburton. Her white dress maintained a phantasmal glow in the moonlight, the powder-blue trim washed out by the silvery blue light. Her hair shone, pulled back in a ponytail held by a washed-out blue ribbon. Her gaze was firm, unaffected by Henry's motion or voice, her neat hands clutching tightly her lethal weapon.

Gasping for breath, Henry got out of bed and stood in front of her. Her eyes neither moved nor blinked and her grimly set mouth never faltered. She didn't seem to notice Henry's faint, polite questions.

Henry could not bring himself to touch her round shoulder or the cold metal of the gun. He trusted that his eyes knew well enough what he was seeing, and that what he was seeing was real.

The little girl holding the shotgun didn't care either way. She stood immobile, unblinking, staring at the painting, until finally Henry left the room and slept once more on his couch.

* * *

If Henry had not recalled the ghostly conversation of the little girl when she was still only a painted image, he never would have thought to rediscover the canvas and easel after a two-year hiatus.

"You *never* paint my picture," she had said before the conclusion had rung out as a single shotgun blast.

After gathering the necessary equipment, including new oils from the art supply store, Henry piled his wares at his bedroom door and fully expected her to be gone—nothing more than the product of an overburdened mind lacking inspiration. But she was still there, standing in the same position, staring at the same spot on the wall, her face as grim as ever. Her eyes did not move to focus on Henry, so he hurriedly shuffled into the room and set up his easel beneath Reginald Arburton's painting of a coarse, simple room looking out onto an autumnal yard.

The girl was as unfazed as ever by Henry's movements, though when he was finally settled and looked out at his subject, he could swear there was the glimmer of a smile near the corners of her grimace.

He didn't ponder the occurrence for too long. Henry knew he had work to do before the girl followed her words with actions and leveled her shotgun at him, the bullets undoubtedly every bit as real as the little girl in the blue-trimmed white dress looked.

Henry painted feverishly right through lunch and dinner, the brush strokes coming back to him like rainfall after a drought. His critically-acclaimed ability to mix colors had not been lost over time, and the image of his bedroom with the nine-pained window took form easily beneath his brush. The girl stood motionless and waited, not seeming the least bit interested in Henry's choice of brush or knife or the amount of paint he daubed onto the canvas.

Called an impressionist by some and a sloppy realist by others, Henry's new work unfolded true to form, but with a distinctly new angle not heretofore seen in his paintings. The lighting was more solid, the lines less blurry, the shadows less overpowering than his earlier periods.

And the little girl, she came out so crisp and clean that when Henry put the final dot of white at the end of her nose and looked up, only to find she had vanished from his room, he felt no sense of loss that he would never see her again.

He turned the easel toward his bedroom door and backed out into the hallway to look upon what would be called the first and last real work of Henry Edgewater's photo-realistic period.

The sheen of the shotgun looked real enough to touch; the girl's ribbon, seen just over the top of her head, real enough to untie; her white dress seemed almost to quiver under the strain of her arms, reflected in the grimace on her face.

And in the lower left pane of the window the girl stood in front of, Henry had painted the top of his own head, his eyes peering silently into the room where the little girl stood.

It had been the only way he could think of to ensure he was not actually in the room with her when he looked at the image. He almost named the painting after his subject, but at the last minute changed his mind, imagining it would be overkill in light of the crisply defined image itself.

But whatever it had all been, the painting, at least, made it stop.

The House on Moon Road

On the scale of things, there are those that are known and there are those so far beyond the reach of human conception as to be utterly and completely unrecognized. This scale is not monochromatic. Between these two extremes lies a vast gulf representing those words that start with negative inflections: Unknown, unexplained, impossible, improbable.

This scale also is analogous to how people approach the very same issues the scale itself describes. At one extreme, we find the skeptics, those people for whom nothing exists save what can be experienced by the five senses: what can be touched, measured, weighed, and otherwise termed "real." Far from them, on the other end of the scale, we come across the believers, for whom a lack of explanation proves nothing, and belief is a very great measure of reality, for if enough people believe something to be true, for all intents and purposes, it is true. For these extremes, never the twain shall meet, but again, the scale is not monochromatic.

Between the skeptics and believers is a cavernous void dotted with *real* critical thinkers, the men and women who do not doubt their senses and measuring sticks out of hand any more than they inherently believe what they think they are witnessing. Herein we find scientists spending tens of millions of dollars searching for the unseen, unknown source of cosmic rays; the unproved existence of dark matter; and the impossibly-small weight of neutrinos. We find entire towns and infrastructures pop up around supercolliders and radio telescopes, which in turn expend a massive amount of resources to operate and sustain.

All in the search for answers to make the unknown, known; the super-natural, natural; and the hyper-real, real.

But to what end? Does it ultimately affect life on Earth to be able to hold an infinitesimal chunk of dark matter? Or find the well-spring of cosmic rays, far upstream in the universal currents? Or determine the weight of smaller and smaller particles? In terms of the Quest— the search for answers—this satiates human curiosity admirably. But what of the questions closer to home? What of the answers to extra-sensory perception? Or super-natural beings that may co-inhabit our space? Would not the definitive answers to these questions do more to affect life on Earth?

What if we could prove that ghosts were real, for example? What would that say about human life and the inescapable problem of physical death? That would be worth more than the weight of a neut-rino, many would say.

And so, like those who are spending tens of millions of dollars looking *out there* for the unknown, the impossible, and the heretofore super-natural, should not some scientists set out to also look for the unknown, the impossible, and the heretofore super-natural *right here*, right under our noses?

All that is required is the right location and a team of scientists willing to go to it in order to spend tens of millions of dollars to search for definitive proof of just one ghost.

The perfect location may, in fact, be the house on Moon Road.

The Folklore

The property's long reputation of historical hauntings stretched as far back as Derrick Ware, who built the domicile in the summer and fall of 1798 and left it as soon as the winter gave way to the spring of 1799. The Wares told magnificent tales of footsteps on the roof, hair pulled by unseen hands, candles that lit themselves, and strange glowing eyes watching from the woods. Even then, there were skeptics, who put it all off to "settlers' jitters"—the kind of hallucinations common to city folk who tried to return to the wild. No matter that the Ware family had been gradually moving west, from new town to new town, for the past 10 years and had—by the accounts of their own relatives back in Boston—"gone native" long since, despite being one of the wealthiest farming families of their day.

Thus the house on Moon Road entered the 19th century under a dark cloud, and sat abandoned for many years, until George Ballach moved there with his pregnant wife in 1805. Ballach lasted seven years in the house, even after losing both his wife and unborn child in the first year. His wife's last words—as reported by Ballach—became infamous and the source of much speculation for decades: "They've come for the baby!" she apparently cried out the night she died and the night the Ballach heir was stillborn. The superstitious called it a blood sacrifice—an offering of appeasement to unseen forces—and offered this as the sole reason Ballach had been able to live there so long. When he finally left, his visage showed only a blank, horrified stare, and he would only whisper, "She finally joined them," if anyone asked what troubled him. To all other questions or comments he remained mute, and spent the balance of his life in seclusion near Philadelphia.

It wasn't until 1825 that the next family took residence, after having the house and property blessed by Father John MacElduff, who admitted to them, as he left, that the area seemed to him "the most damned spot on Earth" and urged them to leave posthaste. "There is a darkness here so foul not even the light of God can penetrate it for long," he was quoted by the family as saying, though he later denied the claim, no doubt fearing repercussions for his lack of faith. In 1850, the last living member of the family lay in the house on her death bed, having been thrown from a horse the day before, and admitted to her doctor that her family's time there seemed to be "filled with more accidents and suffering than average families see," but if there had been specific manifestations, as the lore would have suggested, the tales of them went with her to her grave.

Despite this relatively successful habitation of the house on Moon Road, the property wallowed in probate with no claimants and was eventually returned to the state, which could not sell it again until 1900 ushered in a new age of reason, and Genial "Gene" Mallistad purchased the home. As if echoing the previous turn of the century, however, the buyers lasted only a year in the place, even after spending a good amount of time and energy working to return it to a comfortable, homey condition. The Mallistads left complaining of disembodied voices threatening their lives, claw marks appearing on the floors and walls, a massive wolf-like beast that prowled the woods on moonlit nights, and strange dancing "globes of light" that would hover near the windows and weave through the trees. Technically, the Mallistad family owned the house for the next 44 years, but only because the state had all but given it to them, leaving them free of debt, and the Mallistads had been unable to resell it. Those 44 years were not without activity, however.

Gene Mallistad visited the house on Moon Road every year in the spring, to clean it up, and again in the fall, to cut back the summer brush and prepare it for the winter. Every now and again he would find a prospective buyer and would take them out to see the place, but despite his efforts to maintain the house, one look was all it took to "send some folks running back to the motor car as fast as they could run." Some folks, Gene claimed, pretended to be buyers just to get a look at the dwelling, because the one thing Gene

Mallistad couldn't maintain in his 44-year stewardship over the house was its reputation.

As before, during the 50-year stretch of state ownership, the house on Moon Road was rarely alone. Thrill seekers for generations would sneak onto the property for a glimpse at the ghost of Ballach's wife, or to hear the wails of her stillborn child, or to see the glowing eyes of the wolfman who prowled the woods. The stories that emanated from this combined 94-year stretch served to create the body of literature surrounding the house on Moon Road, not to mention the few tantalizing snippets Mallistad himself let slip from time to time, after too many drinks at the local pub.

Thus the colloquial history of the house on Moon Road was perfected, orally, over the course of nearly a century, and one of the oddest tales surrounded the physical house itself. Despite being left vacant for 50 years before the Mallistads, and unused for the next 44, it never seemed to deteriorate beyond repair. The work Mallistad did before moving his family in wasn't on the scale of rebuilding, so much as it was just a thorough cleaning, some new paint, minor repairs, and re-clearing the land that had become overgrown with weeds, shrubs, and saplings. In fact, Mallistad later admitted that the first time he set foot on the property, he was amazed as how well-kept the supposedly abandoned home appeared. "Even the trees," he said, "seemed to have kept a respectful distance from the house itself. Some of the saplings had clearly been growing in the cleared ground for the past 50 years, but there was still a definite clearing the house stood in, as if something had prevented anything so permanent as a tree from taking root too close, or bringing any harm to the home."

Mallistad often admitted that he "never felt right" at the homestead, and since his family had moved out, he had never spent another night at the place. Any work he did in the spring and fall was done over the course of one long day and amounted to five hours cutting back the clearing, and another five clearing out litter from inside the house and reshingling odd patches of roof or banging in new nails and boards here and there. "We knew kids got in there all the time, on dares," he admitted. "But even they seemed to treat the home with respect. Nothing was ever defaced or damaged, at least not by the kids. I think you can feel it, when you get out there, and you don't want to make it mad." When asked what "it" was, Mallistad usually changed the subject. Most of the lore about the house on Moon Road arose not from Mallistad.

The "kids," however, talked, and their favorite topic was usually claw marks. Before the Mallistad era, especially, talk in the mills, fields, and shops in the vicinity of the house on Moon Road centered on the Beast, as it was called—a great, loping, shaggy wolf-like creature that seemed to be there to guard the woods at night. Many tales surfaced of thrill-seekers who hiked out to the house to spend the night. Many opted to sleep outdoors—since the house felt "too oppressive"—but would find themselves invariably chased indoors after dark by "a massive shadow with glowing eyes that prowled the edge of the clearing and seemed to get closer and closer." Such stories often ended with bumps and footsteps on the roof, "as if a hoofed creature was pacing back and forth," and the inexplicable appearance of claw marks dug into the floorboards near where they had slept.

Mallistad himself verified at least one instance of claw marks in the floorboards that he had to repair "sometime around the first war," and recalled a number of the boards having to be replaced when they had first moved in. Those grooves he had attributed to "worm rot," but something in his eyes, decades later, said he had since begun to think differently of their origin.

As news of the Beast spread—the tales of those who successfully slept outside all night, without incident, notwithstanding—those daring enough to still go out to the house on Moon Road began increasingly to stay indoors. Thus began the stories of ghostly activity, all of which, no matter how distinct from other tales, was attributed to the ghost of Ballach's wife. She was variously a "shimmering apparition in a flowing white nightshirt," a "ghastly demon with glowing eyes, twisted hair, and fingernails like claws," and a "troubled spirit, wracked with guilt and sobbing uncontrollably." Most often, though, she amounted to little more than unexplained footsteps in the old master bedroom, a strange wailing noise, or various knock and raps on the walls and doors.

By Mallistad's day, the favorite pasttime of ghosthunters became the Candle Test. Culled solely from the century-old testimony of the Ware family, kids began to bring candles with them to test the veracity of Ware's claims. True to form, stories emerged of candles that would wink out without so much as a puff of air, or else light themselves when no one was present. As modern scientific inquiry began to captivate popular culture, experiments were conducted with two or more candles—some lit, some unlit—and reports were obtained that spoke of those that had previously been lit going out, even as the others burst into flame. One story in particular summed up the candle tales, told first by Dr. Emil Yathers, a professor of English at the nearest University. In his experience, he, and several stunned witnesses, watched as two candles alternated lighting and snuffing out right before their eyes "with no source of either wind to extinguish them or flame to light them." Being a professor, his testimony weighed more heavily than that of others. After his story entered the canon, Mallistad had to begin allowing time to pick candle wax from the boards in his yearly cleanings.

"It was a relief to finally sell the place," Mallistad admitted in 1944, at the age of 70, when the local paper ran a story on the house's sale. "It was never much trouble to me, but I'm getting too old to care for her any more, and it shows." When pressed on his personification of the place, and if he'd actually warmed to it over the years, his expression reportedly went grim as he delivered what was to be his final statement on the house on Moon Road: "No one could warm to that place, but I think it warmed to me, because I kept her clean. It's the house that matters. The house and keeping people out of those woods."

Camp Asherton

Gene Mallistad finally sold the property—at a break-even price, when one considered the 40 years of taxes he'd paid—to a man who claimed to be a spiritualist. Todd Asherton appeared in town dressed in a black three-piece suit, carrying an ebony walking stick, and took ownership of the house on Moon Road, sight unseen. By all accounts, Asherton was a showman, and it was his urging that developed the story in the paper of the home's sale—a free ad, in other words.

Todd Asherton was born in 1910 to a wealthy family in a town 55 miles north of Moon Road. His father had developed a better railroad spike and spent a lot of his time on the road throughout the state, hawking his wares and making his family quite rich. It was from these travels that he learned of the house on Moon Road, and shared the tales with his family, especially his wide-eyed only child, Todd. In fact, the house on Moon Road became a favorite nighttime story for the young boy, and it no doubt inspired the man's spiritualist leanings. Psychologists could also point out that Todd's interest in the occult was an attempt to force his father to spend more time with him, as the young boy's mind equated his father's travels not with selling goods but with exploring "far off" lands, like the house on Moon Road. The young Todd Asherton unconsciously thought that if he could produce ghosts and stories at home like the ones his father returned with, then his father would have no more reason to leave. In fact, by the time Todd was 10, the elder Asherton *didn't* have much reason to leave—the family's wealth was well established and a traveling sales staff could easily have been hired—but the question of infidelity came to the fore. For the next five years, when Todd's father was home, the time was spent more in arguing with his wife than telling his son stories—providing more fodder for any psychologist trying to prove that the grown up Todd Asherton was little more than a larger version of a boy who missed his father and took the blame upon himself for his father's absence.

It also didn't help that when Todd was 15, his father left for a sales circuit of the state and never returned. Todd—unable to believe the man he'd loved and missed could do wrong—just knew that his father had been in an accident and died, a theory bolstered by the fact that shortly after his father had left there had been a bizarre one-car accident near the house on Moon Road. The car—or what was left of it—was found parked at the side of the road, burned down the the chassis, leaving no trace of its occupant (had there been one). All the authorities knew for sure was that the car had been the same make and model as the one Todd's father had driven away in. Todd thus decided that his father had gone to visit the house on Moon Road firsthand, in order to return to his boy with eye-witness accounts of the happenings there, but had instead run afoul of whatever forces there were and had lost his life.

Todd's mother, on the other hand, proved her case for abandonment in court and was awarded full control of her husband's business, which she then turned into one of the nation's largest and most profitable ironworks. The fact that her ex-husband never returned to reclaim a stake in the new, exceedingly wealthy business was all that prevented her from outright denying her son's version of events, though she also knew that two days before he'd left for the last time, he had taken more than enough money out of the bank to live out the rest of his life quite comfortably—a fact Todd Asherton never knew until he was much older, by which time his own romantic memories of his childhood and father superseded all other notions, no matter the evidence.

At his mother's urging, Todd went to college and studied business, and even though he graduated in the middle of his class, it was obvious he had little desire to take over the ironworks. The "odd hobby" Todd had developed after his father's disappearance, which had been humored by a mother's misplaced guilt, coupled with his education to foment the young man's dream of a spiritualist city. Upon graduating, however, Todd—sheltered as he'd been—found that while his mother had managed to shield him and the ironworks from the effects of the Great Depression, the same could not be said of the rest of the country. Investors were hardly lining up to sink money into a "village full of people looking for something that isn't there."

So Todd took his show on the road and became a transient medium and spiritualist, at a time when unsuspecting "clients" were more than willing to forgo bread and pay instead for the chance to glimpse a brighter future or speak with those lost to the Depression. Moving from town to town—always to the moment when he'd outstayed his welcome—Todd Asherton would, over the next 10 years, hone his act to the spiritualist side, a move that certainly paid dividends when World War II began to take sons and fathers from loved ones. It was thus at the height of his career—when his own earnings far outweighed the money his mother had been wiring him for the last decade—that he decided to buy the house on Moon Road, start a spiritualist center, and settle down to found his city.

Todd Asherton intended to create his spiritualist city in the line—but not the small scale—of Lily Dale and Camp Chesterfield, but knew that first his chosen locale had to eclipse his own less-than-glorious reputation. He had hoped that buying a home as infamous as the house on Moon Road would go a long way to achieving the notoriety necessary to increase—and validate—his personal business and allow the settlement to flourish, only he hadn't realized that the house was little more than a local phenomenon. Outside the county, few people had heard the tales of the house on Moon Road, so for his first few years of residence, Todd spent more time promoting the lore of the place than he did entertaining guests seeking the services of a spiritualist, or wanting to lease land. Accordingly, the truth of the stories peddled by Todd Asherton is open to debate.

After only three months in the house he finished writing his first memoir, *Moon Road: Living in a House That No One Wants*. The wordy subtitle on the front cover of his independently printed book further explained, "Why a modest frontier home has remained empty for most of its 150-year life." The fact that the cover never once mentions ghosts or demons—and indeed mentions "life" and "living" instead—is one of the few shreds of evidence that the showman spiritualist was trying to write a balanced book. "He was, after all, founding a new town," one biographer has pointed out. "He knew that ghosts would be the attraction at first, but his scheme—if you want to call it that—was to get people out to his village so they would fall in love with the locale and want to stay. Tales of demon dogs prowling the woods wouldn't go a long way to achieving that goal."

Thus was Todd Asherton beset with a dilemma that tested his business acumen more than inheriting a flourishing ironworks could have. The young founding father had to at once play up the lore to attract guests, but also play down the lore so as not to frighten them away. This is how he struck upon the theme of *Moon Road*, turning the hauntings not into some malevolent force out to get anyone who came near, but rather as a misunderstood force that could be befriended, if only the right people would come around. Spiritualists, he concluded, were the perfect candidates for this mission: "There are forces here, to be sure, in the woods and in the original house, but any angry manifestation is derived from frustration at not being able to communicate with the current occupants. Like a child who has yet to gain a command of language, the spirits are thus provoked to throw tantrums, which generations of visitors have grossly misinterpreted."

For the next 111 pages of *Moon Road*, Todd Asherton recounted the previous 150 years of ghost stories, many of which were repeated from the stories his father had told him, supplemented with his own observations and interviews with people who lived in the area. His first night on the premises he did the candle test, which resulted in a "self-lighting flame that jumped more than three feet above the candle's wick and scorched the wall of the bedroom." That night, he went on, he heard footsteps pacing around his bed, which always stopped as soon as he tried to establish contact. And so it went—always the underlying plea, woven artfully between the lines: It's not scary here, but there are ghosts, and I need your help to speak with them.

On the one hand, while *Moon Road* can be dismissed as a long-winded advertisement for the Village of Asherton, it also serves the valuable purpose of collecting in one place most of the lore associated with the house on Moon Road—and a discerning reader can always tell the difference. The original stories have none of the flare and show of the tales introduced by Todd Asherton: If the locals said they awoke in the morning to find claw marks on the floorboards, then Todd Asherton would say he woke up to find the maker of the marks watching him, only to spook "the creature" and see it run away before he could make meaningful contact.

Asherton hawked his *Moon Road* book in the same way his father had done business: He took a box on the road and made personal sales. It worked, too. Sales of his book, coupled with his earnings from "spiritualist readings" done at the same time, padded his amassed wealth enough that he could secure a loan to begin construction of the village. His plan was to first build two rows of "camp cottages" in the woods across the clearing from the house, then host weekly spiritualist reunions throughout the summer. As people came and experienced the hauntings firsthand—and fell in love with the place—they would be more than willing to set up their own, permanent residences. These plots, Asherton decided, would be leased to buyers on a ten-year plan: If they stayed for the life of the lease, they'd own their plot of land and home outright. If not, then it would be leased to the next prospective buyer under the same conditions.

In the spring of 1946, ground was broken for the cottages, which amounted to little more than two rows of oversized hotel rooms with small kitchenettes. Midway between the rooms and his house, in the clearing, there was to be a large gazebo built, for camp meetings and spiritualist services. Todd Asherton had lived in the house on Moon Road for almost two full years by that point and told the local paper that, while he had seen and experienced many things, he had not encountered anything "that made me want to pack up and leave." He admitted, however, that he could see how "those less educated in spiritualist matters would be scared off" by the things he'd seen.

This perfectly timed story—and it being the first summer after World War II ended—ensured that the inaugural summer camps in Asherton were fully booked. Construction was completed without a hitch by mid June, and the camp officially opened its doors on July 1, 1946.

Talk in the local taverns did not elicit much interest in staying in Camp Asherton after sunset, however. The construction workers, who had toiled daily for two months to build the cottages and gazebo, refueled nightly in the pubs and swapped stories and the overwhelming opinion that "anyone would be crazy to stay in those woods after dark" (as the foreman said in the same article where Asherton denied the claims). It could be that the foreman was told to play up the sinister edge to the house on Moon Road, but long after

Asherton had come and gone, the stories of the construction crew remained consistent.

Most of the tales amounted to little more than circumstantial evidence, which could be written off as the jitters of overactive imaginations. After all, the entire construction crew had grown up with tales of the house on Moon Road and had the money not been so good (and the Depression still so fresh in their minds), most later admitted they wouldn't ever have set foot on the property. As it was, they did, and came back with glimpses of "shapes out the corner of my eye" and "odd warbling noises from them woods." One crewman even went so far as to say that "the trees we cut down for the cottages cried out, as if in pain." He also admitted that, "everyone heard it, but no one else wants to admit it." In fact, it was said that the woods "buzzed with ill feelings" until the lumber had been returned to the site after being prepared for use in the cottages themselves, as beams, supports, walls, and stairs. Asherton bragged that 90 percent of the trees cut down were returned to the woods in one way or another during construction, a figure often disputed by experts who claim that a construction site would be lucky to get back 40 percent of the trees removed in the form of usable lumber. Whatever the case, the crew agreed that once the cottages and gazebo were finished, the "ill feeling" in the woods seemed to have lessened greatly—not to mention they had, by that time, been working in the woods for two months and had undoubtedly just got used to the place.

The only story of any real form came from the foreman, who recounted how he had once been going over the blueprints with Todd Asherton as they determined where best to place the gazebo (it ended up being offset from the line created by the house and cottages, with a flagpole and flowerbed positioned where Asherton had originally wanted the gazebo). While reviewing the blueprints, the foreman happened to glance up at the house and spot "the most beautiful young woman in one of the windows." He asked Asherton who the young lady was and if there would be a wedding in the camp that summer, but Asherton looked confused. "When we looked back at the house so he could see her," the foreman said, "she was gone. We both ran to the house—I let Asherton go first—but we couldn't find her or any trace of her. Turns out she'd been in the window of the master bedroom, which I guess is where Ballach's wife is said to haunt. It gave me the shivers, and to be honest, Mr. Asherton himself looked pretty shaken, as if until that moment he'd not actually seen anything weird at the house." The foreman's reading of Asherton's reaction was later used to help discredit the body of Asherton's *Moon Road* memoir.

The summer of 1946 was the only time that could be honestly called the halcyon days of Asherton. Before the camp had even opened, a plot of land had been leased under Asherton's proposal, and he had several other prospective clients lined up. Todd Asherton also had a full three months of week-long rentals and was considering extending the season into October. After the first two weeks of camp were behind him, Asherton confidently told *The Spiritualist News*—a national rag concerned with such things—that he was not only sure Camp Asherton would blossom, he was now convinced it would be a fully established village several years ahead of schedule. "Many of our early visitors have already booked ahead for a week or two next year," he explained. "And several people have taken home with them literature on our lease-to-own program. Everyone wants a piece of the Village of Asherton."

But even with a camp full of would-be spiritualists who had come to Asherton expressly for an "experience," the cottages began to prove to be too much. At first the screams of guests that punctuated the wee hours were taken with a grain of salt—the over-excited reactions of deprived spiritualists who wanted to find proof of *something*—but soon they became so common place as to cause a minor panic. What had previously been screams as a result of hair being pulled or hot breath on the neck of a sleeping guest, the last week of July elicited visual confirmation of the source—or presumed source—of the antics. Reports of glowing red eyes began to circulate the camp, as well as guests waking up only to find a "shaggy gray-haired beast" staring at them. The obligatory claw marks were found on the floorboards and, when guests reported "heavy footfalls all along the roofs of the cottages," similar marks also were found on the roofs.

"Those weren't ghosts or spirits," one guest later confessed to the same *Spiritualist News*. "They were demons and things no one should ever have contact with."

By the end of August, half the bookings for September had been canceled and Todd Asherton was forced to shelve any plans for an October extension. To be sure, the vast majority of guests for the first two months had not experienced anything radical—perhaps a few shivers or presumed whispers during sessions at the gazebo, or during the once weekly overnights in the actual house—but the stories of those who had seen or felt something truly odd made a greater impression and spread further and faster. In these tales, candle flames leaped "five foot if they grew an inch" and guests were routinely "chased down like prey" by the gray-haired beast. Walks in the woods, along trails Todd Asherton had cleared himself, turned into nervous treks plagued by "glowing orbs weaving between the trees" and "the distinct impression that we weren't just being watched, but actually *stalked*."

The only reason the stories didn't emerge with such profusion the following year was because, despite being the first full season, lasting from mid May to the end of September, there were only half the number of guests compared to the year before. Many weeks, Todd Asherton found himself entertaining only two guests, who would gladly take him up on the offer to sleep in the guest room of the house rather than stay in the cottages alone. Capacity for the camp was 48 adult guests, allowing for 864 visitors per season. In 1948, only 100 hardy guests stayed at Camp Asherton—and most of them were spiritualists who readily admitted they "dabbled on the darker side." Everyone else had been scared off by report after report in various spiritualist circles, all of which had come to the same simple conclusion: Camp Asherton was not just haunted, it was possessed.

The next few years served only to re-enforce this opinion. Of the guests who were not "dabbling" with demonic forces, most reported feeling like they had "camped for a week just outside the gates to hell." Swirling shapes, glowing eyes, hot breathing, growling, sentient orbs—the cottages seemed to be the epicenter for all that was bad in Asherton, and the house itself was all but forgotten. In fact, one couple admitted that "our overnight stay in the house itself was so restful, we asked if we could spend the rest of the week there. When Mr. Asherton refused, we decided to go home early and forfeit our reservation."

But if there was a specific incident that served as the death knell for Camp Asherton and Todd's dreams of a bustling Asherton Village, it came in July, 1953, when one guest was heard shrieking uncontrollably in the night. When the other guests finally broke in his door, they found the prone and clearly deceased body of Reggie Buckles, a confirmed bachelor whose diary entries from his stay at Asherton revealed the fact that he was secretly hoping Ballach's wife would visit him in a way only a confirmed bachelor could envision. Instead, the claw marks proved to the other guests that he had been visited by the beast, though the coroner ruled his death as "a severe heart attack triggered by extreme fright."

In short, Reggie Buckles has been literally scared to death at Camp Asherton, and Todd Asherton only managed to limp through to June of 1954 before finally calling it quits and closing up shop.

The Moon Road Orphanage

In December of 1955, Camp Asherton and the house on Moon Road were sold to the state to be revamped as a county orphanage. The irony did not escape Todd, who said only that it seemed "a fitting end to my personal history with the house on Moon Road." For their part, the state officials who had bought the land admitted that "Mr. Asherton allowed us to stay with him for a week to assess the place." The result was that they "found nothing out of the ordinary." They felt that Camp Asherton's demise "was due more to the overactive imaginations of people who believe in ghosts, not because of some actual malevolent force in the woods."

The only part of the original land that was not sold to the state was a solitary half-acre furthest from the house and cottages, which had been sold under Asherton's lease-to-own program in May of 1946. It took all of five minutes for a judge to rule in favor of Maria Latitude, who had quietly enjoyed her plot of land for the past nine and a half years, and was not inclined to give up her home for the want of six more months. In fact, after the ruling was handed down, the state agreed to expand her plot to three full acres, "in the interest of giving her sufficient privacy from the residents of the orphanage." When asked by an overly interested media why on Earth she'd want to stay on the possessed land, she simply countered, "I can't imagine why all those people ever left. I have always enjoyed my time at Asherton and find the woods peaceful and relaxing." On the subjects of demons and the stories of the house on Moon Road, Maria Latitude refused to comment and vanished back on to her plot and into anonymity. She wouldn't even entertain Todd Asherton himself, who attempted several times to interview her for what became his second —and final—memoir, *Camp Asherton: The Real Story of My Decade in the Shadow of the House on Moon Road*. This time he not only found a publisher, but the book became a bestseller.

Meanwhile, camp Asherton was completely updated, and very marginally expanded, to be reopened in the fall of 1956 as the Moon Road Orphanage. What happened during the next 25 years is open to speculation, but when the orphanage finally closed its doors, it did so without any fanfare or talk of ghosts or demons. In fact, the orphanage was often heralded as "the state's finest institution for wayward children," posting only one death over its two decades of operations, and amassing a litany of positive reviews for its "cleanliness, beautiful grounds, and well-behaved children." In 1980 the state merely closed all county orphanages in favor of several larger—and more containable—statewide institutions. Thus was the house on Moon Road—most recently the office and home of the orphanage's headmaster—once again abandoned.

However, in 1982 Todd Asherton's career—which he'd continued as best he could with a series of "scientific" examinations of the paranormal—was given a boost with the publication of the 25th anniversary edition of *Camp Asherton*, which was released in tandem with a tell-all by Cretia Dominio called *The Moon Road Orphanage: Monsters at Play*. Cretia had lived at the orphanage for seven years, from ages 11 to 18, and many assumed her memoir was another in a rash of orphan/patient screeds against an outdated institutional system that was ripe with abuse, be it physical, mental, sexual, or all three. Cretia's book, however, spoke of a wholly non-human form of abuse. It was a book the state immediately dismissed as "fantasy," attempting to recast Cretia Dominio as an "unfortunate girl who still has yet to come to terms with the sudden deaths of her parents."

Sadly, for the state, by the summer of 1983 the furor over the supernatural goings-on, at an orphanage people had said should never be built where it was, had reached a fever pitch, and nine other children who had lived at the Moon Road Orphanage had come forward to validate Cretia's claims, making six boys and four girls who wove similar tales of ghosts, poltergeists, and strange "unnatural" creatures running rampant through the orphanage, house, and woods. As Cretia concluded in *The Moon Road Orphanage*, "The grounds were clean because we were told to keep them clean, and we did exactly what we were told, because if we didn't, the headmaster would lock us up with the Beast until we promised to behave."

The state wrote the whole thing off as sensationalism and all but accused the former orphans of jumping on the bandwagon against state-run institutions. And while a case can be made for the financial rewards of jumping on that bandwagon, it is also true that, to this day, not one former "guest" of the Moon Road orphanage has come forward to refute the claims of those who became known as the Moon Road Ten, and nearly 1,000 children spent time at Moon Road during the 25 years of the orphanage's operation. Cretia Dominio did admit that the timing of her book's publication was planned to coincide with the republication of *Camp Asherton*, but also pointed out that she had written it starting in 1965, with the intent of having the place closed down. Completed in 1971, she had been unable to find a publisher, for fear of lawsuits, but once the orphanage had been closed and the headmaster in question had died—in 1981—publishers were more amenable to the prospect, especially considering the Todd Asherton tie-in.

"My only regret," Cretia later said, "is that the timing wasn't right in 1971, to save another decade's worth of orphans from the horrors we saw."

A little digging by investigative reporters in 1982 unearthed the fact that there had only ever been one person who had stayed at the old Camp Asherton for two weeks, every year of its existence: His name was Dr. Rupert Oliono, and he went on to become the first— and only—headmaster of the Moon Road Orphanage, and was actively involved in the institution's founding and location. Dr. Oliono's professional background was in childhood psychiatry, and by all counts, he was an amiable, joyful man, and a pleasure to be around.

Even Cretia nostalgically referred to "Dr. O" as the friendliest person at the orphanage and credited him with a complete lack of corporal punishment at the institution. "Of course," she also admitted, "he didn't need to threaten us with beatings when he could just make us spend a night in the gazebo."

The gazebo had been renovated by the state to become a five-room "separation area" for particularly violent or bad children and, according to Cretia and the Moon Road Ten, became also the nexus of "every truly bad thing that happened there." While stories of footsteps on the roofs of the cottages persisted—the buildings having been altered to become two long rooms full of curtained-off beds, with a cafeteria taking up half of one—the appearances of the Beast seemed to now be fixed wholly on the gazebo.

"The energy in the gazebo was never good," Cretia explained. "Kids were put there because we were angry or frustrated and acting out. I think the fear and negativity attracted the Beast." This is not to say the Beast ever physically harmed anyone, but as James "Scoots" Tresson—one of the boys in the Moon Road Ten—explained, "When you see a massive monster standing in the corner watching you, you have to believe you only survived by accident."

The activity at the orphanage, according to Cretia and the other nine orphans who spoke up, was not reserved to the gazebo, however. The Beast itself was often glimpsed in the woods, along with assorted colored orbs and "wispy, smokey shapes that curled through the trees." These sightings were often preceded (sometimes by a day or two, other times by mere hours) by the presence of a ghostly man walking the length of the "A" building—the cottage row in which Reggie Buckles had died. In fact, the descriptions of the ghost matched descriptions of Reggie Buckles, though Cretia did admit in an interview that the orphans were often allowed to walk the three miles into town to buy candy and comic books, and they often came back with stories of the house on Moon Road, gleaned from curious townsfolk would stop them and ask how life at the house was.

"None of us ever mentioned the ghosts to *them*, though," Cretia admitted. "That was too risky. They could've been sent there by Dr. O to see if we'd blab, and that would mean spending a few nights in the gazebo."

Cretia was undoubtedly wrong on this count, however, because ample stories emerged from the orphanage over the 25 years of its existence, enough so that a "society of concerned citizens" was formed in 1961 to pressure the state into moving the orphanage to more suitable grounds. Only twice did the pressure from this group need release, and both times Dr. Oliono simply derided the protestors as "crackpots who see shadows and call them ghosts." No mention of the Beast or the gazebo ever came from this group, though, so at least Cretia's contention that "we never talked about the gazebo because you could tell by their eyes what they'd seen once Dr. O let them back out" seems to be true.

There was also a sense of reward at the Moon Road Orphanage: If punishment earned you lonely days and nights in the gazebo, then reward earned you dinner and a night in the house itself. "The dinner was really good—Dr. O told great stories," Scoots Tresson said. "But it was still creepy to have to sleep there alone." In fact, Dr. O began awarding the privilege in pairs, when kids started to refuse the honor because they didn't want to spend the night alone. Dinner, it was said, was always candlelit, and oftentimes the candles would wink out, one at a time, in a pattern that defied any eddies of wind, only to reignite moments later, usually with flames twice the size they had been before—an oft-repeated oddity that, by all accounts, Dr. Oliono seemed not to notice, or at least deem worthy of comment.

At night, the orphans said, you could hear "Ballach's wife pacing in the rooms upstairs, searching for her baby." Only Dr. Oliono had a room upstairs (the four permanent "house mothers" lived at the ends of the cottages, and the rest of the staff had homes in town), and Cretia was adamant that it was easy to distinguish his heavy footfalls from those of the ghost. "Sometimes you'd hear them both," she allowed. "You could tell Dr. O was hearing it, too, and he was chasing her from room to room, trying to catch a glimpse."

While most of Cretia Dominio's 200-page *The Moon Road Orphanage* (10 pages of which were pictures from her time there) involved accounts of strange lights and ghostly sounds—along with sightings of the Beast—overall it did little to add anything new to the lore surrounding the house on Moon Road. Its sales paralleled those of the reprint of *Camp Asherton* and, as one reviewer put it, "You need only decide if you relate more to an orphan or a showman, because both thin books seem to have been filled with stories from a common source, and the only difference is the life story that brought each author to live on Moon Road."

The Moon Road Orphanage even contained its own death, though the events couldn't have been more different than the demise of Reggie Buckles. After the build-up involving the gazebo and the Beast, one would have been safe to assume the death involved both, but in fact it involved a picnic in the woods one picturesque autumn day. Cretia Dominio had not been on the picnic ("I was only thirteen then, and you had to be fourteen to go hiking without a house mom"), but she had been a resident of the orphanage at the time.

According to her recounting of the tale—which was verified by Scoots Tresson, who *had* been there—three of the children had been allowed to have their lunches in the woods, along one of the many hiking trails Dr. Oliono maintained throughout the property. The trail they had chosen ended at a creek that marked the border with the property of "that weird Maria lady," and the children had spread their blanket and decided to go for a wade before eating. Suddenly, one of the boys—Jonathan "Jonny" Woodings—cried out that there was a lady drowning in the creek. The others ran over and saw the same thing as he had in the mid-shin deep water: The pale face of a woman whose body seemed to be floating impossibly under the shallow surface, her dress pulled and twisted by whatever currents existed below. Jonny took a step toward the lady, but the others—Melanie Mallick and Scoots Tresson—shouted at him not to get any closer, and began to back away.

"That was when she grabbed him," Scoots Tresson said, his story changing little over the years from the initial inquiry to the release of Cretia's book. "I saw a white hand reach up out of the water and take his, but that lady didn't want help—she pulled him down and held him under." The screams of Melanie and Scoots roused Maria Latitude, who happened to be working in her garden not too far away, "but she seemed to be smiling in this weird way," Scoots said, "so Mel and me, we ran back to the house as fast as we could."

This was the only ghost story to ever officially emerge from the house on Moon Road during the tenure of the orphanage, and Dr. Oliono was able to summarily dismiss it as "the fantasy of two young children who have already had a hard life, seeing their best friend drown and being unable to assist him." Dr. Oliono's point was that tales of "ladies in the water" pulling unsuspecting children under were widespread, especially around "any body of water where children play alone." In his professional opinion, it was the way in which children—"and superstitious folks"—drive home their point and ensure that others don't go near the water. In this case, at least, it worked: Dr. Oliono never made the creek off-limits (though he did begin requiring a water safety class at the local Y), but the children rarely—if ever—took the trail to the creek again, at least not without a house mother or the doctor himself.

After the orphanage closed in 1980, the house on Moon Road again sat vacant, but was overseen by Maria Latitude, who was paid a small sum to walk the grounds and check the buildings weekly, to report anything that needed attention. Still owned by the state, the house and buildings would turn up from time to time under different proposals—from summer camps to retreat centers to forming a state park—none of which ever went beyond committee. It seems that this time the stories of the house—forwarded by Todd Asherton and Cretia Dominio—had finally taken firm root.

Maria Latitude took her job seriously, and often walked the grounds twice a week, but if she ever saw anything, she never told anyone. In town, she was widely—and sometimes seriously—regarded as a witch, the fact that she had lived on the Moon Road property alone for four decades being enough to condemn her as such. However, she never had to report any serious damage or graffiti to the state for their attention. Her reports usually amounted to fragments such as "building A needs paint" or "storm last week tore off shingles." By 1990, the state began to ignore her reports, and in 1993 officially relieved her of her duty. It seemed that no one—living or dead—was interested in the house on Moon Road any more. Some may even argue that the occupancy by so many people for 36 years had been too much for the house on Moon Road: After centuries of sporadic visitors chasing wildly speculative tales, the continued presence of so much living *energy* had spent the spirits' will, and the house itself gave up.

Moon Road Amusements

In 1995 Todd Asherton died of cancer at the age of 85, which news sparked a brief resurgence in both the man and his books—and the house on Moon Road. That Halloween an upstart "amusements" company rented the house and buildings from the state to create a seasonal haunted house, only to discover that people were more afraid of the house and land itself than they were of their rubber-knife-wielding ghouls.

71

The next year, they rented the house and buildings again, this time starting in the summer, for daily tours, capping off the year with a grand finale "night hunt" at Halloween. While the daylight tours were a relative success, the grand finale booked only 10 people, 3 of whom didn't keep their reservations. Either interest had finally waned or people were still too afraid–especially after the tales in the bestselling books—to visit the place after dark. Whatever the case, in 1997 the Moon Road Amusements company opted to eschew its namesake and expend its resources on summer carnivals and a haunted house in a different building, which turned out to be much more financially rewarding for the company.

"The house detracted too much from the games, it was that simple," explained Larry Johnston, founder of Moon Road Amusements. "No matter what we did, people just didn't have *fun* around the house. The energy was too ... heavy, I think." Asked if he, or anyone he knew of, ever saw anything while on the property, his expression belied knowledge, though his short answer was, "No."

Ten years later, in 2007, the property was purchased from the state by a "very wealthy man who wishes to remain anonymous." The first thing he did was to construct a nine-foot high fence—topped with barbed wire—around the full parcel, which turned out to be 40 acres and much bigger than anyone had ever surmised. Apparently he also had met with Maria Latitude, because her home and acreage, it turned out, was fenced *in* with the rest of the property.

No one else has been on the property since, though the talk in town has turned to "those science types" who have come and gone in the last few years.

More emphasis has been placed on those who have *gone*, of course, and who can blame them for that?

The Cottage of Misplaced Time

I

The graveyard was beautiful. Snow clung to the trees like white flesh on bones, and the falling ice had started to form icicles that hung like diamond necklaces from the branches. The expanse was in a remote part of Phillip's Stand, Ohio; a few animal prints criss-crossed silently among the stones. The air was a perfectly crisp January night with the hint of wood-fires, like a soft perfume, dancing in and out of our range of smell. As we wandered deeper into the cemetery the ice turned to snow, the flakes drifting down like the strange white petals of a foreign rose; as the wind picked up, the snow began to fall in torrents.

I reached out and found my fiance's hand, pulling her gently to me and bringing her ear to my lips, "Let's go back, huh, Ellie? This is a bad snow all of a sudden—"

I felt Ellie tug sharply on my arm, then her grasp silently fell away from my hand. I crouched down, figuring she had proved my point by falling, but my searching hands couldn't find her. As suddenly as it had begun, the snow ceased all together, and then I could see that Ellie had vanished. I looked frantically back the way we had come and saw a black path snaking, strangely uncovered with snow, across the whitened land. It led to the decorative wrought iron gate of the graveyard; one of the gates was slightly ajar and a thin triangle of light was on the ground before it, as if a door to a lighted room had been left cracked. I shook my head slowly, furrowing my brow: there was no source of light that could be seen through the gates, only the disappearing expanse of snow. Turning back to the path before me to continue my search, I saw a gaping hole directly in front of me where solid ground had been only a few seconds before. A foul mist clung to the air above it and I realized with nausea where Ellie must have gone.

"Ellie!" I yelled after her, eliciting no response. I was frightened, disoriented, a strange new emotion gnawing in my stomach. Slowly I reached through the thick fog above the hole and I could feel it pulsating sickeningly around my arm, massaging my fingers. As the fog dissipated somewhat I scooted forward along the gravelly path and peered over the lip of the wound, seeing with confusion that it was actually the opening to a musty wooden staircase which led down into darkness.

"James? What's happening?" I heard Ellie's voice, small and lonely, climbing that monstrous staircase to me.

"Ellie!" I yelled again, my voice echoing hollowly back, but she either didn't hear, or couldn't answer, because all I heard in response was a low menacing growl drifting from that cavity in the graveyard. I remained perfectly still, trying to come to some logical conclusion, but always ending up on the same note: I must follow Ellie's voice down that staircase, down which she had obviously fallen. I rose to my feet and sighed, trying to pluck up my courage for her, then finally began my nervous descent of the stairs, not knowing if I was more afraid of walking into what was surely a grave, or of finding Ellie's crumpled form at the bottom.

Both fears were unwarranted, for at the foot of the stairs I found neither Ellie nor a coffin, but rather a tunnel that extended out of the range of an odd red glow that bathed my surroundings. The light sent shivers over me; it was entirely illogical since I was underground and no light—especially red—was leaking from the dark world above me, not even the earlier pinpricks of the stars. I called Ellie's name once more, to no avail, then began to hesitantly shuffle my feet at the base of the stairs. I felt like a small child knowing where he has to go, but deeply afraid of going to it. I could not reconcile an odd snow squall with a hole that led beneath the graves of the nameless dead, and this lack of reconciliation caused a deepening fear.

The tunnel was barely taller than me, and only as wide as the staircase. I gazed along it, to the edge of the glow, narrowing my eyes with decision. I moved cautiously forward, one feeble step at a time, whimpering Ellie's name for reassurance.

The red glow followed my every small step forward, creating a pocket of odd light in the darkness. About a hundred feet down the earthen corridor, dank with the smell of decomposing earth, I stopped and looked more closely at the walls. They were moist; dark, wet earth full of worms and insects like I've never seen before. The most abundant worms had two dots at the end of their perfectly white bodies; eyes, as I saw them, watching me. Eyes that seemed to be laughing at me. I hurried on down the corridor wanting more than anything to just find Ellie and leave that hideous place.

After about five minutes the tunnel ended at a stout wooden door and, unflinchingly, I grasped the cold metal knob and turned it, willing to go anywhere that was away from those worms. The knob squealed in protest, but unlatched the door easily enough, and I pushed it quickly open with my shoulder. The red glow came distinctly to an abrupt end at the threshold of the doorway, making it seem as if a thick, black velvet curtain had been hung to the floor on the other side of the door. There was a constant draft coming from the other side, however, brushing my face like the breath of a summer's breeze. I reached out carefully into the impenetrable darkness but felt nothing in the black air. As I bravely stepped over the threshold I was assailed by the aroma of fresh-cut grass, dim and fragrant, and a soft light slowly filled the scene, like someone turning up a dimmer switch, until the landscape before me was lit with the brilliance of a clear summer dusk.

II

I was in a forest. The trees were about twice the size I was used to and everything was a moist, deep green. The sky was the silent, rich purple of twilight clouds, and a mist hung in the air, more seen by intuition than sight. I was standing on a thick-shag grassy expanse that covered the woodland floor for as far as I could see. When I turned to see where I had come from, the doorway was just a red glow in a hillside, between two trees. Methodically, I turned and started climbing the small hill, deducing that, by all rights, the cemetery should be on top of it, though deep-down I knew that just as it should be snowy (and wasn't), there should be a graveyard (but wouldn't be). It was my last chance at finding some sort of logic in all this and that was the only way to combat the fear that had settled on me; a fear rooted in being confronted with only the illogical. Fear and confusion are the worst emotions we have, and when they are both present and feeding off each other the pressure becomes unbearable.

From the hilltop I gazed out over the forest. It was a deep emerald green throughout, the moisture in the air causing everything to glisten like the landscape had been dipped in glitter. I could hear birds—I assumed—flitting to and fro among the branches, and everywhere was the delicate perfume of fresh-cut grass and clear streams. It was an image of paradise, but still a low dread settled upon me, pushing on my diaphragm like lead: in all this beauty, Ellie was nowhere to be seen. I called for her again, hopefully, and stood transfixed as my voice faded into the distance with no response. Disenchanted, I began to instinctively remove some layers of clothing, since the forest was much warmer than Phillip's Stand had been. As I dropped them carelessly at my feet I noticed a sudden movement as of something dodging out of their way.

I jumped, my heart pounding uncontrollably, as a two-foot tall creature dusted itself off near me. It looked like a manatee, with folds of velvety skin—like whatever had made its covering had been expecting something much bigger—only it had arms and legs instead of flippers and tail. Its motions were extremely human-like and it looked up at me with what seemed to be non-hostile contempt on its scrunched manatee face. It nodded slyly, its velvet skin rustling, then turned and ran off. I shouted after it to stop and when my eyes caught up to it, it had frozen solid at my command. I approached it, sure it could answer some questions, but as I neared I saw that the frozen figure was actually just the weathered stump of a tree: wrinkled and rounded on top; brown, wet, and lifeless. Enraged, I looked around the forest before me, seeing nothing, and I felt sick at being alone and inescapably lost from the rest of my life.

Then, entirely without warning, the ground beneath my feet gave way, and in a whirlwind of black direction, I fell.

III

I felt things in the darkness scratching at me, clawing my face and tearing my clothes. I was falling first through a rosebush, then being pushed through a dandelion. I saw dreams of my fiance, alone, shuddering, begging me to hold her hand. I saw demons, all teeth and drool and menacing laughter. I saw fire and light and rainbows. I felt people handing me money, people kissing me, saw people yelling in horror and disgust at me.

Still, I fell.

77

I tumbled and turned. I was falling deeper, beyond all my sleeping dreams. I saw a Bible before me burst into flames; I saw all the tomes of myth and religion and superstition—pages fluttering, turning into dancing flames.

Finally, I screamed.

I landed heavily on a dirt floor—nothing visible above me to have fallen from (except darkness) and nothing around me to feel, save the rocky dirt below. It stank of overturned sod and I heard the mournful cries of hideous flying things with swooping, leathery wings. A frigid wind had been blowing and it suddenly stopped, a yellow dot like a stage light spot-lighting me from what seemed to be miles away.

IV

I began walking aimlessly, heading as best I could for the source of the light, hoping it would contain some clue as to my situation. The mind has a way of taking care of itself; my mind was beginning to numb, to form a barrier of disbelief around the things that were happening, explaining them as either lucid nightmare or extreme hallucination. The fall I had just taken retreated like the distorted memory of a dream; it was the only way I could cope. It had become a case of either numbing over or driving quickly to insanity, and I knew which path would help me find Ellie, so I trekked on like a zombie returning to its village.

As I walked, silent and contemplative, I could only see dusty images beyond the yellow-orange circle of light I was in; a circle that moved with my every step like some phantom stagehand in the distance was following my theatrics. Occasionally I heard the beating of those leathery wings, but I never heard or saw more of the creatures that produced the noise. Once I thought I glimpsed a moist, khaki wing flit across the beam of light, but quickly dismissed it as I had to: as imagination.

God knows how long I wandered in that half-dazed fashion, tromping over the flat, rocky soil, never seeming to get any closer to the light. I found that darkness—and being stuck in the midst of it—is one of the worst torments to the soul. My mind felt like a butterfly, waiting for the slightest breeze to come and force it into flight. Shapes beyond the circle moved and rallied to let me pass without seeing them; great shapes that made me think of stone monsters, roughly humanoid and strangely chiseled. I tried not to think of the stone beings but instead of Ellie and home. It seemed that the light was deterring the monsters, and if I had given consideration to what would happen if the light went out, the butterfly of my mind would have flown and I would have gone over the mountain.

Finally, after what had been at least an hour of endless walking, I reached a lighthouse from which my yellow-orange spotlight shone. In a flash of curious lucidity it occurred to me that for every step I took toward the lighthouse, the light dimmed a proportional amount so as to always remain at a constant intensity, thus creating the illusion that you were never any closer to the source. It was not an odd or fancy lighthouse, but just like any you see on any coast, save this one had no windows or doors. A quick circumference of the structure showed it to be in a strange state of limbo; it was neither obviously used, nor run-down. A curious gaze far up the smooth, white wall, to the windows at the very top where the light came from, revealed no clues as to its occupants. The glow stayed on me as I explored the new terrain; the lighthouse was beside an ocean.

The sea was lit by an even flare like that of daylight toward dusk, like the forest above, only here it seemed to be a late-fall day. The sea itself contained quite an angry army of waves marching constantly on the shoreline, but when I stumbled upon a rowboat cast far above the high-tide line, I knew instinctively that it was my lot to battle those waves. The ocean seemed my only chance for escape, since I had explored aimlessly for an hour or so, finding only one change in the dark land I'd crossed: the unfathomable lighthouse and the sea I was now before—the sea the light had led me to.

As I stepped onto the stony beach the yellow-orange spotlight stopped, sliced off to a form a half circle that for some reason reminded me of a good dog that had reached the edge of its property and was dutifully waiting in case I should return. The wind had picked up again, not harshly, but cold and dully constant. As I dragged the boat toward the water I was glad that I hadn't had the chance to shake too much of my winter clothing in the forest above. The thought brought me again, momentarily, out of my mind-numbed stupor, and I cast wondering eyes above me, expecting to see in this fall-dusk the roots of trees and clumps of dirt hanging impossibly down and forming the sky. Instead I saw the white and gray brushstrokes of cloud cover and a bright spot over the waves I assumed was the sun, hidden from view. It was curious, but not alarming, as I sank back into my quiet stupor: there were more pressing issues at hand, issues the past and future had no business in.

The sand was rough, more like gravel than true sand, and it took quite a bit of work and back complaints to drag the boat down to the water. The waves, I could see now, broke quite a distance from the shore, growling and tumbling for some time, like a static-filled TV getting louder and louder, until they finally ran themselves out with tentative kisses of my shoes. The first wave to come so close took me by surprise and I jumped back like a child at play, glancing behind myself with embarrassment. It was then that my mouth gaped open with disbelief.

The land I had just crossed was completely gone, the effect being the same as I had experienced at the end of the tunnel, only now on a grand scale: a thick velvet curtain seemed to have been drawn across the edge of the beach, at the high-tide line, for as far as I could see in either direction. I could still feel a slight breeze stirring from the land beyond—could even hear creatures stirring—and I knew that what blocked my sight was no physical barrier, just complete darkness. Squinting, I could just make out the dim spot of the lighthouse like a circle painted on black cardboard, and if I concentrated enough, I could also make out the spotlight it cast, a sliver of color beyond the beach, waiting for me if I should return.

I pulled my eyes from the sight and plucked up the courage to step into the water, dragging the boat behind me. I felt exhausted, as if I was robotically performing this chore just so I could go to sleep and put a strange, hard day behind me. The water was ice-cold, gray, and unforgiving. It hissed gently around my ankles, ebbing and flowing with each new wave. The boat, likewise, would rise and fall with the water, first floating then becoming marooned on the pebbly beach below the waves. Eventually I dragged it out far enough to fully float; I was up to my thighs when a wave had passed, the water pressing against me with numbing precision. I took the chance to turn my back to the boat, holding it in position as I sat over the side, swinging my legs in behind me. As the next incoming wave sucked most of the water away the boat slumped under my weight, its bottom scraunching over the sharp rocks and pebbles below. I dug down for the oars, jostled into position, and began rowing to move myself away from the shore. My legs were drenched and cold, but as I rowed those first few strokes, I noticed dry patches already forming, the water evaporating (thankfully) at an uncanny pace; a pace so illogical I simply ignored it, tacking it to the outside of my numbed mind for later consideration.

Instead, I chose a realistic fear, one I could allow to take up my mind: the fear of the waves and current dragging me back to the beach before I could get away from them. Luckily I was fast enough, tossing on the unrelenting surf, the waves first soaking me as they broke on the boat, then raising me in their swells as I passed the break-line. The water that splashed upon me dried as quickly as before, leaving me dry seconds after the drenching. I had no real idea of where I was rowing to, I was just trying to go forward, away from the beach and the dark land and hopefully to somewhere I could fathom. It was only after I had rowed for perhaps half an hour, the sea having turned black beneath me as the waves chopped and sliced at my boat in the crisscrossed winds that blew first in my face and then on my back, that I broke my dazed dash and stopped rowing, pulling the oars up. As the water dribbled off their ends, I studied the distant shore.

I could see a huge section of the beach I had been on, the lighthouse now a dim glow like the after-image of a flashbulb on my retinas. I saw no signs of life anywhere along the beach. It looked like a lifeless, desolate illusion, the blackness of the land beyond so complete that I couldn't be sure if it *was* land beyond and not just more ocean, the beach nothing more than a long finger of beach stretching into the sea. It was only my own experience that told me otherwise. I turned the boat parallel to the shore, in order to row along the line of the beach until I found something helpful, when I caught a glimpse of something out the corner of my eye, further out to sea: a plain panel door standing in its frame, supported by no wall, bobbing impossibly a few feet away in the rolls of water.

I turned more fully in my seat, thinking my eyes had deceived me, but the sight changed none, the door bobbing by itself, never seeming in any danger of tipping over and sinking. I shrugged and maneuvered to approach it, and it was at that moment—at the moment my mind had just shrugged and accepted this sight as curious but perfectly acceptable—that I realized I had, in some crucial way, come to terms with my situation. I suddenly felt like I could fully function, using new parameters of logic based on this strange world, and that meant I could find Ellie. As I cautiously rowed toward the door my mind slipped back into gear, shaking the zombie-like numbness that had protected me this far.

My first thought was to circle the door, to get a full scope of what I was dealing with, but as I rounded to the far side, putting it between my boat and the shore, it quivered and fell, splashing silently into the water and disappearing. Astonished, but feeling even more brave now that the floating aperture had behaved reasonably, I rowed straight to where it had been, arriving in time to see a few stray bubbles surface in tiny hisses. As I rowed past the spot, trying to get a better angle, it suddenly sprang back to the surface in a frightening rush of water, once more bobbing impossibly between me and the expanse of ocean beyond.

I rowed around it a few more times, the door behaving exactly the same way each time: sinking as I put it between myself and the beach, then rising and bobbing as I came back to the other side again. On my last circle I saw that I needed no more evidence: whatever had led me this far was distinctly telling me which side of the door I had to enter, should I decide to do that. The decision took no time, as the same instinct that had driven me toward the lighthouse, then into the waves, now told me that the answer to my problems lay behind that floating door.

I slowly worked my way closer to it, the bow of my boat inadvertently knocking it with a dull thud against the frame, but the door stayed standing, as sturdy as if it had been set in a solid wall. Once close enough, the motion of the rolling sea scraping my boat against the frame with squeaks and splinters, I reached out and touched the door. Perhaps I had expected some revelation at the simple touch—a sudden answer as to where I was and how to find Ellie—but all I felt was a rough, wood-panel door, a chip of old varnish flecking off at the pressure of my nails.

I pulled the oars into the boat, which was now sideways to the door, rubbing against the frame but not drifting more than a few inches away from it. I scooted slowly across the bench, my shifting weight jostling the boat, and grasped the cold metal knob that gleamed dully in the gray light. It turned easily beneath my grasp, the door swinging silently open to reveal the entrance to a tunnel of earth; a tunnel lit by the same eerie red glow as the last one, and carrying the same thickly moist and slightly rotten sod odor to me. The sense of *deja vu* was nauseating, as the deep feeling of having traveled so far, only to have gone in a circle, sank in.

V

I stepped carefully out of the bobbing rowboat and through the door, half-expecting it to be an illusion and that I was, in fact, stepping onto the surface of the ocean beyond, but my feet hit solid ground and I stumbled to catch my balance.

Ahead, down the tunnel, I could see the staircase coming down to my level, and my first thought was that what had once been a door to a forest now led to an ocean. Upon closer scrutiny, however, I saw that I was now *behind* the staircase and that the tunnel dimmed off into darkness on the other side, as it had before. I crept a step forward, instinctively pushing the door closed behind me, but only when it snicked solidly shut did I think that I may not have wanted to do that. The red glow intensified around me as I spun around to catch the knob and open the door again, but it had disappeared, being replaced by a wall of earth—the dead end of a tunnel.

I turned back around and took a tentative step forward, my heart pounding maddeningly since, as I recalled it, the stairs had taken up the entire height and width of the tunnel: my eyes grew wide with the realization that the stairs would block me like the bars of a jail cell. Whatever force had driven me here had successfully trapped me behind the stairs.

When I reached the stairs, a few slow feet later, I grasped the risers blocking my walk and gazed down the tunnel like a prisoner gazing down his cell-block. I managed to refrain from screaming and pounding on the horizontal bars, but only because I knew no one would hear me. I looked up and saw the sky above, through the hole in the ground that led to this odd world of strange events. I was so infuriatingly close to freedom—but, for all I knew, miles from Ellie. I looked to my left and right and saw nothing but the same abundance of those red-eyed white worms, almost audibly squidging and burrowing in the moist earthen walls. The idea grasped me that all I had to do was follow suit: dig an alcove in the dirt wall and squeeze through to freedom. All I had to do was dig through that sour wall with my bare hands, serrating God knew how many of those hideous worms and insects with my nails. As my vision tunneled to the worms, they became more detailed, their ridges and bumps showing up in astonishing relief on their segmented bodies, my mind zooming in further for even more repulsive detail. They writhed, and I could well-imagine a tiny mouth, with tiny, stalagmite teeth, opening and closing like the jaws of a piranha. If I had felt chided by them before, now I felt they were about to burst with cruel, malicious hilarity.

I began to feel sick and backed away from the stairs, the walls seeming to turn into nothing but a writhing white mass of worms with insane red eyes and hungry mouths. The cloud in my mind became thicker again, numbing the edges, and I shied from each wall like I had just realized they were drawing closer; trying to suffocate me in a terrible death of worms. When my back came up against the wall behind me I screamed, and my mind broke into action for itself, leaving conscious fear and recognition behind. I ran forward, falling to my knees at the base of the stairs, and began to dig frantically with my hands at the right wall. I was so afraid of the worms and the smell and the light that I had ironically become heedless of them in my mania and was only mindful now of getting away as quickly as I could. As soon as my canine scratchings had dug a hole that seemed large enough, I forced myself through. More of the wall came crumbling onto me as I squeezed into the alcove, but I had reached the point of no return and I just kept pushing and pushing, forcing myself to the other side.

Finally I popped out and went sprawling onto the ground. The thought of turning and scrambling back up the stairs flashed through my mind, but then I thought again of Ellie...and saw that my nose rested inches from one of those accursed worms, the floor beneath also covered with the squirming, biting creatures. I screamed again and jumped up, pounding the dirt from my clothes and shaking violently to rid myself of the diseased soil, at the same time trying to run down the tunnel to the door. When I thankfully reached it, I threw myself against the wood, searching for the knob with my left hand. I found it and turned it, my weight forcing the door to spring suddenly open, and I went sprawling again, but this time onto the soft, green grass of the warm forest floor.

VI

I lay there for a few moments, recomposing my mind, just taking in the smell of the grass and the breeze perfumed with the sweet secretions of foreign flowers and trees. I rolled onto my back and looked at the doorway I had come through. The aperture made it look as though the hill was bleeding. But I was too thrilled to have wound up back in the forest to worry about how that red glowing doorway looked.

In fact, as I lay on my back gazing up at the purple-blue sky, it concerned me more that even though I had been gone at least two hours, the time of day in the forest appeared not to have changed by a minute. I realized that time must flow very differently here, and that this euphoric feeling of summer twilight could be mine forever if I simply stayed where I was. I began to nod off, a smile creasing my lips, and I may well have lain on the floor of that misty, twilit forest for hours, but for Ellie's distant voice drifting to me through the misty air. The plaintive sound shocked me out of my comfortable reverie and I sat bolt upright.

"Ellie," I breathed.

My head was filled with the early morning fuzz of recent sleep, and I assumed I had been dozing for some time; when I looked at my hands the dirt encrusted with the bodies of the worms was completely dry. I wrinkled my nose with disgust and stood and wiped them off as best I could on my jeans. I took off my sweater as well and shook it out, discovering only a few dried streaks of the muddy wall on it. Then I slung my sweater over my shoulder and began to walk away from the door, diagonally to the left, toward Ellie's voice and toward where I could see a groove that I hoped contained water slicing through the grass.

The forest was indescribably beautiful: fresh, serene, convalescent, the sounds of wildlife twinkling in the air around me. I cast a furtive glance over my shoulder at the hill where I had fallen through to the lighthouse, hoping I would find no more such surprises, at least not until I had been reunited with Ellie. Shortly I came upon the groove I had noticed, and it indeed turned out to be a crystal ribbon of water, so I knelt to rinse my hands in its delicious lapping trickles. Small, silver fish darted along below the surface, dodging my hands. I rinsed my hands then dipped them down and brought some of the clear water to my lips to drink, not realizing how thirsty I was until the first drops slid soothingly down my throat.

After relieving my thirst I stood and hopped across the shallow stream, hurrying in the direction of Ellie's cry through the silent majesty of the lush trees. Every now and then I would glimpse birds in the air; sudden bursts of darting colors: blue, red, yellow. Occasionally a human-like creature would jump from bough to bough, or tree to tree, high up in the green canopy. I heard chirpings and chatterings, child-like gigglings that reminded me of raccoons, and unseen teeth gnawing at the bark of the great sentinel plants. Yet even with this teeming, foreign life, I felt strangely calm. At times I almost forgot why I was wandering through the forest, tempted to simply lie down and gaze up at the bruised twilight sky draped like a sheet over the branches far above. But I kept moving on, dodging massive tree trunks every now and again, or scampering over boulders that seemed to have been aesthetically placed by hands, long enough ago for them to have grown thick coats of damp, fluffy moss.

I must have traveled for quite some time, but the light never diminished nor intensified, remaining always like the time of long summer days gone by when my mother called me to grudgingly return home to my bath and bed. At times the sensation was so intense that I felt as if I *was* ten again, dashing through the woods between my friend's house and my own after a hard game of backyard baseball. It was these instances of complete recollection that got me running, lest I should be late for my curfew—not to mention the TV shows I loved—and then grounded indefinitely from something necessary, like my bicycle. I would run then, as a boy, ducking under low branches, the wind combing my hair, being drawn deeper into the rhythms of my feet, foolishly wondering if that girl in homeroom even knew I existed. Then I would catch a glimpse of my hand pumping in the air and it would look old, the ring Ellie had given me catching a stray ray of light, and I would realize where I really was and who I was running after. Once the snap of reality was so great I almost cried, feeling like a kid callously thrust into the adult world, having skipped the important nostalgia-filled days of junior and senior high school; having been fitted instead with a collection of fading memories that seemed more like a movie than a life. I felt robbed, cheated, and slightly jaded, but the feelings passed reluctantly as I thought of Ellie's smiling, innocent eyes crying with abandonment, her small mouth curled down in fear, her scared voice quivering out my name into that wilderness of beauty and horror. My legs sped up a notch at once, as if to escape the wistful longings of the past, and I ran on.

Eventually I reached a clearing and stopped at the edge of it, hands on knees, catching gasps of air to regulate my breathing. The blood was pounding to my head. It felt like I had been running for over an hour, but time was so slippery that I soon gave up trying to calculate it. In front of me, across the clearing, I saw a small thatch-roofed cottage, its chimney puffing out a fine tendril of white smoke. Beside the front door was a pile of logs and a wheelbarrow. Hanging under the windows to either side of door were boxes of the most intensely colorful flowers I had ever seen. All harmless appearances aside, though, something subconscious in me stirred, and I knew, without a doubt, that I would find Ellie inside that cottage.

VII

I walked cautiously across the clearing until I reached a stone path that led to the front door. I trotted up it and brought my hand up to knock. It was only then, with my fist poised near the door, that I realized how angry I was. I took in a deep, calming breath, smoothed my clothes as if to straighten my thoughts, and thought that I should not take out my fears and irritations on whoever answered, since they may be entirely innocent. I rapped politely on the door. A squat, bald, old man who looked strangely like a tree stump answered, eying me suspiciously.

"Umm—yes—" I said, bringing my hand up to cover my mouth as I cleared my throat. "I'm—uhh—looking for someone..."

I trailed off, but the old man just stood before me, hunched, with one bushy eyebrow raised curiously. He was wearing a heavy beige shirt and leather vest, along with thick brown pants and large black boots, and I was surprised that he wasn't dead of heat exhaustion, especially with the fire he apparently had burning inside the cottage. I myself had long since stripped down to only my T-shirt and jeans; my sweater and thermal top now tied precariously about my waist— and I still found it warm, though not unbearable. The old man seemed quite comfortable in such temperatures, however, almost as if to him it was cold.

"A girl?" he suddenly asked, and my eyes grew wide with anticipation.

"Yes, that's right, a—"

"From there?" he cut in to ask, his crooked finger pointing over my shoulder, back the way I had come.

"I suppose," I agreed, turning back to him from my glance in the direction he pointed. There was now an old woman in the doorway, wearing the same outfit as the man had been, standing in the same hunched manner, only she had flowing white hair and a face that may have once been beautiful. She was pointing in the same crooked way as the man had been and she gazed at me with a brief, strangely knowing smile.

"How do you want me?" she asked in a voice that sounded just like the man's had; a voice that could easily pass for masculine or feminine, depending on which sex was producing it.

"Excuse me?" I replied, slightly taken aback. "What happen—"

"I am Eshwar—how do you want me to appear?"

"I don't understand... Where's the man I was talking to?"

"It's just me, dearie. Do you prefer a man or a woman? I am neither, but..." As the woman's voice trailed off her face stiffened and squared and her hair shrank back, along with her chest, until the bald old man stood once more before me. I gaped at him.

"Well?" he asked. "What do you deal better with? A man or a woman?"

I shook my head in brief amazement and I snapped my mouth shut.

"Umm, no offense, but I just want to find Ellie—"

"The girl?" he asked again, pointing his crooked finger once more. "From there?"

I didn't take my eyes off the man, glaring at him to stop stalling, and he began to change again. The transformation stopped cold half way, with the scraggly hair and semi-softened features of a person somewhere between a man and a woman, when Eshwar heard, as well as I did, Ellie's voice from within the cottage.

"James? Is that you?" She sounded afraid but relieved. I looked past Eshwar into the cottage but couldn't make anything out.

"Oh?" Eshwar said. "You know my present then?"

"Present?" I asked in disbelief, taking a step toward the door to push Eshwar out of the way. The creature's firm hand halted my movement, and it smiled happily up at me, its harsh green eyes glistening.

"That's correct, stranger: present. Mine. I found her."

"Look," I said, failing again to force my way into the cottage. "She's not something to be found or traded or given. She's not a *present*. She's a *person*, and she's my fiance."

"So you claim ownership, then?" Eshwar gleamed evilly.

"No," I growled, getting angry. "I don't *own* her—"

I gave a good shove to Eshwar this time, moving the creature enough to stumble into the cottage. The home was small—two rooms—and in the corner of the largest room, beside a small fire, nestled between shelves of books and pots and jars of leaves, there was a cage, from which Ellie peered out at me with relief and dismay. Eshwar let out a small cry, spinning around to face me again.

"Get out!" it ordered, forcing me to turn from Ellie. "I want to be alone!"

"Fine," I replied. "Let her go and we'll leave you be!"

"Not like that," Eshwar spat with contempt. "I want to be alone with my new pet—"

I hurried across the small room to the cage. When I touched Ellie's fingers a tear slipped from her eye, but her face remained set and determined.

"Stall," she commanded. "I'm almost out." She said it so discreetly, without seeming to even move her face, that I wasn't sure if I'd heard her or read her mind. Her eyes looked haggard, but her spirit was undeterred, so I turned back to Eshwar to carry out her wish. I felt Ellie's calming hand reach out and touch my shoulder.

"So, Eshwar," I began stiltedly, fighting back my anger and frustration. "Is this all your doing?"

"What do you mean?" it asked, genuinely shocked. "She came to *me*, in the tunnel. Fell right in my lap."

"She fell," I agreed, moving the conversation to a crude table decorated with a single flower in an earthen vase. "But not for you." I sat facing the cage and Eshwar sat across from me with his back to it. I caught Ellie's sly smile, then brought my attention back to Eshwar.

"Well for who else?" it asked, smiling at me like I was an idiot. "She fell into *my* lap."

"Not on purpose," I explained, not minding the ignorant circle of the conversation, since it bought Ellie time.

"Yes, yes," Eshwar muttered, eying me nervously like it had found a hole in its own logic, after all. "Well, you know, the Borders *are* acting strangely now. Letting all sorts in." Eshwar's face set and it looked at me pointedly. "But did you go to the graveyard on purpose?"

"Graveyard?" I asked, momentarily confused; it felt like I had been in the forest all my life.

"The graveyard...over there," Eshwar pointed, roughly in the direction of the red door between the trees. "The graveyard in Phillip's Stand?"

"In Phillip's Stand?" I clarified, understanding now, but wasting time.

"That's what you call it I believe," Eshwar answered. "Did you go there on purpose?"

"I suppose we did, yes."

"Why?"

I honestly had to think for a moment, and I cast a curious eye at Ellie, who was still fiddling noiselessly with the lock on the cage. Her face described determination, her eyes glassy with the seeds of frustrated, close-to-the-goal, tears.

"Ummm," I said, snapping back to Eshwar's attention. It sat staring at me as if hypnotized. "We went because of the ice storm. To walk in it."

"So you came on your own! You're *both* mine!" Eshwar shrieked joyfully.

"Hey," I agreed, sitting back in the small chair and throwing my hands up. "If that's the way you see it..."

"But let me ask you," I continued quickly, stopping Eshwar's thought just as it opened its mouth. It shut its mouth again with an audible click and considered me curiously. "Where are we?" I finished. A question creased Eshwar's brow as if it couldn't understand how I could be so stupid.

"You're in Perendjo, don't you know?"

"Oh," I replied, truly dumbfounded. "And this is all Peren— uhhh—*that* place? The forest and the lighthouse—?"

"You've been to the beach?" it cut in, shocked.

"Yes..." I agreed suspiciously.

"What's it like?" Eshwar wondered, excited. I heard a quiet click and saw Ellie's face light up with a triumphant smile. I glanced back at Eshwar, but it hadn't heard, apparently entranced by the thought of the beach and the lighthouse.

"Well," I said, almost forgetting what I was saying. "It's very pebbly and dark, and the sea was cold and fierce—have you ever been there?"

"No," Eshwar said, shaking its head violently. "She won't let me. Not my place. Besides, the Golgantry scare me—their wings—" Eshwar's face screwed up in revulsion and I tried to reconcile what it had said with what I'd seen. I thought of the wing I had glimpsed in that strange orange light, and had the sick feeling of finding out, in hindsight, that I had been inches from some disaster. Eshwar must have seen my shocked face.

"You *saw* them?"

"Yes," I intoned, mesmerized by my memory and the meaning Eshwar had given it. Eshwar shuddered, feeling for me, and I noticed out of the corner of my eye that Ellie had slipped out of the cage and had taken a length of rope from a hook beside it. She had expertly fashioned a lasso, and as Eshwar grabbed its chair to move closer and hear my story, she pounced and slipped the loop over its head, pulling it tight to trap its arms at its side and its body to the chair-back. Her face had been a study of vengeful anger: teeth clenched, eyes flashing, movements nimble.

Eshwar shrieked with surprise and I leaped up, sending my own chair flying. Ellie, meanwhile, quickly passed the remaining length of rope several times around Eshwar and the chair—even once or twice around the seat, to anchor its twisting legs that flailed danger-ously in an attempt to escape. As Eshwar pistoned its legs below the knees, rocking the chair, and pumped its small hands open and closed into fists, I moved to Ellie's side and steadied the chair as she tied a knot behind Eshwar's back. The creature shrieked again, rocking the chair harder, so I merely pushed with its rocking motion, spilling Eshwar and the chair onto its side. Still Eshwar fidgeted, causing the chair to spin in maddening circles such that it bumped into things.

"Come on!" Ellie gasped, smiling proudly at her work as she grasped my hand and jumped over the spinning creature on the floor. I dodged with her to the front door, and in one impressive wave of motion, she threw the door open and I ran through, with her in tow, slamming the door again behind us. As we ran down the stone path across the clearing we could hear Eshwar shrieking frustratedly inside.

"The sea! The sea!" I heard it yell as we entered the forest on the far side of the clearing. "I want to see the sea!" The last shriek was exceptionally horrible, calling to memory the leathery wings and strange noises of things Eshwar had referred to the Golgantry... I clutched Ellie's hand more tightly and ran a little faster, back along the creek's edge to the door between the trees.

VIII

We stopped sometime later, the cottage now many bends of the river behind us, its chimney-smoke no longer visible by any stretch of the imagination. Ellie hadn't wanted to stop at first. We'd hardly spoken as we jogged through the trees and grass, and her wide eyes told me that she was terrified from confusion, as I had once been. Before, she'd been channeling all her energy into her escape, and any thoughts of where she was, or how she could possibly be there, had been shelved in lieu of necessary focus. I understood her fear, but I was also plain tired out from all the running.

"Let's just catch our breath for a second," I pleaded, and tugged Ellie down onto a flat, moss-covered rock beside me. "I'll try to explain as best I can..." I panted. Ellie looked around objectively, her frightened eyes following the path of a bird, or else the flight of one of the strangely humanoid creatures far up in the distant canopy, then rested apologetically on me again, with a weak smile. In that smile I saw my own insanity, and I knew that this was how mad people viewed the world: beautiful, yet dangerous; normal, but not possible.

"It's beautiful," she whispered, casting another quick glance around at the sparkling emerald trees and the lush carpet of grass. "But it's so...so..."

"I know," I whispered back, hugging her to me. "It's a menace. Eshwar...the bird-things...and none of it makes any sense..."
Ellie broke my embrace. She wiped small tears from her eyes but said nothing, and we both spent several minutes in contemplative silence.

"Whew!" she finally gasped, like a person overcoming nerves and just saying what's on her mind. "It sure is hot!"

"Yeah," I agreed, trying to sound normal. Ellie took off her sweater and tied it around her waist.

"Where's your coat?" I asked, trying to keep her talking. Despite what I'd said, I had no idea of how to explain any of it.

"Eshwar took it," she sighed heavily.

"Oh. Right."

Ellie sighed heavily again and watched another bird dart through the trees. I could tell she was a ball of anxious energy, sitting still only because she thought it made me happy. She wanted only to go home. I did, too, but at the same time I found myself lulled again by my surroundings; and now that we were out of its cottage, I didn't even fear little Eshwar popping up unexpectedly—assuming he'd managed to untie himself.

"What was it like?" I finally asked. I stood slowly and motioned for to walk beside me, an invitation she gladly accepted, slipping her hand comfortably into mine.

"What was what like?" she asked as we ambled on. Her countenance was dazed, but she was doing well at hiding it. She exuded a feeling of deflation, a feeling of tired recognition that things would never be the same and all she could do was get used to it.

"Eshwar," I said carefully, trying to judge if this was the best approach, after all,. "I mean, falling or whatever happened..." Ellie was silent. She sighed heavily, following the ground below he feet with her eyes. I didn't think she was going to answer, but I could see by her face that she was just trying to put events in order for herself, first. To her, the time had whizzed by in a frozen emotion, now released in one deft blow, falling on her like a sack of sand.

"Well," she finally said. "I remember wanting to sit in the graveyard for hours—it looked so pretty with the ice and the snow. And I remember you pulling me close and saying that we should go back, and I was about to answer when I fell." I think she was telling herself, more than telling me, what had happened.

"It was just that sudden," she explained. "I fell down the stairs and I felt stupid because that was exactly why you'd wanted to go back, and then I was afraid I'd broken something. I had just begun to stand up when I felt someone grab me. It was Eshwar, and before I could ask who she—it was a woman then—was, she threw a sack over my head and knocked back down, tying it around my ankles. I screamed out to you and tried to thrash around, but she was very strong and suddenly I was being dragged quickly away, my head bumping along the ground. Then I was lifted and carried over her shoulder, I suppose, but it was then that I passed out."

A tear oozed from her eye and I wiped it away in a weak attempt at understanding. I squeezed her hand reassuringly.

"I was terrified," she recalled, stifling her tears. "I thought I was too old to get kidnapped and I couldn't imagine what an old woman wanted with me. By this time I was lying on the ground, but I had the distinct impression of being inside. It was warm, so I imagined we were in the woman's house, and I began to cry a little because the sack was still over me.

"The next thing I knew my ankles were untied and I was jerked out of the covering, but before I could move or regain my composure, I heard the cage door clang into place and the lock drop. I leaped to my feet, and there was Eshwar, smiling on the other side of the bars, only now he was a man. That was very confusing, on top of everything else, and I just gaped at him. As he turned to do something else, I watched him transform back into a woman, and I just couldn't believe my eyes." She shrugged. "So I guess I didn't. I concentrated on a way out. I knew this wasn't just a kidnapping...I even considered that I was actually still a crumpled form at the bottom of the stairs, having a comatosed dream." She smiled at me then, her eyes glistening with tears, and snuffled in a deep breath. "I guess you came just in time, because if I had of escaped, I would just have run blindly..."

"So what happened to you?" she asked. "And where did Eshwar say we were?" She looked at me and smiled suspiciously. "And are you sure this isn't a dream?"

"I'm not sure of anything, to be honest."

I told her about the hole and the tunnel with the worms and the red light, and how I had come to the forest only to end up falling through a hole myself into some world somehow *below* the forest. I tried to describe the terror and images of my fall, of my hours stumbling through the dark sea-world with the great leathery birds, and she shuddered in all the right places, but I knew, to her, it was just a story. I explained about the sea and the impossible door, and my imprisonment with the white worms in the red tunnel, and how I escaped and ended up once more in the forest, where I fell asleep, waking up only when I heard her call for me. Finally, I tried to describe how it was running to her, how I had slipped into some memory-spell and had believed I was only ten, running in the summers of youth, and how disorienting it was to discover that I was not ten, and that I did not know, really, where I was, and that I was afraid I would never find her again.

When we arrived at the red door between the trees, relief swept over both our tired faces, and we trotted faster, like ponies in the home stretch. It wasn't until we were a few feet away that I noticed the stump that looked kind of like a hunched old man, and I squeezed Ellie's hand, bringing us both to a sudden halt.

IX

"Well, well, well," Eshwar said, rising from where he had been sitting against one of the trees of the doorway. "If isn't they who think they can just tie Eshwar down."

Ellie shot me a terrified look. It was almost angry, as if I, or someone, had promised that this would not happen.

"Move out of our way, Eshwar," I demanded, but my voice lacked any real conviction.

"No," he decided. "First you must show me the Lands Below."

"What?" I asked, understanding only that he was offering some form of deal that may secure our freedom.

"The Lands Below, friend," Eshwar explained companionably, taking a few business-like steps toward us. Ellie tugged on my sleeve, which she held tight in her fist, and I could feel her trying to decide whether to hold her ground, back off, or just bolt.

"What's he talking about?" she whispered frantically; rhetorically.

"The Lands Below?" I clarified.

"That's right," Eshwar pointed up the hill that the red door was set in. "I know where the entrance is—I saw you use it. But you must first guide me through the Lands Below if you want to be let go."

I shook my head slowly. The last thing I was going to do was risk my life down there again, especially with Ellie in tow and a creature I didn't trust along for the ride. All I wanted to do was go home.

"No," I said, trying to sound knowledgeable. "You have to go alone."

"I don't think so," Eshwar replied, but he seemed uncertain, so I drove my wedge in further.

"Yes, it's true," I nodded enthusiastically. "There's only one light in the lighthouse. As long as you stay in its beam, you'll be fine."

Eshwar considered what I said very carefully. "What about the Golgantry?"

"Golgantry?" I clarified, not understanding at first. Ellie tugged on my sleeve again, and when I glanced at her, her eyes were glassy and wild with terror. Hurriedly, I continued my bluff, "Oh, the *Golgantry*. Well, I barely knew they were there. I heard them, but they stayed out of the light."

"Hmmm," Eshwar paced, apparently oblivious to the real threat Ellie posed to him. Her eyes had looked as they had when she had pounced on him before, and I knew it was only my calmness that was preventing her from doing the same now. Eshwar stopped and supported his chin with one gnarled hand, narrowing his eyes at me.

"What else is down there? Does Perendjo go any lower?"

I shrugged. "I didn't find it if it does. All I found was the door, which brought me back here."

"Where's the door?" he snapped, his eyes becoming excited.

"In the sea."

"Yes," he growled. "I want to see the sea."

Ellie relaxed just a touch and let go of my sleeve.

"Well..." he began anew, pointing an accusatory finger at us and narrowing his eyes to dangerous slits. "I would still—"

And I will never know what Eshwar's final proposition was to be, for at that moment Ellie had simply had enough: she lunged around me at the little creature. He shrieked and tried to duck, transforming instantly into a woman in an effort to confuse its predator, but Ellie managed to hooks its collar and pulled it back to her harshly, throwing it on the ground. Her teeth were clenched in a violent pout; her eyes concentrated on the strange figure's shocked face, which had become a man's once more.

"Wh—?" Eshwar managed before the wind was knocked out of him as he hit the ground. I backed up a step, gaping with disbelief.

Ellie put a foot under the creature's chin, holding its head in place, then knelt down with a knee on his chest. Eshwar flailed madly, but Ellie merely hunched over and grasped his branch-like arms at the wrists, pinning them to the grassy floor. A sliver of drool leaked from the corner of Eshwar's mouth, and its eyes darted from Ellie to me, asking someone to help him. I just stood there, gaping.

"Now you listen," Ellie growled. "We're leaving and you can't stop us. You do whatever the hell you want when we're gone, but if you get in our way again, I'll kill you."

I believed her, as did Eshwar, by his face, and a chill ran up my spine. It made all the arguments we'd ever had pale to nothing more than a child's tantrum. This was real anger: primal, dangerous, brought on by real pain.

"Yes," I heard Eshwar gasp through his diminishing air supply; his fear seemed tangible in the air around them.

Ellie sprang up and stood glaring down at the figure threateningly. Eshwar squirmed a little, rolled onto his side, and coughed harshly, holding his throat. He shook his head to clear his thoughts and rose slowly, brushing himself off with wary glances at Ellie. He turned and walked slowly up the hill, taking a few tentative steps to test and see if Ellie would pounce again anyway, then he ran, darting up the slope to the top of the hill, changing on the way into a woman.

Once she reached the top, she turned and looked back at us with such sadness on her face that it almost made me feel guilty.

I nodded slightly, to be polite, I guess, and then Eshwar turned and vanished, falling through the hole to the Lands Below. I wondered briefly what sights Eshwar would see as it tumbled down the to the world below.

Timidly, I reached out and took Ellie's hand. She squeezed mine tightly, a tear slipping from her eye. I squeezed her hand back and smiled weakly, assuring her that she had done the right thing, when all was said and done, then I tugged her lightly through the red door between the trees and we dashed madly for the stairs and the cemetery in Phillip's Stand.

The graveyard was just as we had left it: drowsing under a thick, new snow with crystalline icicles hanging from the trees. We quickly put our sweaters back on, then we walked up the black snake of a path toward the gate and the short walk home.

As we left the cemetery, Ellie glanced back in, a strange smirk on her lips.

Pitæthi

Hugh Pippin lent precariously over the rim of the well and listened more closely for the sounds to reach him. The sun was warm on his back and as sweat slipped down his neck it tickled him, engulfing his body in a spasmodic flit that straightened him up. He sucked in a breath and narrowed his eyes at the horizon, as if he'd intended to sit up, regardless of the tickle.

"Murmurs," he whispered, his head cocked like a dog watching its can of food rotate on the can opener. Hugh's head slowly lowered again, bringing his ear closer to the noises that leaked from the well-hole.

To the casual listener it would have sounded like wind whipping in gusts through a tunnel, but Hugh was no casual listener. He, like his father before him, and his grandfather before that, called himself a Listener, the ominous capital "L" enough to have the family shunned by the local Ladies' Church Auxiliary. No, the Pippins had never been your casual listeners.

"Hugh?" a woman's voice called from the house. He stopped what he was doing long enough to offer a stilted wave across the weedy backyard.

"What are doing?" she asked more pointedly.

"Listening," he hissed, and on cue the whipping winds from the well moaned more loudly, like air rushing through old vents and rattling dead leaves on the other side.

To humor him, Hugh's wife stood at the back door with her arms crossed and strained her ears. Her husband was a dull bump in the long grass maybe a hundred feet away, still with his hand held up, fingers splayed, asking her to shush. She could hear nothing; maybe the wind slamming against the eaves of the old house.

"Hmph!" she finally decided and spun on her heel, letting the screen door slam shut behind her. It was hot alright, and she half-wondered if the sun hadn't baked her dear husband's brain. He'd been going soft, as they say, for a couple of weeks now.

"Just like his father," she tutted, stalking across the kitchen and grabbing the phone on the wall. She dialed a number and put the receiver to her ear, rolling her eyes impatiently as the other end rang a third time.

"Doris?" she asked rhetorically when the phone was finally answered. "Rebecca. What are you doing?"

"Oh, just some cooking," Doris answered slowly. She knew that Rebecca Pippin only called for one reason, at a time when there was housework to be done. "What's wrong?"

Rebecca sighed as if she hadn't realized anything was until Doris had asked.

"Well, it's Hugh again."

"Listening?" Coming from anyone else, it would have been a shaded, demeaning question, but from Doris it was a real concern.

"Yeah...he's at the well again."

"Why don't you ask him what he's doing?"

"He just tells me to shush—"

The screen door creaked open and Hugh stepped into the kitchen with a very dour expression. He saw Rebecca on the phone and nodded once at her, absently, then moved across the room and into the hallway, opening the basement door.

"Uhh...can I call you back, Doris?" Rebecca asked hurriedly. "He just came in."

"Sure," was the reply, but Rebecca hadn't actually waited for it before she hung up. She ran over to the basement door and looked down the stairs into the darkness. When Hugh didn't turn the lights on first, it worried her.

"Hugh?" she called.

"I'm working, honey!" he called back happily.

"On what?"

"You know—my *work* !"

Rebecca sighed and straightened up, crossing her arms decidedly and chewing her lower lip. Hugh's work involved the same thing his father's had, and, apparently, the same thing as the infamous Grandfather Pippin. It was a continuing process, passed on from generation to generation of the recent Pippin line. It was also a process that had driven the other two Pippin men mad, leaving them in a bewildering dementia that had lasted until they died. Rebecca was worried her husband was now well on his way down the same harried course.

When she'd married Hugh, ten years before, he'd been a fun-loving, but desolate, man. Early on in the relationship she'd met Hugh's insane father and had learned of the Pippins' leaning toward dementia, but just as snow is forgotten in summer, Rebecca hadn't been able to imagine the same fate awaiting Hugh. She had heard the talk, too, of the family madness, but had written it off as the gossip of jealous old maids, which it mostly was, but even gossip usually has a kernel of truth, as Rebecca had found out two years down the road when she'd first caught Hugh "listening."

What he was listening for, however, had never been satisfactorily answered, in Rebecca's humble opinion. *Them, You know,* and *I hope we never find out* were hardly real answers to such a simple question. She'd tried to find out for herself once, covertly, when Hugh was away, but the dusty old tomes he kept in his basement "workroom" hadn't elicited any coherent answers.

At first glance they'd appeared to be nothing more than a carpenter's mathematical doodlings, but upon closer study Rebecca had discerned certain markings and abbreviations that had abhorred her for no good reason. With a certain amount of awe and horror, Rebecca had been able to distinguish the diagrams of buildings which, along with a larger map that showed where each building was located, described an entire town. Above some of the buildings—toward the start of the collection of three tomes—she had seen scrawled in a stilted hand "Proved," and on the others where "Proved" had not been added, the original word still remained: "Speculated." Halfway through the third tome the handwriting had changed to a hand she'd recognized as her husband's, and upon a brief glance back again, she'd noticed certain layouts where her own husband had crossed out "Speculated" to clarify, "Proved." The whole thing had left her so unsettled that she had never again looked at the books, or even set foot in Hugh's workroom, and had not thereafter tried to imagine what he was up to when he disappeared for hours into the basement.

She shifted her weight now to the other foot and sighed again, but kept her arms crossed. Lately he'd been going downstairs a lot—with the lights off—and when he did eventually resurface, it was always with a glassy-eyed stare that saw, but did not register. They were close, he'd whispered one night the week before, almost as if he'd been talking to himself. His eyes had seen her for one fleeting instant, then he'd shaken his head to clear his thoughts and had looked back down at the corn on his plate.

"Who's close?" she'd asked, but he hadn't said another word. He'd simply given her a grin that said he'd take care of everything, if she'd let him.

"Not to worry," she breathed, gazing down the cold flight of creaky old stairs. The familiar rainbow patterns of light were flickering on the walls and floor, emanating from Hugh Pippin's workroom with the disturbing absence of any sound whatsoever. Rebecca sighed again and slowly turned away, unable, still, to break her nerves and walk down the steps to simply look and see what her husband was up to.

The prismatic glow whispered over Hugh Pippin's smiling face. His eyes were closed and appeared completely relaxed, but not sleeping. On the desk across from the recliner he sat in, the third tome was opened to a page only half filled with writing. Almost looming over it, standing on a two-inch tall pedestal, was a crystal pyramid, from which the colored bands of light emerged. The source of the radiance was apparently internal, as no other light in the whole basement had been turned on, and the bands flickered in such a way as to denote that the source was rotating within the pyramid. A slight chuckle came from Hugh's closed lips and his smile widened briefly in response, then relaxed again to a more natural position.

"I've heard the murmurs," he said softly. "I'm hear to see them."

He chuckled again, then suddenly his expression fell completely, leaving his face like a blank slate. He stirred in the recliner, the shifting of his weight popping the chair upright, with the footrest still extended. Hugh didn't seem to notice: the rainbow glow from the pyramid stopped without warning and his body didn't move again for several hours.

* * *

It was completely black when Hugh opened his eyes, but from the shrill blast of wind on his face, he knew that he was outside. He could smell a woodfire burning somewhere, the scent almost overpowering in a world where his sight had been rendered useless. Hugh took a step forward, slowly, his hands out, groping for the statue he knew was there. Once his fingers had found it, he let his hands work down the long, cold, tendril of a stone arm that ended not in a hand, but in a slow taper that finally rounded off. Hugh was smiling broadly.

"Line up with the arm," he mumbled to himself, turning in the direction it pointed. He walked forward three steps, stopped, and turned to his left, then walked on again, thereby passing the odd statue. Every ten steps he announced a number, counting up as he walked down the street by memory. Over the last fifty years the Pippin men had mapped out most of the streets of Pitæthi, but had yet to enter all of the buildings their work had assured them were there. It was a slow process, but Hugh was certain he was getting close now.

"Fifteen..." he mumbled, moving slowly forward, "...sixteen...seventeen..."

He stopped and turned to his right, then began to walk forward again, his arms outstretched once more, and groping. Just as he'd expected, after eight steps his fingers found the rough wood of a door. He ran his fingertips carefully down it, smiling more broadly, until they distinguished a chilly knob sticking out of the splintered surface. He closed his fist around it, then slowly turned the device, unlatching the door with a soft click. Weak yellow light burst from the cracked door and Hugh blinked twice rapidly as his eyes adjusted to it. He chuckled softly to himself then slid through the door and into the room.

"I've heard the murmurs," he said with another light chuckle. "I'm hear to see them."

The door snapped closed behind him.

The room was lit with the yellow glow of candles, though no candles were to be seen amongst the sparse decor. At a rough wooden table sat an old man with puffy white sideburns and an impatient demeanor. The walls held no coverings, and apart from another door behind the old man, the small square space was completely uninteresting.

"Hmph!" the old man declared, shaking his head slightly at Hugh. "Took you long enough to find me!"

"Grandfather?" Hugh guessed, judging by the few pictures he'd seen.

The old man sighed, then tried to smile, an expression that did not suit his visage. "Sorry to snap, son. Guess I forgot how difficult it is from your side."

"But...you're dead, aren't you?"

"I suppose," he chuckled naturally, then reconsidered. "To one way of thinking. But surely you didn't come here to talk about me?" Hugh, amazed, simply shook his head *no*.

"Well," Hugh's grandfather decided, pushing his chair out on scratchy legs and standing, "I'll get them..." He stepped the short distance to the door beside him and opened it, his countenance one of near-impatience. Beyond, Hugh saw more cloying darkness, but also what appeared to be the faint, distant outline of a moon.

"Where's that...?" he whispered, more to himself than anything. His grandfather glanced over with a sly smirk and winked, then leaned out into the darkness and made a strange guttural noise that sounded as if the old man was clearing his throat, except that it had a peculiar cadence that belied language. Moments later Hugh heard a fluting cry echo from the darkness beyond the door, and the flapping of leathery wings. His mouth twitched into a nervous grin as he recognized the noise from his previous wanderings in the black streets of Pitæthi; it was a wet sound that made one think of wings holding up thick beasts that by all rationale should not have gained flight. All his adult life he'd been working for this—as had his father and grandfather before him—but suddenly he was not so sure he wanted to meet the living inhabitants of Pitæthi.

Grandfather Pippin made another guttural charge, which was quickly answered by the trill of the flute-noise, and followed almost instantly then by two or three more flute-like replies. The wings' disturbances grew louder, until finally Hugh heard heavy feet take purchase on the ground just outside the door.

"Only one of you?" the old man said with a curt nod. "It's my grandson."

"Where's my father?" it suddenly occurred to Hugh. "Why isn't he here, too?"

"Your father," the old man replied skeptically, "prefers the forest above, and the company of his own kind, in Lithari."

"Lithari?" Hugh asked with genuine bewilderment. "But I thought that was just a simple city—?"

"It is," his grandfather growled slowly, glancing at the door as it opened a bit wider, pulled free from his grasp by something outside. He stepped back and pushed the chair in to the table, then smiled at Hugh and took in a deep breath.

"The Golgantry," the elder Pippin announced proudly as a creature stepped through the aperture into the yellow light. Hugh sucked in a stilted breath, but tried his damnedest to hide his surprise.

"Hello..." he mumbled, with a slight bow.

The creature's skin crackled like dried leather as it walked. It was the color of wet bark, and seemed almost to be a walking tree, except for the leathery wings that flapped unconsciously behind its torso. As the creature shrugged its shoulders to better fold its wings, Hugh noticed the arms were tendrils of branch-like flesh that ended not in hands but rather, like the statue he had only ever felt, in a thin taper that rounded off to a smooth stump. With a quick glance, Hugh noticed that the creature's legs were the same way, the stumps leaving tiny round depressions in the soil behind it as it moved past the table, toward Hugh. The younger Pippin took in another quick breath and looked to the face—or what he assumed to be a face—for eyes. He found none, just a rounding off of the torso a foot above the shoulders, bringing the creature's full-height to some seven feet, the same veined-and-tendoned pattern of its body continuing onto its head. Two of the thick tendons moved apart on the top of the creature's head, and Hugh got the sensation that it was about to speak, when his grandfather cut it off.

"The Golgantry built Pitæthi," his grandfather explained with pride. "They have no eyes, as you can see, it being pitch-black in the Lands Below. But they can hear...and speak some English, luckily."

"Very lucky," Hugh mumbled; he could see why his dad would prefer the company of other people in fabled Lithari, the great city at the edge of the forest of Perendjo. That's where the Pippins had been striving to go all these years, by way of Pitæthi and the Lands Below— why Grandfather Pippin had opted to stay on the first rung, Hugh could not, at that moment, guess.

"I'm glad to meet you," the Golgantry suddenly said in a voice that sounded like a tuning fork dipped in mucous. "Your grandfather is proud of your progress."

"Thank you..." Hugh said as if guessing at the correct response, then he turned to his grandfather, "Have you been to Lithari, then? Is this the way?"

"Lithari?" the Golgantry coughed. It lapsed into a momentary trill of its true fluting-noise, the sound intense and piercing in the small room. Outside, beyond the now-closed door, Hugh heard others that must have accompanied it flute a quick reply.

"These Golgantry have sedentary brothers in the forests above," the elder Pippin explained apologetically, then added. "They never go up there."

"Oh," Hugh replied, flicking a quick grin at the quiet Golgantry. "If you want to go," the old man offered, "they won't hurt you. All you have to do is follow the lighthouse to ocean."

"The ocean...?"

"Yes...there's a door in the sea that will take you to Perendjo."

Hugh shrugged, unwilling now to be so adventurous, "I don't understand...maybe next time."

"Of course," the old man offered with a small, polite nod.

"But why...?" Hugh began, then turned to Golgantry. "Why did you call to us?"

"Your grandfather listened," the creature responded in its strange twinkling trill. "And he taught you how to listen...and the other, he taught. We have been talking for a long time. Some of your kind hear better than others."

"Now you have us," Hugh stated politely, "what can we do for you? Grandfather...what do they want?"

Grandfather Pippin shrugged. "The same as all of us—to explore mythical lands they've only known through fables. They've heard of our home—"

"*Our* home?" Hugh spat incredulously. "But if they can't see—!"

"We can hear, taste, and feel, young Pippin," the creature trilled;

Hugh shot a horrified glance at his grandfather.

"But they can't just waltz down the streets of New York City, can they?"

"I'm afraid they only want to rediscover what was once their home..."

"What?" Hugh gasped. "*Re*-discover—?"

"And reclaim," the Golgantry added almost as an afterthought, "what our stories say is ours."

By some miracle, Hugh Pippin managed to open the door and leap from the room, then run blindly back along the course he had taken to his grandfather. Above him he heard leathery wings take flight, but if they intended to hurt him or try to stop him, the Golgantry thankfully failed on both counts.

Hugh burst into the kitchen awash with sweat, his face bright red and his heart beating rapidly in his heaving chest. Rebecca dropped the glass she was washing into the sink and ran to her husband's side, convinced he'd had a heart-attack.

"Hugh! What is it?"

He took several deep breaths, consciously trying to calm himself down and slow his breathing. He was mostly successful, and after another large gulp of air, he grasped his wife's shoulder not only for support, but also as a way of comforting her.

"I'm okay now, Rebecca..." he gasped. "But you have to listen to me. They're coming...they want to take it all back..."

"Who is?" she asked painfully. "What are you talking about, Hugh? And what do you get up to down there?" She led him across the room to a chair and lowered him carefully into it, then turned and poured him a glass of water, which he took thankfully and drained in a few big gulps.

"The Golgantry," he replied serenely, scanning his wife's face for any signs of comprehension. "I had no idea..."

His eyes were wide and bright, and Rebecca ran her fingers through his hair soothingly, trying to smile in the face of an obvious breakdown.

"What's this?" she asked sweetly, humoring him as she would a child. Had Hugh been less concerned about what he'd recently learned, he would have sensed her tone and clammed up, but instead he mumbled on.

"My grandfather's was working to let them back in...and he got Dad and me into it, too..."

"Your grandfather?" his wife asked, scrunching her brow with disbelief.

"Yes," Hugh nodded, meeting her eyes for just a second, his own widening briefly with realization. "But he must need someone already here, on this side... And my father never found him..."

"Honey," Rebecca said slowly, with all seriousness, bending down beside him and taking his hand in hers. "You're scaring me, hon. Your grandfather's dead—*and* your father—"

He cut her a look and narrowed his eyes suspiciously, running a loose tongue over his bottom lip. He grunted and seemed to reach some conclusion, then narrowed his eyes further and shook his head to clear his thoughts.

"I know that," he finally snapped, standing up with such force that his chair toppled over behind him. Rebecca jumped to her feet, backing away a step. His face had lost its wistfully transfixed stare and he had obviously become aware who he was talking to.

"Never mind, honey, I'll take care of it."

And before she could respond, Hugh Pippin dashed out the back door and ran straight to the well, crouching down beside it and cocking his ear attentively.

The Dog and the Red Room

I know all about the last painting in Irene Burgman's last show: Number 22, "Nicholas," a beautiful painting of the artist's dog against a background of deep blue and purple velvets that look real enough to grasp. I know all about it because I was there when she painted it, and for this reason I also know why the painting wasn't on the curator's show-inventory list, or why there was no date on its back. I know all of this because of the dog.

I don't recall when I first became aware that a dog appeared to be following me. I was out and about one day, doing errands, when I noticed the soft clink of the tags around its neck; a sound that I seemed to have been hearing for some time, but hadn't fully registered as following me until that moment. It sounded quite close, so I looked down with a smile to greet my new companion, but I saw nothing there; nothing behind me, either. Shaking my head, I continued on.

The sound continued as well, sporadically, like wind chimes blown by an unfelt breeze. It was almost as if the dog—if indeed it was a dog—would only make itself known when I had fully dismissed, and nearly forgotten, it. Every time I heard the tags I would stop and look around myself; every time I would see nothing but my own foolish shadow mocking my movements.

My errands took me on a foot-journey of about forty-five minutes, but it wasn't until I neared my home that I fancied I heard the precise click of claws on the sidewalk behind me, along with the quiver of the tags. I stopped once more, this time turning to the sound and bending over as if to greet an actual dog.

"Here, boy," I offered, holding out my hand for the animal to smell. I heard the scuttle-click of its claws and could imagine the dog doing a nervous dance before me, unsure of whether or not to approach. I got the distinct impression that it was a mid-sized dog, even going so far as to envision a black Labrador. It was quite gentle, even harmless, and I barely jumped when something cold and wet brushed against the thumb of my dangling hand.

"That's it," I said, recovering from my mild shock. "What do you want, boy?" Most people ask dogs serious questions which, of course, go unanswered, but seeing as this dog had already displayed itself to be anything but an average dog, I allowed that it may break some aural, as well as visual, norms and respond to my question. In a way, I suppose it did.

Just below the knee, where pants hang out in a straight line, I felt a tug on the fabric. A playful, but insistent, growl accompanied this ghostly pull, so I instinctively straightened back up, ready to move.

"Where to?" I asked in the tone reserved for animals and small children, and I heard a small bark in response and the excited back-tracking of claws away from me.

"Well don't run off!" I cautioned, glancing around for any spies. "I won't be able to keep up!"

The possibility of insanity flitted across my mind like the sudden dart of a spring bird, and I considered that acquiring a ghost-dog was surely the least harmful form of the disease. Then the dog barked lightly again and began to click slowly away, stopping every so often to, I imagine, cast a glance over its shoulder at my progress. I quickly followed the now-constant click and jangle back down the street the way I had just come. I tried my hardest not to look as if I was following something that wasn't there, but the only person I met began to wave, then seemed to think the better of it, giving me instead a curious look. I just smiled politely and hurried after the ghost-dog.

I was led right back into town to a house in the midst of businesses. It is an old structure with a grand porch and wood siding, and may well be the last remnant of the town before the city. I had often admired the building as I passed it from time to time; the wood carvings hanging from the gutters and around the gable windows are an artistry the new, material world seems to have forgotten. Only twice before had I actually been inside the house: The lower floor now housed an art gallery, and the upper floors, as I understood it, served as the curator's apartment and storage areas.

Inside it was cool and dark and, as I had expected, between shows. Various covered paintings were leaning against the walls, waiting to be attached to their respective positions; I could hear the curator in the back somewhere, perhaps hanging some of the pieces for the new show. The dog, however, had no interest in the back, trotting instead up the stairs to the second floor. The staircase itself is a work of art, sweeping up out of the small foyer in a graceful, winding arch, giving the space the illusion of grand size, but never had I entertained the thought of going up them. They were not roped off, but to ascend them seemed a violation of some unspoken rule, since neither did they have any notices inviting the public up.

I followed the sound of the dog with my eyes, along the curve of the stairway, until my gaze caught the room at the head of the stairs—a room bleeding an odd red glow that was the only light seeping into the upper floor. The effect was at once disturbing and calming, and I found myself entirely unsure of what to do. As if to solve my dilemma, the dog barked again from directly in front of the room, and the light seemed to momentarily intensify in response to the noise. I wet my lips nervously and cast an ear into the gallery: The curator was still hanging paintings and I could hear no one conversing or moving about in the small coffee room at the back. I looked up the stairs again, at that darkness sliced through only by the red glow. Placing a steadying hand on the banister and swallowing my nervous guilt, I began my ascent.

The risers creaked casually under my weight, telling tales of time-wear to all who cared to listen; I rose slowly, not wanting them to talk too loudly. Ahead of me I heard the dog's excited, honest patter; in fact, I may have been repelled from continuing up because of the red luminescence, but with the dog skitting about, it somehow lost its sinister edge and I managed to fully ascend the staircase.

The door was open, allowing the light to spill forth, and I could see that the sign on it read, "Storage"; within I could hear the dog clicking on the wooden floor and I took a bashful, curious peek in. I could see a black Labrador plain as day dancing excitedly around an old woman with a cane who was teasing the animal with a treat. I turned to sneak back down the stairs, filled with a strange mixture of guilt, serenity, and foreboding, but then the woman looked up at me, smiling, and allowed the dog to finally snap the treat from her fingers.

"I saw you walking by earlier," she explained. "So I sent Nicholas after you." The dog barked proudly at the mention of its name and wagged its tail, gazing at me.

I moved cautiously such that I was fully in the doorway. The red light made it impossible for me to clearly discern color, but it appeared as if the woman had on a light blue housecoat decorated with dark blue flowers. She shifted her position and tapped her cane once on the floor, smiling again. Her short, white hair reflected the red light, much as her soft, white, wrinkled skin did, and the eyes behind her glasses shone happily.

"Come in, won't you?" she asked. I silently obliged. A brief look around showed me that the room was bare—no source for the red light that I could see—save the two of us and Nicholas, the dog. The only window had a heavy curtain drawn across it, and a glance at the overhead fixture proved that the usual light source—though red, as a preservation technique for stored works—was turned off. When I looked back at the woman I noticed that, where the room had been bare seconds before, there now stood an easel set up with canvas and paints.

"I need your help," the woman said, drawing my attention back to her. "I am Irene Burgman; that's my show the curator is setting up."

"Oh," I said, my voice sounding odd and hollow in the room.

"I'm too old," she continued. "I need you to hold the brushes, because I never painted Nicholas..."

"I'm no painter!" I replied, slightly confused; my voice sounded too loud, too full in the red room, but the woman didn't seem fazed by what I had said, or how loudly I had said it. Nicholas sat down, panting, his eyes still carefully watching me.

"I don't need a painter," Irene said nicely with a bright smile. "I just need someone to hold the brushes—I'll tell you exactly what to do." Her smile broke when I didn't respond and her expression dropped. "Please, young man, let me finish my work...I just have to paint Nicholas."

I sighed and smiled, shrugging and moving quickly to the old woman. What harm could there be in appeasing an aging artist who was probably too arthritic to hold her own brushes? All my suspicions, all my cares about the odd lighting and the former ghost-dog—all the things any person in that situation would normally think of—fled from my mind as if the woman's grandmotherly smile had hypnotized me in some way. I was so consumed with pleasing the old lady that I hastily sat down and prepared the palate, as per her careful instructions, as she stood sideways to me, pointing with her gnarled old finger, but never touching anything.

She quietly told me exactly what to do—all her secrets, I imagine. How to hold which brush or knife, how much color to mix, where to put it and how heavily. She gave explicit directions on every detail of the piece, but never once did she touch me or any of the tools. When I would glance at her from time to time she would be smiling proudly and reassuringly, and Nicholas would add an excited little bark and patter in place beside Irene Burgman. After about a half hour I began to see his form appearing out of the dark background of the canvas: Nicholas was lying, head on paws, face gazing alertly at the viewer. Only twice did Irene find cause to shriek a horrified "No! No! Not there!" and then flustered about, telling me how to fix my mistake. Yet even in this frustrated state, she touched nothing.

Within an hour the painting of Nicholas was complete, and I could tell that the color and detail were exceptional. I felt no pride of creation, however, as I fully understood that I had merely been a tool of Irene Burgman's, no more worthy of credit than the very brush I held. As I stood and backed away from the work—which I had signed with her signature, "Burgie," flubbing the "B" slightly—I began to feel a deep admiration for the piece, and I knew that it was as much the work of Irene Burgman as any of the other pieces downstairs.

"Thank you," I heard her say from behind me, with tears in her voice. I turned to offer my thanks to her for allowing me to be privy to her artistry, but the room was empty; neither she nor Nicholas were anywhere to be seen or heard. Confused, I looked back to the painting, but the easel and tools, too, had vanished, leaving in their place a canvas covered with a cheesecloth, leaning against the wall. A corner, bearing the signature of the artist, was exposed, and it was only by seeing the signature's smeared "B" that I knew it to be the piece I had seconds ago completed. I instinctively went to remove the cloth from the canvas, lest it destroy the wet oils, but all at once the hypnosis—if such there had been—was broken, and as I backed up several steps, toward the door, I began shaking my head, convinced that I had entered some realm of insanity so deep as to seem real, yet knowing just as surely that I was not insane at all.

I turned and bolted out of the room, bounding back down the stairs, almost tripping up on the pile of folded cheese cloths at the foot of them. I saw that the show was now completely hung, and from the back room I could hear the curator talking to somebody. I walked unsteadily toward the voices and found him conversing with a young brunette girl who looked to be in the process of leaving; neither noticed me at first, which was just as well, as I was trying my best to erase a look of horrified realization from my face. Their conversation ended at that moment with loud "so longs," as if to indicate that I could safely enter without disrupting them.

"You look lost, friend," the curator said as the girl brushed past me with a shy glance and smile. "Coffee?"

"No—thanks," I replied, wanting to ask my questions and leave.

"Umm...Who's show is that you've just hung?"

"Oh...Irene Burgman's her name," he answered, motioning for me to sit with him at the window table. I followed him over, but I did not sit, my mind trying to whir through what I needed to know.

"And...she's...here?" I guessed, trying not to sound too distraught. He narrowed his eyes at me and sipped his coffee, his head twitching with mild disbelief.

"Nooo...I'm afraid she'll miss her own show... But surely you've heard?" He waved at the girl who had been inside before, as she walked past the window outside, back up the alley, motioning to us that she had no clue what she'd been thinking to go out the front way.

"Heard what?" I asked, trying to sound curious, not afraid. The curator turned his attention back to me and sighed, his expression a tad suspicious.

"She died last week, you know... Strangest thing really, because her dog died not two hours later. She was famous for loving that dog." He smiled affectionately, but I just gaped and took a step back, covering my mouth slowly, my eyes wild with impossibility.

"Oh, that's very sad," I gasped, catching my breath and managing to marginally recompose myself. The curator cocked his head with concern.

"Okay?" he asked.

"Yes, yes—fine," I stammered. "I—uhh—I have to go now, I think." And then I very rudely turned and dashed down the hall to the front door, casting a glance over my shoulder as I left, to the room upstairs.

It was completely dark, and the door was shut tight.

The Ghost at the Gatehouse

Miles stirred in his slumber. He could hear music—slow, somber, methodical music—playing somewhere in the distance. A funeral procession, by the sound of its mournful cadence. His head lolled to the other side and a low moan escaped his lips—presumably the music outside was entering into his dream. He coughed distractedly and began to awaken, his hand unconsciously reaching for his glass of water, but the groping fingers were stopped short by a wall instead of finding the glass of water on his nightstand.

Miles came fully awake in a rush, sitting up quickly to determine where he was. He hadn't risen more than a few inches before he cracked his head heavily on something very firm, but padded. He opened his eyes more widely, only to discover they had been open already, and was greeted still by a choking darkness that not one dot of light penetrated.

Somewhere he could still hear the music and he realized that if it was indeed a procession, it wasn't going anywhere.

Must have reached the cemetery, he concluded. He stretched out his hand to explore his surroundings.

It took Miles brief moments to deduce that he had been kidnapped and entrapped, apparently as the bartering chip for a common thief's prosperity. In fact, Miles rather thought he had it all figured out: He had been kidnapped by a grave-digger (and probable grave-*robber*, as well), taken to his place of employment, then cunningly concealed in a coffin to await the arrival of the ransom.

Brilliant, thought Miles, *Except—*

He listened intently for a moment. The music had stopped, but now he could hear—he was *sure* of it—the low tones of a solemn voice talking. He couldn't distinguish specific words, but the sound of a voice speaking slowly and quietly, just out of earshot, was unmistakable. His captors, no doubt, discussing their plans. Miles strained his ears to hear them.

This darkness really is thick, he considered as he settled his head back down on the pillow, *Quite inspiring.*

Again his thoughts were interrupted, now by the sound of beautiful, feminine voices singing a requiem. Whoever's funeral was going on, they must have been *very* important. He tried to think of the other prominent members of his society, but couldn't recall a single one who had appeared to be ailing.

Those damn cars, Miles decided. *Must've claimed one of them.*

And then it struck him, a thing so obvious that he felt a fool for not having thought of it first: If there were mourners nearby, all he had to do was bang and make a lot of racket. Surely *some* one—the chauffeurs huddled together smoking, for instance—would hear his cries and come to his rescue.

He knocked lightly on the wood above his head, testing the sound, and found that although the satin trim would allow him to knock quite heavily, the wood was admittedly much thicker than he had imagined. The sound that returned to him was not the hollow ring of the top of a box, but rather the dull, embedded *thump* of a cellar wall. Frowning, he tried again, this time a little bit harder. Again, he was greeted by a dull pounding that even *he* could barely hear. Panicking, he pounded both hands on the coffin and even tried to give it a series of good kicks, too. He stopped when he heard a splintering sound.

I'm through! I've rescued myself!

But it was just a small crack, barely discernible with his fingertips through the satin interior.

Very nice coffin, he considered, *to put a snatched-person in...*

For reasons unknown to him, other than he was now piloting himself on some survival-instinct, Miles began to feel around again, hoping for a hammer the idiot kidnappers *must* have left in the coffin with him. His fingers did indeed find something, but it was not a hammer. It was the smooth, cold neck of a bottle. A heavy bottle, Miles discovered as he hefted it.

Like a fifth of whiskey, in fact—

Miles froze, bottle mid-heft, a look of dawning horror creeping across his face in the impenetrable blackness of the coffin. The bottle was most assuredly a fifth of whiskey, just like the kind he'd always joked he wanted to be buried with.

"Panic" is hardly the word for the instinct that consumed Miles' body and mind at this point of discovery. He dropped the bottle—quickly forgotten—and pounded, kicked, and screamed for all he was worth, even banging his head on the coffin lid, for that extra ounce of noise. All to no avail. When he was finished—worn out—the stillness was as pressing as the darkness. The funeral had clearly dispersed, leaving Miles six feet from the rest of his life.

* * *

Miles Abernathy was cool. He'd always taken pride in how well he kept himself, even under the direst of circumstances, and this calm he maintained until the last breath left his body.

Miles considered the situation carefully and came to the only logical conclusion he could: He was stuck. Even if he managed to fester the crack above him enough to dig a hole, it would only bring six feet of earth down on him. (He had, in fact, tested this theory after discovering that he had made quite a dent in the coffin lid, with his previous panic. He had cut through the satin with his favorite pocket knife—at least they'd buried him according to his wishes—

and managed to poke the blade through the crack, rotating it to slightly widen the gap. He had been rewarded with a tiny dusting of dirt, most of which had fallen in his mouth.) And certainly no one would hear his cries, since an entire funeral had missed them before. They had unfortunately stopped burying people close to the surface, with little silver bells, since the end of the plague had supposedly also ended the occurrence of people being buried alive. In short, Miles knew damn well that he was truly, in every sense of the word, *stuck*.

There are two options here, he explained to himself. *Well, no, actually three. I could slit my throat or wrists with my knife. I could wait until I suffocate. Or...*

And a smile crept across his lips...

I could crack open this bottle of whiskey and have myself one last party. If I'm lucky, he mused, *I can drink myself to death!*

Seeing as Miles hated the thought of pain and had always been paranoid of suffocation, he settled on the last option.

* * *

Miles could hear music again, but this time, when he opened his eyes, he could see people. Lots of people. A gala ball, by the looks of it. He smiled broadly and raised the bottle to his lips, taking another swig, most of which spilled down his shirt-front.

"Miles, old boy!" a voice said as a hand clapped him on the back. "You've had too much to drink, I'd say!"

"S'okay, Rojjer, rilly, 'm fine..." He hiccoughed and emitted a low-key belch, looking sheepishly around himself like a small boy.

"Well, well, Miles," Roger replied with amusement. "Just don't drink yourself to death, old boy—!"

Everything went black and with a start Miles cried out, his fuzzy mind taking a moment to connect the blackness with where he was:

on his back in a stain-pillowed bed, a half-empty bottle of whiskey standing dutifully at his hip with one, weakening hand grasping its neck.

He giggled weakly, as a cornered man often does, and sent a message to his hand to bring the bottle closer to his lips. His arm twitched, but his hand ignored him for the time being.

"Jus sit raht thar, Misser Hand. Jus fine..."

He burped softly and giggled again. "That o-fenn you, Miz Walkens?"

"Not at all, Miles," she replied haughtily. Miles' eyelids fluttered open.

"Mary!" he exclaimed, entirely sober again. "I was looking everywhere for you!"

"And why's that, Mr. Abernathy? Do you have less moral things in mind?"

Mary Walkens feigned a blush and hid behind her fan, her come-hither eyes the only thing Miles could see of her face. They were in the farthest reaches of his garden, as usual, and Miles sat down on the bench next to her.

"Why, Miss Mary," he breathed. "I've never known a lady to be quite so forward!" He scooted closer to her on the bench, taking in a deep breath of her delectable fragrance. Peaches, he thought. Mary Walkens *always* smelled good enough to eat. He put an arm around her waist, and she dropped the fan to her lap and brought her face closer to his.

"What would my husband think?" she whispered, not entirely joking.

"How lucky I am, I imagine..." and before she could say another word, he closed off her mouth with a kiss.

"Mary..." he whispered.

"This isn't wrong," she smiled, reaching out and pulling his face back to hers. "We married for security, didn't we? And then we found...love."

"Mary," he smiled. "I do love my wife. I would never hurt her, in a million years—"

"There's love, Miles, as I've said a thousand times, and then there's something... *deeper*, isn't there?"

"More animal?"

"If you say so."

"Undeniable?"

"We only have one chance, Miles. We have our security—"

"NO!" Miles cried out, pounding on the lid of the coffin again.

"NO! PAMELA! I's zorry. I's zorry..." The tears came more strongly as he relaxed back into the coffin and found the neck of the bottle—miraculously still standing—beside him. "I di luv oo, Pamela. I di...I di..."

There was just about a quarter of the fifth left when Miles woke from his delirium with more lucidity. He scratched his nose—or tried to, anyway—and wiped a floppy hand over his mouth, realizing that after all the parties he'd attended, he'd never been this drunk in his life.

"Bez time now, s'pose..."

He raised the bottle again and poured a swig over his face, coughing as a few drops managed to slide down his throat. He thrashed his head a little for no good reason and settled the bottle back down beside his left hip, his hand still on it, only now holding it up at a precarious angle.

"Waz ah dreamin?" he asked, fully expecting his wife to reply. "Pam'la? Waz ah? I 'member drinkin from a boddle... Die fall a'zleep? Hadda ah-vul dream..."

* * *

The fine lines between dream, hallucination, and reality are sometimes indistinguishable, one from the other. It is only through one's surroundings that a safe assumption as to the cause of a particular vision can be attributed. Miles found himself in a dangerous position, indeed. Here he was no longer sure if he was asleep and dreaming, awake and dreaming, or had already awoken from a terrible nightmare to discover what the conventional would label "reality."

Miles was watching his mother from his crib, but with all the clarity and consciousness of an adult. He squirmed again as he heard her voice, unable, it seemed, to control his body himself.

"Mother?" he queried, but it of course came out, "Ma-ma."

"Hush, Miles, darling. Mama has some work to finish."

"Ma-ma."

The Oedipal side of Miles' mind realized for the first time how very beautiful his mother was—or had been, since, to his knowledge, the dear lady was long dead. He wondering fleetingly if this was the cause of his sometimes-debilitating attraction to women, then shook his head to clear the thought. Only a Freudian thinker would be puerile enough to blame every adult action on some latent, childhood sexual experience, be it real or imagined.

"Mama!" he declared again, and felt an uneasy pull in his groin as the beautiful woman turned from what she was doing and lent over the crib.

"Are you hungry, Miles, dear?" she asked sweetly, smiling and standing straight. She brushed her hair casually over her shoulder and unhitched the left-hand strap of her dress, then slowly began to undo the buttons on the blouse beneath. Miles squirmed uncomfortably, unable to prevent an adult smile from forming on his baby lips. His mother had by now all but fully exposed her left breast, and she bent down and grasped Miles under his chubby arms.

"Stop fidgeting, Miles," she demanded, settling the child on her left hip and using her right hand to adjust her clothing. "Go on then,

Miles," she soothed. "I really have to finish my ironing." She bounced him softly on her hip, using her left arm to move his small mouth closer to her. "Go on..."

Miles jumped back in horror, stumbling and falling from the end of the bench, landing solidly on his bottom.

"What on earth are you doing!" Mary Walkens exclaimed, hurriedly covering herself, then scooting down the bench to look at him.

"I—I'm sorry, Mary," he stammered. "I don't know! I just had a sudden urge to...well, throw up, if you must know—"

"You've had too much to drink again, haven't you?" Mary asked slyly. She straightened her back and ran a sultry hand up her front and over her breasts. "Or does my body offend you?"

Miles stood and shook his head, clearing the nausea from his throat. "No, Mary, quite assuredly not!" He smiled at her. "I can't explain...I just felt sick, for absolutely no reason..."
He sat down again beside her as she refastened the buttons on her dress.

"Well, it can't be the guilt," she decided, almost talking to herself. "Not by now."

"Maybe it is," he sighed. Miles turned to look at her, but she had turned away from him and was gazing serenely down the garden path.

"Mary?" he asked. "Did you hear me?"

"Yes, Miles, I heard you," his mother replied, turning back to face him. "But I don't see why *you* should feel guilty about your father—"

Miles shot up, his eyes flying open, and cracked his head—hard—on the lid of his coffin. He was vaguely aware that the bottle had fallen over, but by this time it didn't matter. All the precious whiskey that was left lay in the side of the bottle, in no danger of spilling out the neck.

He moaned and rubbed his head, the world still spinning, even though some deeper, untouched part of him knew that was quite impossible.

"Juz a dream..." he stated quietly, scratching his scalp and burping softly. "Gotta stop drinkin like iss..."

He dropped his head back down on the satin pillow and sighed heavily, then sighed heavily again, his lungs still unsatisfied for air.

"Oh God..." he breathed, pulling in another ragged sigh. His fingers found the bottle again and he brought it to his lips, amazingly managing to down one more tiny swallow. "Waz happun da me? Very tard..."

His arm flopped down, leaving the bottle resting against his neck as his head lolled in the other direction, his chest rising and falling slowly; heavily.

* * *

Miles walked up the road to his house, his legs dull and throbbing stalks below him. The carriage had flipped over just down the road, but his head felt ready to explode from the effort of the short walk back. He could see his gate now, but there was a strange man standing at it. As he got closer—and managed to pull his vision into focus—he discerned a beard, and wise, old eyes.

"Mister Miles Abernathy," the man said, smiling broadly. "Had a nasty tip down there, eh? How's the horse?"

"Dead," he croaked. "I managed to crawl up the embankment..." His legs gave way and the old man hopped around the half-closed gate to help steady him.

"Are you a friend of Pamela's?" Miles asked as he felt the surprisingly strong man hoist him back to his feet.

"No, no. Not really."

"Then just help me up the walk to the house, if you don't mind—"

"Oh, I can't do that!" the man exclaimed, pleasant in his denial.

"Very well, then I'll do it myself," Miles decided, trying to take a step through his gate. The man's strong hold stopped him.

"Can't do that, either, I'm afraid."

"Why not?" Miles asked, confused, but too weak to offer any physical resistance.

"Miles, you lived your whole life in that garden—" Miles shot the man a look to see what he meant, but the face was stony and silent. "—and now you want to go back into your house."

"But it was my mother's fault!" he exclaimed. "I was far too old to have feedings!"

"Now listen to you, Miles! You sound like a blasted Freudian!" the man admonished. "It doesn't matter who's to blame, does it? You had the choice set before you, and you decided which road to take."

Miles stirred on his satin pillow, raising the bottle one last time and pouring the remaining whiskey over his face. He coughed once, but that was all.

"I zee i' now!" he breathed in his slumber. "My mama..."

"Sit down here a moment, Miles," the old man offered, leading him to a bench that sat tucked into the hedge at the front of Miles' property.

"I was too old," Miles whispered. "Now I see it... It never occurred to me before..."

"It really doesn't matter, anyway," the old man sighed. "That was quite a nasty bump you took. They probably think you're dead."

"No!" he wailed. "*I'm not dead!* I want to see Pam-la..."

"What about Mary? Perhaps you should go into the garden and wait for *her?*"

"No," Miles whined, beginning to cry. "I think I'll just wait here... Explain to Pamela. She'll understand, won't she...?"

132

The man shrugged and stood up, walking away down the road. "You could be waiting forever, Miles," he called over his shoulder.

"*Forever.*"

Kittens Hollow Sound

Between Green Lake and the large inland sea called Lake Harper runs the medium-sized Muskingham River. As the water nears Green Lake, it cuts into a deep valley and forms the sound known as Kittens Hollow. If the topography of the area was studied in cross-section it would look like the flat surface of an ocean with two solitary waves, and Kittens Hollow would be in the trough between the rollers, almost as if the walls of the hollow had heaved themselves up quiet suddenly around the river, like the shrugging shoulders of some primeval beast that had yet to relax its motion. Other than at the hollow, the hills that formed the phenomena were quite gradual, creeping up from all directions, slowly piling foot upon foot as if to fool the careless traveler, with the intent of spilling them over the lip of the comparable cliff of the valley and into the sound below.

Kittens Hollow runs about five miles in an east-west direction, and the train we were riding on plugged morosely along the northern lip of the valley, looking forward to the descent toward Green Lake and the bridge which marked the end of the sudden rises that created the valley, where the segment of the river called Kittens Hollow Sound once more became the Muskingham proper. There we would be taken back east, along the edge of the sound on the floor of the valley, into the station at Kittens Hollow. The rails then continued on from the valley, back to Lake Harper. A course along the northern rim was necessary to make a loop the train could corner comfortably; nevertheless, the view alone was spectacular enough to warrant such a dangerous trip.

134

My wife, Elizabeth, did not necessarily agree, as with one glance out her window over the depths of the hollow, she hurriedly turned her face away and buried it in my shoulder, clutching my arm dramatically.

"I can't look," her muffled voice explained from within my coat.

"Well don't, then," I agreed, straightening in my seat to get a better view over her head. The sun, setting in the west over Green Lake, cast long orange rays into the sound, lighting the waters with their fiery glow; a distinct ribbon of color cutting through the emerald blackness of the valley walls.

"It's really quiet beautiful," I breathed, moving my arm in an attempt to unbury Elizabeth's face, but she wouldn't have it, tightening her grip and shaking her head in negation.

"Don't care," she replied resolutely.

As the train came down off the rim, the gloaming over distant Green Lake seemed unreal, as if only the echo of some ancient past humans had never witnessed. The engine carried us around a left-hand bend, toward the bridge at the mouth of the sound, cutting off my view but lighting the compartments across the aisle, much to the joy of those passengers, judging by the clamor of excited cries and whispers.

Elizabeth finally resurfaced, her curiosity aroused by the others' excitement, and glanced hesitantly out the window. We were crossing the bridge now, and the train's reflection ran over the surface of the water; a black line cutting across the red-tipped waves. The wheels began to screech as the vibrations of the track slowed, and I noticed that the train had turned right, to continue on along the river to Green Lake, as opposed to heading east through Kittens Hollow.

"I thought the train went into Kittens Hollow?" Elizabeth said, turning to me as if it was my fault that this apparently was not the case.

"It did," I declared, pointing to the dull silver-glint of tracks disappearing back into the darkness along the valley floor. A brief knock came at our cabin door, and the conductor stuck his head in with a bright smile and a brief nod.

"Folks heading into Kittens Hollow?" he asked.

"Yes," I replied, standing expectantly.

"I'm afraid you'll have to get off here, then," he said jovially, straightening and opening the door for us. "There's a taxi waiting, only the train doesn't go down there any more."

"Really?" Elizabeth wondered. "Why not?" We collected our suitcase and bags and moved to the door, the conductor taking Elizabeth's wares and nodding for us to lead the way down the aisle.

"Not worth it," he replied loudly, so we could hear him as we walked to the door at the end of the carriage. "Kittens Hollow all but shut down a few years back, when the new resort opened out at Green Lake. Go out to the left there," he indicated as we reached the end of the carriage. "Watch your step."

We disembarked into the care of a taxi driver only too happy to see a living fare being handed to him. He was old and would have been more at home on a fishing boat, I imagine. He smiled a toothless grin and rubbed the stubble on his chin, helping Elizabeth off the train and onto the road below, then he took my bags and quickly loaded them into the taxi, turning and taking the rest from the conductor.

"Heya," the taxi driver nodded to me as I stood watching him, then he waved to the conductor, who nodded back politely and shut the door. I watched as he moved to the other side of the carriage and waved his hat out the door for the engineer to see, and the train, with a jolt, began to move again toward Green Lake.

"Whe're ya staying?" the taxi driver shouted as the engine picked up steam behind us.

"Do we have a choice?" I asked, and he winked with a shallow shake of his head.

"Not really. If ya don't wanna stay in the hotel, ya can always sleep in the street!" He laughed at his own joke and winked at Elizabeth, then turned and opened the cab's door for us, ushering us into the back seat. He closed the door without slamming it, then got into the front and started the motor. I turned in the seat and watched as the caboose of the train made the graceful bend off the bridge and disappeared into the encroaching night over Green Lake. The sun had vanished now, leaving enough light to bruise the sky, but not much else. When I turned back as the taxi started to move, I was slightly shocked at how dark the road along the river's edge was. Our driver was hunched slightly forward in his seat, his attentive gaze hopefully saving us from going off the road and into the sound.

"So what're you folks doin' in Kittens Hollow, anyway?" he wondered, his eyes never leaving the road.

"Oh, I heard there were some good business opportunities out here," I replied. "My wife and I are thinking of opening a shop."
"Gettin' away from the city?" he guessed, his eyes flicking briefly to the rearview mirror.

"I s'pose," I sighed, putting my arm happily around Elizabeth and giving her a squeeze. "The city's not any place to raise a family."

"Sure 'nuf," the driver agreed. "And there sure are a lot a businesses up for grabs..." He trailed off and considered us momentarily in the mirror, then nodded as if whatever question he'd thought of had been answered. "I guess you're independently wealthy?"

"Yes..." I replied slowly. The cab took a few lurches over some rough road, and our driver clutched the wheel more tightly, cutting the conversation off for the time.

"'Bout another mile," he said absently a minute later, as if he could sense our unrest. "Sorry I gotta drive so slow..."

"Quiet all right," I replied. "Better than going for a swim, I'd say."

He chuckled lightly, but said nothing as we hit another few bumps in the road, the cobblestones obviously deteriorating the closer we got to Kittens Hollow.

"How did it get its name?" Elizabeth wondered after a few seconds.

"Kittens Hollow?" he asked rhetorically. "Or Kittens Hollow Sound, or Kittens Sound," he mumbled on, almost waiting for us to argue with him. When we didn't, he spoke up again. "Mr. Arthur McMurdouc founded the place, and not too long after he'd put the tracks in up on the north rim—to get the building materials to his town, of course—a freight company asked to use the line. Back then the Kittens Hollow line just came down from the main line and then back over again, but for whatever reason the main line was blocked and the only way to get the freight through was to use McMurdouc's by-pass—they still call it that, even though it's a real line now, going down beyond Green Lake."

He paused and brought the cab to a stop in front of the only building with any lights on—our hotel—then turned and looked back at us as he finished his tale.

"Anyway, seems some kids had put a whole box of kittens on the tracks up there, either as a prank or because they'd been told to get rid of 'em. S'pose it don't matter too much, cuz when that freighter hit it, they say all you could hear was them kittens yelling and scream-ing..."

He stopped with the grisly details when he caught sight of our horrified gazes.

"Yeah, well, Mr. McMurdouc changed the name right then and there from McMurdouc's Hollow to Kittens Hollow." He nodded once to put an end to the tale, then turned and opened his door, leap-ing from the cab to then open our own and usher us out into the cool night that had slipped over the sound. He was smiling broadly, as if his expression could wipe the horrible tale from our minds.

I looked around at the run-down buildings and pot-holed streets before me, barely visible under the weak glow of the hotel's lights, and instantly understood why the property was so cheap: No one in their right mind would think of opening a business in such an obviously unused area, unless, of course, they enjoyed bankruptcy.

"Not much left, is there?" I asked out loud. Elizabeth put her arm around me consolingly and gave me a light squeeze.

"Not since Green Lake was developed," the driver agreed, unloading our bags.

"'Fraid there's no porter at the hotel."

"Yes...well that's all right," I replied, jolted out of my reverie and reaching for my wallet. "What do I owe you?"

"Train company paid it," he said with a shrug, so I gave him a bill anyway.

"Well, here's something for your trouble, then."

"Thank you," he said with a light bow, taking the bill and stuffing it into his shirt pocket.

"Guess you must be from Green Lake?" I suddenly realized with another glance around at the deserted streets.

"Yes, sir," he agreed, turning back to his cab. "Not many people come here, and those that do don't really need a cab. Call us when you're ready to leave," he added as an afterthought, handing me a business card. Then he climbed back into his cab and started the engine, driving in a slow circle around us to head back the way we'd come, leaving my wife and I standing in the middle of the road with our luggage.

"Do you think that story was true?" Elizabeth asked as we carried our cases to the hotel's verandah. She dropped her over-laden bag the second we stepped foot onto the porch, the vibration causing a small sifting of dust to rain down from the slat-boards overhead. I brushed my shoulder and smiled at her whimsically, then shrugged.

"Maybe...don't see why not."

"Howdy, folks!" an amiable voice piped up suddenly from within, the door flying open a second later. A hunched old man stood grinning at us, nodding his head slightly every so often as if agreeing with his own remark, since we had made no response.

"Hello," I replied, extending my hand, which he gripped loosely with arthritic joints. "Reggie Ainsworth? From upstate?"

"Yes," he winked, grinning over at Elizabeth. "I've been waiting for you—this the wife?"

"Yes—Elizabeth."

"Oh, I'm sorry," he suddenly deferred with a slight bow. "I am Arnold Makesmith, proprietor of Kittens Hollow's finest hotel." He swept his arm wide with the announcement, then glanced around himself, his smile slowly dropping. "Well, Kittens Hollow's *only* hotel, really..."

"It looks very nice," Elizabeth intervened hurriedly, lighting Arnold's face with a renewed vigor.

He glanced around again nostalgically. "Well, it's gone downhill a bit since we first opened, but it's still the only place to find a comfortable bed."

"And that's exactly what we need," I replied. Arnold made as if to grab our suitcase, but I politely waved him off—no use causing his crooked form more suffering—and picked it up myself, following him into the foyer of what had clearly once been quite a grand establishment.

It was only two floors, and the main staircase greeted us the instant we walked inside, sweeping up out of the hardwood floor of the lobby with the grace of a ballerina. Immediately to our left was the check-in desk; to our right lay the dining room. To the left of the main staircase, beyond the check-in desk, was a sitting area with sofas and chairs, as well as a large fireplace that was invitingly ablaze. The decor was mostly rich woodwork and fine tapestries, but time and the elements had caused the hotel to lose its glimmer; the wood was grayed and brittle, the tapestries faded and nubby, and I glanced at the fire again, nervously, wondering how quickly a stray spark could consume the entire building.

"Here she is," Arnold Makesmith said proudly of the hotel, then he turned and scurried behind the desk to check us in. He winked at Elizabeth and opened a crusty ledger, running his yellowed finger down the column until he presumably reached our name.

"Ainsworth," he announced. "You'll be in room 27, up the stairs to the left."

I saw that ours was not the only name written in the ledger and asked inconspicuously, "So we're not the only guests?"

"Oh no, sir!" he exclaimed happily. "We usually have about ten or so guests at any one time." I raised my eyebrows curiously, and he added, "They come to get away from it all, don't they? And that Green Lake Lodge is *very* loud."

"Well this is lovely," Elizabeth marveled sincerely. "I can't imagine why anyone would choose one of those sterile old lodges over this."

Arnold shrugged and slid a paper over the desk to me. "S'pose they don't really want to get away, do they? They just want to change the names and faces for a spell."

"I suppose," Elizabeth agreed as I filled out the indicated lines on the paper, then signed the bottom.

"Would you like to pay for the room now or start a tab and pay when you check out?" he asked professionally.

"We'll start a tab," I decided, and Elizabeth nodded her agreement, though we both glanced into the empty dining room. "Assuming there's reason to?"

"Oh, yes," Arnold said, handing us a pamphlet. "That's the dining menu. Breakfast starts at 7, lunch at 11, and dinner at 5 o' clock sharp. We also have a small pub," he indicated a door tucked neatly in the corner, beneath the staircase. "That opens at 2 in the afternoon and closes some time after midnight, usually."

"Superb," I announced, then bent down for my bags as he scurried back around to us, the key in his gnarled hand.

"I'll show you to the room," he explained. "Since the staff is kind of thin just now."

We followed Arnold up the creaky staircase, the banister worn and smooth from decades of hands running over it; the small square of carpet on each riser faded and yellowed from its original royal maroon. At the top we followed him to the left. There were a few rooms that faced onto a landing over the foyer, but the hallways disappeared either way down musty corridors that smelled of age, but not, thankfully, rot, and although the lobby wall had many windows, with a view of the sound through the darkness, I didn't imagine the dingy hallway to be much brighter even in full daylight.

We reached our room soon enough; it was almost the last room in the hallway. Arnold ceremoniously unlocked the door and pushed it open, holding his arm out to usher us in.

"Your room," he declared, then smiled and nodded affirmatively, leaving me in the odd position of wondering if a tip was expected or would be an offense, since he wasn't really a bellhop.

"No tip," Arnold suddenly said, holding up a hand to stop my protests, should I voice any. Clearly, he was used to the dilemma and turned his cautionary gesture into a slight wave, then handed me the key.

"Breakfast at 7," he concluded. He winked knowingly and shut the door, leaving us to our own devices.

* * *

142

I heard a soft clicking at the door and rolled over. It felt like I'd just gone to sleep, and I assumed Arnold Makesmith had forgotten to tell us something important, like he didn't really have a dining staff, after all.

"Mrph..." I mumbled and opened my eyes. The glowing hands of the travel alarm clock we'd brought were cocked at a picture-perfect right angle. It was three a.m.

There was another soft clicking at the door, three short bursts of three clicks, and I realized unmistakably that someone was knocking, and actually using the decorative brass door-knocker.

"What?" I choked out gruffly, then coughed and threw back the covers. The chill air instantly nibbled at any exposed skin and I shivered dramatically. Elizabeth stirred and said something, but did not wake.

I padded over to the door and grasped the knob, then thought the better of it and put my face against the door to peek through the pee-phole. The hallway beyond was empty, bending off in fish-eye fashion to either side. As if to dispute what my eyes told me, however, three short clicks came again and I leaped back, my heart racing in my throat.

"Who is it?" Elizabeth asked groggily, her whisper frightening me in the height of the moment; I spun on her, ready to pounce, and she recoiled slightly, then smiled and rubbed her eyes.

"What are you doing?" she demanded, rephrasing her question.

"You hear it, don't you?" I shrieked madly, causing Elizabeth's face to drop; she grinned curiously.

"Yes—the knocking?—so who is it?"

"There's no one there," I replied gauntly, rushing to her side. She started to shake her head to say that I was lying, then narrowed her eyes.

"Maybe we just heard something else?"

I turned and watched the door for several seconds, daring the knock to come again. There was no more sound from the hallway, however, and the chill of the dark night started to seep into my bones. I turned back and smiled warmly at Elizabeth, then stood and moved back around to my side of the bed, sitting down on the soft mattress and swinging my legs in, under the covers.

"You're probably right," I said to her. The radiator across the room began to tick and hiss as it filled with hot water, as if to prove my wife's conclusion. I pulled the sheets back up, over my ear, and buried my head down in the pillow to go back to sleep.

At three-fifteen exactly, according to our clock, the clicking of the door-knocker sounded again. This time I shot into action, leaping from the bed and hurrying across the room, smashing my face against the over-polished surface of the door to get a look at the hallway through the peephole. As I had expected, the hallway was apparently empty. I took a step back and undid the lock, then flung the door open. There was no one standing there. I stuck my head out of the room and looked either way, but saw no prankster scurrying off. The hallway was colder than our room, however, and as a large puff of exceptionally cool air brushed past me, I quickly turned back and shut the door, slipping the lock into place thoughtfully.

"Anyone?" Elizabeth wondered.

"No," I mused.

"Go back to sleep," she replied tiredly, and this time I managed to do just that.

* * *

The moment Arnold saw us appear at the top of the stairs the next morning, he bounded from behind the counter to greet us, a broad, arcane smile on his face.

"Mr. Makesmith!" I called happily as Elizabeth and I walked down the last few stairs. The odd little man shifted his weight and nodded at us, like a grinning dog.

"I didn't think you'd be joining us, sir," he explained, taking my elbow momentarily and guiding us toward the dining room. "Your table's waiting."

"Oh," I replied with a certain degree of shock, especially when I saw that there were several other people having breakfast already, none of whom seemed to be receiving the same level of service.

"Mrs. Ainsworth... Sir," Arnold said with a tone of announcement. "If you'll have a seat here." A waiter appeared behind each of us, pulling out our chairs and seating us in a very professional manner.

"Do you treat all your guests with such distinction?" I asked with a sly grin. Mr. Makesmith winked back and patted the waiter who had stayed to take our order on the arm. The waiter grinned, too, as if sharing the joke I had just made. I glanced at Elizabeth, but she seemed as in-the-dark as I was.

"I understand you're here to see about the McMurdouc estate," the hunched old man replied. "That makes you very dear to us."

"Estate?" I wondered, trying to fathom what rumor had been circulated about our visit.

"Kittens Hollow, sir? You wish to buy some property?" he explained.

"Ah!" I agreed with dawning realization. It had probably been years since any serious investor had ventured down the dilapidated old road with the intent of sprucing the place up. To them I must have been as precious as gold, for many of the same reasons. The last thing they wanted to do was scare us away.

"Well," I acquiesced. "I came to look around, yes."

"Very nice," Arnold Makesmith nodded with a nimble bow.

"And we wish to make you as comfortable as possible."

"Really, it's not necessary," Elizabeth voiced for both of us.

"Coffee, ma'am?" the waiter blurted, springing into action as if realizing he had fallen asleep while standing over us.

"Yes, please...or no. Tea, please," Elizabeth responded.

"I'll have coffee, thank you," I said, and the waiter scurried off toward the kitchen.

"Enjoy your breakfast," Arnold said softly, taking his cue. He was still half-bowed, and backed away a few steps before he turned on his heel and disappeared into the lobby.

"I think they see us as a renewal of Kittens Hollow," I whispered once he was out of earshot. "But I suppose if we come and make a success, others are bound to follow, and then Kittens Hollow will be back to normal—"

I cut myself off as I saw the waiter returning with a teapot and coffeepot, and smiled nicely back at him.

"Thank you," Elizabeth said quietly, to which he bowed slightly after he'd unloaded the pots to the table.

"Have you decided on breakfast?" he wondered casually as he poured our first cups, and only then did I see the menus before us.

"Oh, no, not quite," I answered, so the waiter bowed lightly again, then silently turned and left us to our decisions.

* * *

When we stepped onto the porch after breakfast the view took my breath away. A slow mist rolled off the sound in front of us, lit by an early-morning sun that peeked over the hill to the east, just off from rising directly over the "V" of the hollow. The water that broke through the mist lapped in a golden flow, fed by the sun's rays, moving slowly toward Green Lake in the distance; if I squinted, I could just make out the bridge that spanned the sound at the entrance to the lake.

But if the sound and hollow was beautiful in the light of day, the rest of Kittens Hollow, in stark contrast, veritably shunned being looked upon. The cobblestoned road that ran along the bank of the sound for the length of Kittens Hollow was pot-holed and crumbling, and in places was nothing but dirt covered with gravel. The buildings that ran in a row along this avenue, facing the sound, were rundown: the timber that showed through the peeling paint was gray and tired, and in places broken windows attested to the fact that most of the stores were empty, and had been for some time.

One continuous verandah led to the east, until naked eyesight could no longer distinguish if it ended or just kept going endlessly. To the west, toward Green Lake, it didn't extend nearly as far, with maybe five more storefronts before the walkway ended suddenly in what looked to be a small dump. For all intents and purposes, the whole of Kittens Hollow was one long building that ran a good length of the sound, some stores extending into two stories, like the hotel, while others had just the one.

"Where do people live?" Elizabeth wondered, and I squinted across the sound at the hillside, scanning for homes, but not seeing any.

"I don't know..." I mused. "I'm sure there are apartments above some of the stores...and maybe further back, toward Green Lake, there are houses? Or around Lake Harper? We know there are houses there."

"I suppose," she nodded, but seemed uncertain, as if resigning herself to having to live in the present poverty, if we indeed decided to open a store in Kittens Hollow.

"Let's look around," I offered, taking her hand. "Maybe it's not so bad." She smiled to brighten her spirits as we moved east, toward the distant, unseen end of the verandah.

I don't think the hour of day accounted sufficiently for the still-ness of the town; our footsteps echoed hollowly along the boards, rattling loose dust from the eaves overhead and scaring the odd bird or scurrying animal. The first three storefronts were completely empty, the last two devoid even of whole panes of glass in the windows. At one time, I could tell, they had been grand and beautiful—bay windows that looked out on windowpots of plants and pedestrians resting for a moment on rustic benches, while still more people wandered past. Now those people all walked the halls of the Green Lake resort, I assumed, and the empty windows stared blankly across the road to the sound, like the eyes of a child left alone, wanting only to be brought back into the fold and hugged.

"It's depressing," Elizabeth mumbled, glancing at me apologetically.

I nodded. "Yes...but there's an air to it all. Ancient grandeur or something—"

"You're so romantic!" she chided, sliding her hand from mine and stopping at a window.

"What is it?" I asked.

I turned and stopped beside her, peering through the window, and saw a small group of people sitting before a fire, drinking tea.

"Well—see?—there's life on this planet, after all!" I declared, moving for the door, but Elizabeth hurriedly grasped my hand and pulled me softly away.

"No...Reggie..."

"What? Don't you want to see what these people want in their town?"

She shrugged, her lips twitching a quick grin. "What if they don't want anything? What if they just want to be left alone to...die?"

"Bah!" I declared with a laugh. "If I'm too romantic, then you're far too dramatic! They're *people*—they must want to see Kittens Hollow thrive again!"

She nodded and allowed me to tug her to the door. The knob squeaked painfully beneath my hand, and if I had been hoping for a stealthy entry, that plan was quickly demolished by the noise. All heads—maybe six of them—stopped talking and turned to face us. A chill crept inexplicably up my spine, as if I were a solider in the conquering army trying to fraternize with the defeated natives.

"Hello!" I called, waving as Elizabeth slipped behind me, grasping my coat for dear life. "My wife and I were just passing by..."

I stopped and lowered my hand, hoping someone would say something in response. No one moved, then finally a man rose and smiled widely. "Are you that Mr. Ainsworth, from the city?"

"That's right!" I said, moving across the room with my hand extended. Elizabeth let go of me and stood near the door looking quite nervous. The place was apparently a tearoom, and as I moved further in I saw a deli-bar at the back of the room. The main room, where the door and bay window were, was empty of furniture, and the six patrons were all huddled sensibly in a dug-out seating area that surrounded a fireplace. The man stepped up and greeted me on the bare boards of the entrance room.

"Glad to meet you!" he said, taking my hand. "Arthur McMurdouc."

"McMur—?" I began to wonder, but his face held an expression that said it would be rude to question him over his veracity. His clothing indeed decried wealth, as did that of all the patrons—albeit fading, soon-to-be-moth-eaten wealth. I tried to smile, then let go of his hand and motioned to Elizabeth.

"My wife, Elizabeth."

She smiled quickly but never took her eyes from Arthur McMurdouc.

"Won't you join my friends?" Mr. McMurdouc said to her. "I'd like to show Mr. Ainsworth what Kittens Hollow has to offer."

"Uhh...no, thank you," she replied graciously, backing up a step.

"Reggie, I'll just go back to the hotel and wait for you, okay? I feel light-headed...."

"Yes, all right," I agreed with concern, moving toward her.

"I'm all right, honestly. I just want to lie down."

"Yes..." I agreed again, my hands still held out to comfort her as she backed through the door with a weak smile. I watched as she hurried past the bay window, with another weak smile as she glanced in, on her way to the hotel.

"I apologize—" I said, turning back to my host. My breath caught in my throat.

Arthur McMurdouc stood smiling at me in a room that blazed with life. The once-grayed walls now held all the rich detail of the original wood, and the area around the fireplace was packed with people drinking tea, smoking, and talking in uproarious tones. The seating—that wasn't taken—was a plush red, and the barman looked haggard with having to deal with all the business. Indeed, the floor I was standing on was now filled with tables and chairs, and still more patrons, eating tea cakes, laughing, and carrying on. Mr. McMurdouc slid up beside me and put an arm around my shoulder, turning me back to the door Elizabeth had just walked through, motioning for me to join him as he went outside.

"No need to apologize, Mr. Ainsworth," he replied jovially, holding the door open and allowing me to pass through it, back onto the walkway. I glanced over my shoulder as he joined me, closing the door behind him, and through the dusty, crusted window I saw a completely empty store, as gray and rundown as I had expected, but then he had his arm around my shoulder again and was leading me down the promenade, further from the hotel.

I felt dizzy for a moment, and surreptitiously closed my eyes, rubbing them slightly. When I opened them I had another jolt, as I the street before me was now busy with traffic and the promenade was bustling with people that we had to weave between as we made our way along it. Everywhere was resplendent with fresh paint and decorative wood accents; the boards sounded firmly as the footfalls padded along them. A barge of some kind was slipping past the whole scene on the sound, and in the distance I heard a train whistle blowing as it moved along the high rim of the hollow far above us, bringing more people to Kittens Hollow.

"As you can see," Mr. McMurdouc almost shouted above the din, "we are capable of bringing quite a crowd to Kittens Hollow. I think any business you open would do very well here indeed!"

"Yes," I agreed distractedly, trying to take in the sights, sounds, and smells that suddenly assailed me in this previously-barren town. I saw mothers, dressed in great, hooped dresses, shuffling children before them while their husbands marched pompously behind, puffing on grand cigars or loping pipes. The roadway was completely cobblestoned and the horses' hooves and carriages' wheels made a romantic click and rumble over the surface as taxi drivers called out to careless pedestrians who were in danger of being trampled. Around us, the tiny bells of countless stores jingled carelessly as the doors were continually opened and closed, their tiny jangle echoing over the water, describing the commerce of the town.

"It's a beautiful place, isn't it, Mr. Ainsworth?" my host declared, stopping and sweeping his arm grandly to denote the expanse before us.

"It is," was all I could think to say. We were about to move forward again when through the bustle a young boy moved purposefully toward us, carrying a large, old, box camera.

"Your picture, Mr. McMurdouc?" the boy asked rhetorically. "For the paper?"

"Of course!" the jovial man cried, planting his arm firmly around my shoulders once more. I tried to smile as broadly as he did while we waited for the flash, which detonated quite suddenly and explosively before our eyes, blinding me for an instant. I felt dizzy again, and my knees buckled slightly; I grabbed at McMurdouc for support, but my flailing hands couldn't find purchase, and I fell with embarrassment to the planks of the verandah beneath me. From behind me I heard footsteps hurrying over, then felt a strong grip take me under my arms. I smelled Elizabeth's soft perfume and opened my eyes to her concerned form, crouching down before me, her delicate hand on my forehead. All around her, Kittens Hollow was as silent as a corpse, its graying timbers and peeling paint again describing a scene of slow rot, not affluence.

"Reggie?" Elizabeth cried, helping me back to my feet. "Oh, God! Are you all right?"

"Yes...I...you saw him, right?"

"Who?"

"That man—McMurdouc?"

Her face looked horrified for an instant as she fought back confused tears. "I saw them all, Reggie, that's why I left. But then...well...I just came back out for a moment to see if I could spot you—to see if he'd been real—and you were weaving like a drunkard..."

"Alone?" I assumed.

"Yes," she whispered. "Reggie, they were never there."

* * *

When we returned to the hotel, Arnold Makesmith watched us with an expectant grin.

"Enjoy your walk?" he asked, and I could swear he winked. I separated myself from Elizabeth and wandering slowly over to the deskman.

"Yes," I said slowly. "Say, were you knocking on my door last night?"

"No, sir," he denied categorically, nervously rubbing the back of his neck.

"Do you know what's going on around here, Mr. Makesmith?" I snapped.

"Going on, sir?"

"Yes—is this town haunted?"

Elizabeth grabbed my arm and pulled me away from the desk with an apologetic smile at the crooked old man.

"Honey," she said, "why don't we go and relax by the fire for a minute or two?" Then she whispered under her breath. "You sound like a mad man, Reggie."

I let her pull me away, over to the fireplace, which was thankfully ablaze. We sat down on the couch across from it and I felt truly winded, as if from a great exertion.

"Sir?" Arnold said quietly, having snuck up behind us. "Mr. Ainsworth? Missus? Would you care for a drink—tea, perhaps?" Elizabeth glanced at me over his choice of beverage, then we shared a briefly mirthful grin.

"Yes," I said quietly, settling my head back on the couch. "Tea would be fine, thank you."

"Me, too," Elizabeth agreed. Arnold Makesmith smiled warmly, then scurried off to the dining room with our orders.

"It was beautiful," I whispered distantly, my eyes closed and remembering.

"What was?" Elizabeth asked.

"Kittens Hollow...in its day. It was beautiful..."

Elizabeth said nothing in response, but I could tell that she was also smiling.

* * *

When I crawled into bed that night, nothing could have felt better than letting my body's weight float free on the cushioning of the mattress and pillows. Indeed, though the day had been lackadaisical after the events of the haunted morning, I discovered upon lying down that my frame had been carrying the full stress of my mind over the affair the whole time. Trying to forget something so grand and inexplicable had apparently been taxing work; Elizabeth, too, sighed deeply as she lay down and drew the covers over herself.

"Odd day," I summed up. She grunted her assent and rolled onto her side, curling up next to me as I lay on my back, staring at the darkness above. I glanced toward her through the murk, but could tell by her body's state that she was relaxed and falling asleep already.

"We'll leave tomorrow," I decided quietly, more to myself than anything.

"Will we be back?" she asked sleepily, her voice muffled by my shoulder.

"I'm not sure..." I admitted, falling silent as my mind cleared, until finally I was aware of nothing. Not too long later, it seemed, a firm hand roused me from my slumber, shaking my shoulder lightly. "Mr. Ainsworth?" a man's voice said near my ear. My eyes shot open and I jolted to wakefulness, sure that Mr. Makesmith was in our room waking me for only one reason: The hotel was on fire.

"Makesmith!" I demanded. I could see a form that had backed off a few steps, but the darkness allowed for no details; the figure, however, did not have the decrepit, hunched form of the hotel's desk-man.

"Mr. Ainsworth," the voice said again, calmly. "I want to show you something."

"Who are you?" I cried, throwing back the covers and sitting on the edge of the bed. I checked Elizabeth quickly, but she still lay quietly curled up and sleeping.

"She won't wake..." the man explained.

"What have you done to her!" I shrieked, leaping to my feet and reaching for the light. The man shot across the room and stopped my hand on the switch before I could turn it; the weak light from the curtained window illuminated a vague outline of his face that seemed, oddly, familiar.

"It's me, Mr. Ainsworth...Arthur McMurdouc."

"Wha—?" I gasped, pulling my hand away from his. "Mr. McMurdouc?"

"Yes—from the tearoom?"

"Oh God," I breathed. "Why are you haunting me?"

The apparition laughed softly. "I'm not here to scare you, sir. I'm here for your help."

"Help?"

"Come with me, please. Let me show you something."

Grudgingly, I followed him to the door of the room, which, though I saw it was still locked, he deftly opened, motioning for me to follow him out into the hall. As soon as I stepped over the threshold I realized I was no longer in the hotel at Kittens Hollow.

In front of me, the movement of the muddy Muskingham River lapped near McMurdouc's shoes in the moonlight. The delicate tinkle of the liquid at his feet served in perfect contrast to the peeper frogs and crickets that thrummed and chirped in the dark woods around us. The moon, like a tired glass eye, beaded down in crystalline simplicity; a low wisp of cloud flitted across its surface as a barely-glimpsed shadow. When I looked over my shoulder I saw not the open doorway to my room, but simply more woods, breathing in a thick summer night heavy with humidity. I sighed and turned back to the enigmatic ghost before me, and fully accepted that he was guiding my present dream.

"Yes," he toned to the peeper frogs, his wide eyes scanning the dark thickness of trees. Save for the moon above, and its silver-threaded reflection in the slow-churning Muskingham River, McMurdouc was encapsulated in complete darkness. The heat was almost oppressive; one could veritably see the moisture hanging in the air, waiting only to fall.

The apparition adjusted his hat and wiped the sweat from his brow in one fell swoop, then stood still, eyes wide, shoes flexing in the dry grass and dust of the cracked earth at the river's edge, producing a soft, crinkled whisper of noise. He glanced at the water momentarily, with a wistful expression, then snapped his head around and met my eyes.

"Green Lake is a sacred place," he said pointedly. "I built in the Hollow so as not disturb its shores. Eventually, I hoped to have enough to buy up the choice land so that it could not be developed. But the Resort beat me to it."

"Sacred?" I queried. "In what way?"

"In the way that certain areas are, Mr. Ainsworth. Maybe its only sacred in the way the sunrise, at the summer solstice, peeks right between the walls of Kittens Hollow and along the river, here, to Green Lake. Maybe its the wildlife. Maybe its the *energy* of the place," he finally stressed with inference.

He motioned to the expanse before me, drawing my attention to the east, where I could now see the distant black valley walls of Kittens Hollow heaved up against the horizon as the first rays of sun shot like a beacon from the mouth of the sound, expanding over us toward Green Lake in a massive orange blanket, while the clear sky above displayed the splendor of the universe, unimpeded by the lights of the city. If the faithful were searching for evidence of God, I realized in my dream of Green Lake, they were covering it up with their roofs and searching for Him, fruitlessly, inside their churches.

McMurdouc turned back to face the river, now suddenly dark again and out of the moon's path. Slowly, he made his way to its bank and plodded west along its peaceful side, humming, it appeared, to the natural music of the peeper frogs and insects. Gradually, I followed his darkening form, my bare feet padding softly over the cracked, dusty bank; the warm dirt beneath my soles was a strange comfort I could never hope to match again.

I had learned long ago that sometimes it is better to simply follow and learn, rather than hamper the teacher with questions. All would be told to those who cared to listen; all questions would be answered before the final turning of night. Sometimes asking questions merely fills the silence of discovery with ungraceful clatter in the hopes of an early finish. There was much I did not understand and many questions I held, but I also understood the difference between wonder and questioning. So often the journey is worth more than a hundred answers. Faith, I suppose, is the knowledge that some questions are unimportant.

McMurdouc stopped near a crude footbridge that spanned the river and gazed up at the stars in the space above the water. I followed his gaze and noticed that the Milky Way echoed the course of the Muskingham River as it ran across the landscape to fall silently into the waters that would, eventually, make up Green Lake, still miles away.

He stepped forward and walked over the bridge. My eyes had adjusted to the near-complete gloom of the forest by the time he struck off on the other side, along an old path through the trees that had many years of footprints over it. He wound through the forest, steadying himself now and again on a tree trunk, or by momentarily grasping a branch that hung in his way, and soon enough we emerged from the woods and looked up through a natural clearing to the stars and moon that gazed down from above.

With a certain sense of trepidation, McMurdouc motioned at the moon, which was sinking quickly, almost lost by its angle over the trees. Hurriedly, he paced to the center of the clearing where stood a single, white statue of a woman, her left arm clutching a massive tome while her right arm held her hand out-stretched, its palm facing up toward the western horizon. By the glow of the moon, the statue's finely crafted body and flowing robes shone with eerie iridescence. As I walked a slow circle around it, smiling in spite of myself, I could hear a low music, like a soft flute whispering in tones beyond recognition; a casual, glowing lilt that flowed with the energy of its own resonance.

Arthur McMurdouc stopped and bent over near the statue's out-stretched palm, his expression dropping with concentration. Slowly, he relaxed and closed his eyes, his earlobe momentarily brushing the stone surface, and I understood that the sound was the music of the moon singing in Sophia's hand.

"Some places are just sacred," I heard him whisper. He put his fingers on my elbow, pulling for me to move closer; his touch made me aware that I, too, had closed my eyes and had been in the trance of the peaceful world around me. When I slowly opened my eyes to smile at him, I found myself back in bed. Elizabeth was fully dressed, standing over me like a mother, with her hands on her hips.

The last remnant of the dream that buzzed in my head was of McMurdouc as he walked off toward the head of the trail that led back to the river. Stopping several feet from the opening, he turned back and looked over his shoulder, smiling a thank-you to me, then returned to his course, leaving me to memorize the revelations of the moon.

* * *

Elizabeth threw open the curtains, revealing a sunlit view of the trees on the imposingly-close valley wall; the scene looked almost unreal in the odd lighting of a sun whose rays were barely able to penetrate the hollow at such an early hour.

"It's beautiful!" she smiled gleefully.

"What time is it?" I asked rhetorically, glancing at the clock.

"Little after eight," my wife replied anyway, moving over to my side and pulling the covers from me.

"We'll miss breakfast," she explained, then turned and looked out the window again. I rose and snuck up behind her, putting my hands on her hips and lightly kissing her neck.

"You like it?" I wondered, hypnotized myself by the tree-en-shrouded slope of the valley's hill; the branches were rustling myster-iously, the leaves ready to turn color and fall, especially, I figured, after last night's chill.

"I love it," she replied, resting her head back on my shoulder. I moved my hands around her, clasping them over her stomach.

"Think we can run a business here, though?"

She shrugged. "Obviously some people still come here. It's quiet..."

"Yes," I agreed. "It'd have to be a quiet business, too."

She turned on me, her face with a playful expression. "And what *other* kind of business were you thinking of opening? A nightclub with topless dancers?"

"Why not...?"

She hit my shoulder with her open palm and shook her head. "Go and get ready for breakfast," she said, then chased me into the bathroom.

When I was dressed and came back out she was sitting in one of the chairs, gazing wistfully out the window.

* * *

Elizabeth was at the counter settling the bill with Mr. Makesmith while I stood by the fireplace looking over pictures of Kittens Hollow in its heyday. My dream would not let me go, and I wondered if it really was possible to revive the town and fulfill what I had learned was McMurdouc's vision of a privately-owned park system around

Green Lake. I could certainly imagine pilgrimages to see the sunrise on the summer solstice every year, and perhaps that's all the advertisement I would need to get the plan underway. Once you attach something so significant—even sacred—to something, people tended to rally around preservation.

"Reggie?" Elizabeth asked, walking up behind me and breaking my reverie. "Ready to go?"

"Sure," I replied thoughtfully.

"Will we be back?" she wondered hopefully as my eyes fell on the last picture. It was from a historic edition of a Kittens Hollow newspaper and showed Mr. Arthur McMurdouc posing with "an unknown investor" on the busy promenade beside Kittens Hollow Sound. I smiled broadly, with only a brief shiver, as my eyes locked onto the eyes of a picture of myself, standing beside McMurdouc.

As we left the hotel and headed for our waiting taxi, out the corner of my eye I caught Mr. Makesmith watching us. I turned to him and smiled as we passed through the door, and he winked, his face carrying the same esoteric expression that had previously seemed so out of place.

"Yes," I finally answered Elizabeth. "We're going to come back and buy the whole damn town."

Oizus

This is where I got off the train last time.

This is where I always get off the train.

It's a dusty station out where the tumbleweeds are the only friends to greet you. Once the train-whistle air has vanished, you may catch the lonesome screech of a raven, or you may hear the wind trying to gently whisper your name.

The first step along the platform is the hardest. You just want to stand there forever, staring across the silver tracks at the vast blue sheet of sky; staring at the crescent moon waiting to fall off the western horizon, once night has made it glow luminescent white; staring at the animals that are brave enough to scurry through the scrub, badgering the dirt with their noses, pushing pebbles in a spray of tinkling noise.

Eventually you will have to move; the first step along is the hardest.

The tired planks will echo with the hollow sound of your foot-shuffle as you turn and bend to pick up your suitcase; a hand still in your pocket, not yet exposed to the tepid air, will surface for counter-balance.

Then you begin to walk, casually, heedless of time, for time no longer has meaning. A breeze may kick up, basking you with grit, but I'm sure you'll not notice, this first time. Your footsteps will appear to follow you, just a little behind, like you were trying to catch yourself. You may even spin around on your heel, convinced you're being followed, but the raven will screech its laughter as only a tumbleweed heads across the tracks.

So you walk on, the tracks to the left, the old dusty building to the right. The woodwork is rough, but painstakingly placed to produce the perfect union of the artful and the useful. Maybe you will run a hand across its side, catching splinters like the prickles of a messy face. Maybe you'll stare too long at the bench under the window, wondering if you should sit and wait for the next train, knowing you better not. In time, you will think to enter the squat pavilion.

The first thing you'll notice will be the smell: the scent of old wood in the prime of existence, mixed with a moist smell of dirt and a light undertone of cleaning supplies (if the Watchman has cleaned recently).

You will most likely put your suitcase down just inside the door, and as your eyes adjust to the dim interior, you'll take in the row of back-to-back benches down the center of the room, nestled between two stout pillars. You'll see the boarded-up concession stand and the empty dining tables and chairs. Then you'll notice the Watchman sitting behind the ticket window, reading his paper.

He'll be a balding man, with just a ring of gray hair on his small head. His eyes will be intent on the paper, whether at horror from what he reads or just stupidity, you can't be sure. He'll have on a blue work-shirt and jeans, his black boots propped on the desk before him. He may glance at you, but he won't move until you speak.

"Excuse me," you'll say, and he'll look around his paper at you. After eying you with great suspicion, as is his job, his feet will slide to the floor with a dull thud, then he'll fold his paper and come to the ticket window.

"Wanna know 'bout the next train?" he'll wonder, his piercing blue eyes jumping over you. He'll reach for a slip of paper, miss, lick his thumb, and try again, this time successfully.

He'll slide the paper to you and you'll see that it's blank. His face will crack into a sympathetic grin, having seen your expression many times, and he'll say, "Ain't no more trains comin', m'fraid." He may cough into his hand—a dry-throated wheeze—and if he sneezes, he'll produce a floppy white handkerchief from his pocket with which to blow his nose.

You'll ask more questions, but the Watchman will only shrug, finally returning to his paper, putting his feet up, and not hearing another word you say. Even so, you will more than likely feel calm, taking the blank slip of paper he gave you and wandering back over to your suitcase.

After sliding the slip of paper into your left front pocket, you'll bend and reclaim your luggage, dragging it to the end of the bench farthest from the Watchman, across from the doorway on the street side of the station. You'll sit, nervously, leaning your elbows on your knees, watching your hands, and you'll wait for whatever comes up next, maybe casting a secret glance at the street.

Soon you slide your feet under you with a graceful swipe, and stand. The Watchman may regard you curiously for a moment, or he may be in the back checking on his coffee. You will not even think about your suitcase, but rather just walk purposefully out the opening between the windows, to the street beyond. You will stand and survey the beige, cracked earth before you, with its stray green stubble placed rarely in some of the rivulets dug by the last rain, now since long forgotten. You may stand like that for minutes or hours, because the land beyond is mesmerizing.

A thought will occur shortly, and you'll wonder exactly where it is that you are. You will stumble half-backwards, mostly sideways, into the dust of the street, always keeping an eye over your shoulder for the sign on top of the station. Soon you will break the shadow of that housing, and the sign will appear below the hanging crescent moon: "Oizus." You will nod, unsurprised, and turn back to the baked land ahead.

So this is where you will be. So this is where centuries of people have trodden, their footprints brushed away by the breath of the wind. And although it looks as if it rained recently, no one has ever seen a drop fall, save the Watchman, who may have been too busy reading his paper to see it. This is where you are going, where it is necessary to live and tell, to pass on the Being to the future, to rage on in the dust and beat back the past. This is what you must do and where you must go.

The road beside the station is covered with inches of dust, but no tire tracks, and the crossing is easy. The other side is hard, like cracked granite without the comfort of a shine. The land has been callused, and the vegetation is stronger.

You will begin to walk across this waste in no particular hurry, your hands hanging limply beside you, swinging to keep your balance. The sun will appear warm on your neck, but it must not be, for every time you involuntarily rub the spot, it is cool. Sweat will, however, form on your brow, but when it runs to the corners of your mouth, your tongue will taste no salt, but instead refreshing water that reminds you of a mountain spring spilling over soft rocks.

You will walk like this forever, never losing track of the time you have forgotten, never getting bored of the same cracked view ahead and to the sides, until finally you will see more green—continuous green in front of you, like a field, but lush, like a forest. When you arrive at the edge of the cracked land, you will find yourself looking down on a full growth of trees, for as far as your eyes can see. A forest begins at the bottom of the cliff; the trees are very tall, the new ground they are rooted in perhaps miles below.

Suddenly you will be very thirsty, and when you turn around to see all that you have accomplished in your walk along forever, you will see the station at Oizus, just across the street; yet any step toward it for water will cause the vision to retreat a step, to taunt you, and you may try to catch it for hours, always returning, unfulfilled, to the forest at the edge of the cracked land. The exercise will show you only one thing: your sweat has turned sour, and your thirst burns hotly in your throat.

Once back at the land's edge you may stand and consider your options, or it may occur to you instantly, but soon enough you will feel the urge to jump into the emerald canopy below, and this you shall do.

You won't fall far before you begin to float through the crisp autumnal air. You may flail as if drowning, kicking your feet and gasping for composure, but soon you will realize this does no good, then you will merely float; oblivious, serene.

You will only float like that, unmoving, for a few minutes, then your thirst will press you to action, and you will fall, suddenly, simply. You will rocket to the trees, maybe with your arms spread in cliched bird-dom, maybe at your side like the arrow you have become. Falling will feel intense, but not unworthy, and you will dip into the trees of olden times, the wood brandished with ancient life and secret knots like eyes. Whipping through the branches, dancing with the leaves, you will come to fires and smoke twirling slowly skyward, the cliff a long-forgotten memory, miles back and farther up.

You may find him immediately, being pulled to his fire, or you may sit by yourself, content to wait, having landed on this soft-grassed earth beneath the green canopy, drinking from the cup beside the fire; the cup that never empties of quenching water. Either way, he will come. A small man with one crossed eye; short, straggly, gray hair; teeth too big and crooked; arm bent unnaturally; a tired gait to his walk. He will come. He will tell you he is a survivor of the forest, the guardian of life, but he'll wink, and you shall be left uncertain.

Sometimes he asks, but soon he will have your cup, sipping from it appreciatively, nodding at the vintage flavor, asking if your thirst is slaked. Answer, and he is gone, grinning healthily in the blink of an eye.

The fires, though comforting, you will leave behind. They will diminish before you turn your back on them, having watched them down to ashes; having sunk lower on the eyelids and taken a nap; having forgotten to move on for the moment, content to sit in the dying heat and whisper good-bye to paler shades of shadows hanging from the trees like Spanish moss; wondering what stories the firs and oaks and witches' circles hold quietly in their sap-filled lives, guarded like the warm baby of an angry she-wolf.

There will be plenty of time to consider these things as you walk through the woods, circled by the birds, following no paths, nor getting lost. On you will walk, marking your progress by the sun that fails; by the stars that wink out of the pin-prickled sky; by the chill that comes to cloud your breath.

It is nightfall, and the time feels right. The air is thinning, lit by the silver face of the moon hung like a ghost in the branches. Fall with full leaves, a strangeness too beautiful to be brutal. A smile may crease your lips, a serious persuasion of honesty, for ill or all.

You can't help but stop and take everything in: the branches heaving languidly in the darkness, fading out the silver dots above, bowing contentedly toward you under the pressure of the winds. Somewhere an owl will cry, a wolf will howl, and if you're fortunate enough, you will catch the mechanical graunch of the elk: a high-pitched timbre-wail piercingly melancholic, sinisterly taunting.

On the eve of the elk's voice, a tear my roll down your from your eye, with a whiff of smoke and leaves in the still air. Here is the wilderness. Here is that one old captured moment twisting through the trees. Here is a loneliness so complete as to scar. Standing at the foot of the sky, looking up, you will come to know that nothing is staring back, yet the trees are listening—and you'll listen to what they describe to you.

Sunrise, next morning, on the wet ground, the gentle smell of dirt is refreshing as your pillow. You will rise, sprinkles falling from your hair, and gaze deeply into a waterfall, ahead through the trees, glittering down like shards of glass. You will listen to its sound—its delicate hush of whispers in the pool below—and you may consider where it was last night, when so much was ignored and everything was drawn into you.

Standing, muscles cramped, a bird will scour the air with its cry, and you may catch a glimpse of its figure darting off, high above the trees. The canopy will look inviting, and a wish comes, to be up there again, flying. The waterfall beckons, and you will be drawn to its lull.

Its radiant splashes will soon cover your head, running down your arms, over your chest, into the pool. It will be cool, taking you off in eddies and spirals of mirrored thoughts. The station at Oizus is far away, but you have yet to leave its shadow.

Finally quenched, you will wade from the spill to the shore, maybe taking a few gulps of the silver-clear refreshment. The rocks look like waves below, golden fish darting between your legs, and so hypnotized, you will miss the figure as he takes your clothes, all hunched and crookedly cautious. The discovery will leave you outraged, searching the perimeter for the thief. Eyes as sharp as eagles' claws, you will find nothing but emerald bliss. You will rise out of the water, look cautiously for spies, then slip onto the land. At first it may feel wrong, but strangely comfortable, vaguely familiar, and soon enough it will feel natural.

Scouting your surroundings, you find the urge to go up again, and decide to climb the rock beside the waterfall and once more stand above the forest. Placing your feet gingerly in mossy cracks, fingers digging into strange crevices, you will work your way up, the sound of the falls crashing farther and farther away below. With a last effort you will haul yourself over the rim, sprawling face down in thick, moist grass. Your angle will make the blades appear huge, like leaves standing up; an ocean of green you could almost swim in.

Rising to your knees, you will study the field stretching in all directions beyond your sight. All except behind you, where the falls descend, but you won't look back now, not even when you realize no river feeds the falls below. You won't look back, though the urge may twinge your soul, because in front you see nothing but a sprint through sun and grass. Arms stretched, so running, you will never feel that way again, embracing all of nothing, the breeze cooling your naked body as it dances, circles, and jumps, but always moves forward. Then the dances will end, and as you regain your capacities, you will stop dead in your tracks.

Ahead lies a dusty hut, silver lines stretching in either direction along the ground before it. Your eyes will wander over the familiar surroundings; your heart will miss a beat.

The sign on the hut says "Oizus."

And you can hear a train coming from the right, may even see its white puff of cloud on the horizon.

Disheartened, you will run to the station, stopping at the line where grass becomes parched earth, at the lip of the embankment to the tracks. A glance will show you the train, puffing closer. You will stumble down the embankment, the rocks hurting your feet, the tracks burning your soles as you dodge across them. On the platform stands the Watchman, knowingly. He'll nod at your suitcase, smile at your nakedness, then tap the suitcase with the tip of his old boot.

You'll move quickly, and by the time you've changed and re-turned to the platform, the train will have arrived and the Watchman will have disappeared. The doors of the carriage are open, so you toss your suitcase in, your clothes rigid with constraint. You'll grab the rail and start to pull yourself onboard, but something will catch your eye, emerging from another carriage.

This is where I got off the train last time.

This is where I always get off the train.

Arthur Dodd's Last Measure

To the audience it may have seemed like Arthur Dodd was watching angels—at least that's how his mother used to describe Arthur's long preoccupations staring at things no one else could see. But that was sixty years ago, when he was a child and such imaginative explanations were necessary. Now he was simply old, and that was explanation enough.

He heard the woman next to him cough lightly and rustle her sheet music in an effort to draw his attention away from whatever it was above the stage that had caught his eye, but Arthur ignored her, just as he had done for the last 20 years. The moth circling the stage lights like a tiny planet was infinitely more fascinating. It looped and twirled in a tight dance, and Arthur could almost hear the strings swell and brass demark as the music only he could hear described each sweep of motion or turn.

As Arthur watched, the moth made an excessively sharp turn and hit one of the lights far above the stage and fizzled, spiraling down in a cramped circle that brought the creature very nearly onto Arthur's head. He dodged just a hair's breadth and it instead bounced off his shoe and came to rest in the shadow of his music stand.

Around him the other strings tuned and whined in random syncopation. Arthur Dodd lowered his bow to the floor and prodded the hapless insect, now either thoroughly stunned or dead. His brow furrowed in concentration as he poked the moth. Its wings were spread but unmoving, the hair-like legs twitching almost in time with Arthur's jabs. He grimaced slightly and poked a bit harder—surely the poor thing had not so easily expired?

"Arthur," hissed the woman next to him—Regilia Smith, first violin (as she always introduced herself, no doubt even in the company of strangers at a grocery store). "What are you doing? They can see you."

Arthur had never concerned himself with the auditorium beyond the stage—it was the only way he could keep from quivering with nerves. He didn't look now, either, nor did he glance at Regilia Smith. He prodded his moth once more, then slowly sat up as the house lights dimmed.

"Sit up straight," Regilia admonished with a toothy smile, knowing full well that Arthur had not physically been able to sit straight for at least 10 years. He took a deep breath and didn't even try to humor her. After 35 years with the orchestra, even trying to sit up seemed as pointless as everything else. What was one more concerto or symphony when he had left a trail of bent-backed performances behind him—a long career that had seen more than one Regilia Smith in the seat to his right but had left him always the proverbial second fiddle?

When the conductor made his entrance Arthur was looking at the lights above the stage again. He didn't even see the maestro greet Regilia then bow to the crowd, and when that first serene note of the first measure shimmered from his violin his eyes were fixed on the immobile form of the moth at his feet.

* * *

"You seem poorly, Arthur," a lanky man said to him backstage after the concert. He held a small case for his tympani mallets like a jewel thief escorting his prize to a fence.

171

"I'm all right," Arthur replied, smiling, but the sparkle of his eyes was dimmed and his skin seemed to be clinging to his face in a last effort at life. "Just a little tired. Worried about my dog—she's old, you know. And then there's Regilia—"

"Ah! Understood," the tympanist replied with a bob at the waist and a smile. He leaned in secretively and added, "She is, of course, blaming you for the lack of emotion in tonight's performance. No one believes her," he added hastily. "I mean, it's not *your* job to keep emotions high."

Arthur chuckled lightly and patted the man on the shoulder. "Actually, I think that's why I'm so tired."

"How's that?" The tympanist's eyebrows quivered with curiosity, as if the muscles were too weak to fully raise them.

"I used to care," Arthur shrugged distantly.

"Hey, you've done this long enough to know we all have off nights."

Arthur tried to smile gratefully but it looked more like a wince. He sighed and dropped the ruse, patting his friend's shoulder again. "It's Christmas Eve—I just want to get home to my dog."

Arthur winked then tapped his violin case and turned to the exit.

* * *

"Helix?" Arthur knocked the snow from his shoes then stepped inside and shut out the cold. "Helix, old girl," he called a bit more loudly. "Did you miss me?"

There was a slow click on the linoleum in the kitchen, then a graying black mutt tottered into view, her tail low but wagging happily. She nudged Arthur's hand with her nose and offered his fingertips a slow, methodical lick, then sat down and yawned widely, almost expectantly. Arthur coughed into his fist—a low rumble in his lungs that strained his throat.

"We're a pair, aren't we, girl?" he mumbled, sliding off his shoes. He put his violin down and shrugged off his heavy winter coat. "Too old to be walking in the snow, eh? How about some hot cocoa?" Helix's eyes glistened happily at Arthur as she diligently followed him into the kitchen. Outside, the wind rattled the panes and made the small home creak and groan, its timbers full of weather-worn duty. Arthur poured some water into the kettle and lit the ring beneath it, then turned from the stove and shuffled over to the thermostat—it always seemed cold to him these days, no matter what the temperature was set at.

"Well anyway," he mumbled, rattling out another cough as he saw that the temperature was a balmy 72. "At least we're home, eh?"

He turned and saw Helix curled in her favorite corner of the couch. She caught his eyes and flicked the end of her tail once, then smacked her lips, shut her eyes, and went back to sleep. To her left, in the window, Arthur's small Christmas tree glistened with fairy lights, its diffuse glow masking the gray in Helix's coat. For a moment she looked young again; barely a year old, and Arthur grinned widely as he recalled the day he'd brought her home. She'd been sick then—full of worms and infections—but she'd still managed to hop to her feet and excitedly jump up Arthur's leg whenever he came near her.

The kettle began to whistle, breaking Arthur's reverie. He shuffled back into the kitchen and poured the water over some cocoa mix, then turned off the light and used the glow of his Christmas tree to find his way to Helix's side.

"Ah, we've had a good run of it, though, haven't we, girl?"

He lowered himself onto the couch with a groan and watched the snow drifting down outside, sparkling silently in the white rays of the streetlamp.

"We had a good go..."

Arthur reached out his hand and touched Helix, tickling the side of her tummy. She didn't flinch or try to lick his fingers or even open her eyes. Arthur put down his cocoa on the endtable beside him and gently shook her.

"Helix?" he breathed, his eyes hot with tears, but still she lay motionless. "Ah, God bless you, girl," he said around a large sniffle.

"Thanks for waiting for me to get home."

A tear finally welled with enough weight and slid down his cheek, followed in quick succession by two more; great drops that glistened like icicles. Arthur Dodd had wanted nothing more than to sit with Helix on Christmas morning and watch the children outside play with their new toys.

"Wait for me, girl," he stammered, trying to hold back the tears. The effort only made him cough, the pain in his chest and throat tightening in response. He slumped back on the couch, put his head back, and closed his eyes, his fingers still twitching on Helix's side.

* * *

When he awoke from the dream he called to his dog, but there was no animal close at hand to answer his summons.

That Helix wasn't curled up on the couch beside him was no great surprise—she often slunk around at night, snuffling off after some morsel of food or in search of a modicum of trouble to keep herself occupied.

But the dream had beckoned Arthur Dodd to take her on a walk, back behind the sheds and garages of his neighbors, to the alleyway of grass cut through the trees at the end of his subdivision; trees that, in an era of encroaching suburbia, still wandered off into the hills and back country of the pioneers, sparsely sprinkled with the odd farmhouse or vineyard or ancient homestead gone to ruins, devoid of the life and gaiety brought by human occupants an age ago.

The dream had beckoned and Arthur Dodd had woken up, his neck stiff from sleeping on the couch, his hot cocoa stone cold and forgotten. As he came to his wakeful senses and mumbled his summons, Arthur realized Helix should still have been on the couch beside him, curled in the exact position she had been in when she'd entered her final sleep.

"Helix?" he called again, excitement rimming his voice as he sat up. He coughed hoarsely once and stood up, despite the rattle in his bones. He could hear the teeth of winter ripping at the walls and shaking the windows, and didn't relish the thought of chasing his dog through the woods at the behest of some half-remembered dream that even now was fading, just as the pale light of the full moon would soon be chased from the sky by the dim promise of a Christmas morning sun.

Arthur padded into the kitchen, fully expecting to see his dog dramatically sniffing her empty food bowl, but she was not to be found in the kitchen, nor on his bed where she normally curled up on the pillows and fell asleep.

"Helix?" he tried once more, now afraid that his companion had come back to life long enough to slink off somewhere private, and he'd missed his chance to see her once more. Arthur checked the den to no avail; nor did the guest room hold any answers.

Then he heard a small thud, as of a paw bending the aluminum of his screen door in just the way Helix had done to let him know she was ready to come back inside. That his dog—smart though she was—had not only opened and closed his back door, but also had first unlocked it, seemed highly unlikely, yet Arthur Dodd found himself standing in the back entryway in a crumpled tuxedo, mouth agape, considering just that likelihood. The wind pounded a few waves against the walls, but as he stood perfectly still and concentrated he heard it again: The precise and careful thud of Helix's paw against the back door, followed this time by a short, discreet yap that demanded entrance.

Arthur moved to the door as quickly as he could, only dimly aware that he had to unfasten the locks before opening it. Helix barked once more with joy and backed up a step as Arthur opened the door and let her in. A single, fat tear glistened in the moonlight on his face as she crossed the threshold, and Arthur realized three details simultaneously: He knew Helix had been curled up on the couch next to him in the light of the Christmas tree; her black coat now shone with white highlights because of its sheen, not age; and Helix dragged her leash into the house, it being fastened to her collar, waiting only for Arthur to grasp the other end and follow the advice of his dream.

"Helix? What on Earth happened? How did you get outside?"

Helix jumped up and licked his hand, her paws resting on his left thigh, her back legs stretched with youth and musculature. She pushed off and sat down before him, emitting a low, excited whine of anticipation, her eyes sparkling with life and intelligence. Arthur Dodd bent down slowly and scratched her ears, realizing as he did so that her fur was warm to the touch—she must have been outside for only a few seconds, perhaps no longer than it taken him to awake, rise, poke his head in each room, then discover his pet on the other side of a tightly locked door.

Arthur sighed and stood back up (ignoring the twinge in his back), smiling and trying not to think too much about the situation. If he could keep whatever magic this was in force for a few more hours, he may yet have his wish of sitting in the front window with her and watching the children play.

"Well, Helix Dodd," he said; her ears perked up and she cocked her head and wagged her tail slowly. "I suppose I had better get ready and take you on that walk."

The simple fact is that Arthur Bates Dodd was not a man to often ignore the promise or arcane knowledge of his dreams, least of all when some force had managed to revive his dog and place her on the outside of a locked door, leash in tow and ready for a stroll. Added to that fact was the night on which it had all transpired. Had it been just another wintry night, Arthur may well have removed the leash and crawled back into bed, dream or not, but this was Christmas morning, the starlight still shining before the sun had peeked down over the crystalline Earth, and if his mother had taught him anything it was that the only real magic left in the world was in the nethertime between sundown on Christmas Eve and sunrise on Christmas morning.

Even more than this was the full moon and Christmas snow—it was surely a time when walks through the woods could illicit all manner of miracles. To be sure, Arthur had witnessed one such event already, so he hastened into his coat and furry snow boots so as not to miss even the dimmest glimmer of magic still held resonant in the pre-dawn air.

"All right, old girl," Arthur asked as he opened the door and followed his dog into the thin winter of a timeless night. "Where to?"

Only once they had reached the grassy avenue cut through the woods by the city planners—soon to be a road, no doubt—did Helix stop pulling and allow Arthur to catch his breath. Past his neighbors' snow-covered humps of wood-piles and dilapidated rough-hewn sheds Helix had tugged him, along the easement between two quiet streets, the backs of the comfortable homes silent in the snowy darkness. Sometimes they heard a dog bark or scavenging animals scurrying from their path, but Helix had not been dissuaded and Arthur was not about to admonish her for tugging too hard, despite the icy tightness in his lungs.

When they finally left the neighborhood and entered the avenue cut through the small wood, the animal cast a furtive glance back at Arthur, as if apologizing for her behavior. Helix still plodded onward, but whatever force had drawn her out of their house was now clearly satisfied that, with all the distractions of neighbors and sidestreets and alternate routes out of the way, Arthur would follow the only course left open to him and would continue of his own free will into the woods.

And Arthur Bates Dodd did just that.

His was instantly transfixed by the smooth fall of snow that had sprung up, clouding the sky as the flakes silently tumbled from the heavens like diamonds through the trees; the iridescent covering glowed spectrally under the muted moonlight, stretching as a blue-white sheet into forever, the long avenue like a great white tunnel capped by the black vaulted dome of the sky. His footfalls made no more sound than a soft crunch; the lone call of an owl was quickly absorbed by the insulating snow, leaving Arthur alone in the woods with Helix at his side, her coat shining like the trunks of the leafless trees, standing in stark contrast to the world around them.

As they walked, the clouds thinned again and the snow stopped, allowing the starshine and moonlight to add a sharp silver lining to everything, which glowed as if lighted from within. Arthur kept moving behind Helix, his knees aching—he didn't remember this avenue, which they had walked down many times, to be so long. But the stillness and solitude of winter soothed him and he didn't mind; dreaded, in fact, the thought of soon emerging from the other end in another neighborhood. Yet when the end came into view, Arthur saw not the flashy windows and shiny siding of modern upscale homes, but instead, as if carved into the very landscape, the sharp angles and dormers of a Pioneer-era congregational church, the ruins of which Arthur had heard stories about, but had himself never found. He stopped for a moment and turned around, to see how far past the upscale homes they were (and how he had missed them), but saw nothing except an unbroken expanse of trees and snow behind him, sleeping happily in the moonlight. When he turned back, there it sat, a quiet monolith with a blank stare, dark windows for eyes, its stairs rolled out like a tongue, the snow already cleared from them as if to allow safe access for the early faithful.

Helix pulled anew at the sight of the humble cathedral and Arthur allowed himself to be forced forward by her. The pair stopped just before the first step, Helix looking expectantly from Arthur to the church, and Arthur gazing expectantly at the spire that loomed above them. The moon's light etched deep shadows over the surface of the cross's tower, in contrast to the ivory sheen of the white-washed siding that glowed from the south and west, but hung in darkness elsewhere. The cross itself, situated resplendently atop the spire, brooding over every tree, hill, and homestead, was black like the sky behind it, the copper having long since weathered to a dull memory of its former self. Arthur knew the cross was there only by the faintest trace of shining black against the black sky, glistening almost imperceptibly, like a distant cluster of stars barely visible to the naked eye. Even through the dulling motion of time the cross found light with which to shine, however feebly, and Arthur was touched by the resilience of human endeavors to praise that which we hold sacred.

Arthur was touched, but more so by the hand of time itself, for though the church looked far from ruined to him, he knew that even this hallowed ground would one day give way to make room for a new road with more houses and a strip mall. Arthur was touched by this faded glory, still standing tall against the stampede of progress that considered holding onto the past an impediment to advancing, as if that which was worthy from the past could not be brought into the future unchanged. Arthur closed his eyes for a moment and thanked whatever force had so far spared this forgotten holy site, and prayed that its protection would be sustained.

He opened his eyes and brought his gaze back down to the church's door, at which point Arthur Dodd saw that he and Helix were not alone. At the top of the stairs a small man in a dashing gray tuxedo grinned kindly. Helix sat beside Arthur and shifted her front paws excitedly, her tail wagging against the ground, curling wisps of snow into the air.

"Moongazing?" the man assumed, smiling more widely. He stood with his hands clasped behind his back and offered Arthur a small bow, the moonlight glinting off his bald pate, surrounded by a ring of puffy, gray hair.

"What's that?" Arthur checked. He began to climb the stairs toward the man, Helix bounding as far ahead as her leash would allow.

"Didn't you notice the moon tonight? It's bigger. Well, closer, really." The man pointed over Arthur's head. When he turned to look, he saw that the moon had dispersed the snow clouds. Its white eye indeed appeared swollen—brighter, larger, perhaps even closer.

"It's at perigee," the man explained in the kindly tone of conferred wisdom. While Arthur had been transfixed by the moon, the man had moved to Arthur's side, and the sudden closeness of his voice gave Arthur a start. Helix sat obediently looking up at the man, her tongue lolling from her mouth, her eyes smiling. The man smelled vaguely of mothballs, but his face shone brightly with life and vibrancy.

"It's closer," he said again, with a wink. "It's been many, many years since the last full moon at perigee, and many, many more since that happened on the solstice."

"No wonder it was so bright, even through the clouds," was all Arthur could think to say. The man nodded once and smiled broadly.

"Well, come into the church, friend ... Moongazer, stargazer, snowgazer—whatever you be, any man who braves the secrets of a winter night is a friend to me."

"I didn't know this church still had a congregation," Arthur said as they walked up the steps, Helix beating them both to the top. "In fact, I'd heard it was in ruins."

"Oh, it's still here," the man acknowledged. "Though the congregation is not, so much."

"Do you often come to church this early?" They reached the massive rectangular wooden doors and the man silently pushed the left door open far enough for them to enter.

"On Christmas morning I do," he replied. "I like to get it ready for them and clear off the stairs." He glanced again at the moon as he spoke, then ducked through the door and waited for Arthur to follow.

"Oh—my dog?" Arthur suddenly realized, pulling Helix short as they entered the vestibule. The man just smiled and slowly closed the door behind them.

"Don't worry, Mr. Dodd, Helix is as welcome here as anyone." Arthur's face went blank at the man's congenial use of his name, after no introduction, not to mention the name of his dog, but something in the way he smiled and walked into the church stopped Arthur from making a comment. He could hear the organist warming up already, plying the keys evenly with long-practiced, habitual forethought.

"I'm sorry," said Arthur, catching up to the man, Helix seemingly at home jogging between the pews with him. "I didn't properly introduce myself. I'm Arthur Bates—"

The man turned and grinned with a strange twinkle in his eyes that stopped Arthur short. "Helix told me who you are," the man said. Arthur, stunned again, said nothing and allowed himself to be led to the first pew, where the man sat down and offered his guest a seat.

181

Had Arthur felt any sense of malice about the place, or his enigmatic host, he would certainly have bolted back down the pews in horror and not have slowed his gait until safely back behind the locked door of his house. But as he glanced around at the Christmas greenery lit by the warm glow of candles, which sparkled off the brass ornamentation, Arthur felt nothing even close to ill will. In fact, with Helix—his most trusted and discerning companion—sitting obediently at their feet, allowing the man to pet her, Arthur felt not only welcome, but somehow right at home. The man's eyes glistened merrily in the candlelit church and he smiled widely at Arthur again.

"Do you know why tonight is so special?" the man asked. Arthur glanced around the relatively plain church for signs of a Nativity, but saw nothing save the evergreen garlands and white candles, echoing the spectral glow of the moonlit windows.

"The solstice is almost over, Arthur," the man continued. "Tomorrow will be three days hence and the sun shall begin her journey east again—but for now, time still belongs to the moon. And do you know what else?"

"No," Arthur managed to breath.

"When the moon is full at the winter solstice, the Willowfolk climb the highest trees and leap into the heavens to replenish their supply of moondust, which they use to create our most meaningful dreams. Even Helix dreams, Arthur," the man added, as if testing him. "And with the moon at perigee—well, the Willowfolk can just collect that much more."

"Willowfolk?" Arthur wondered. It was a tale he'd not heard before, and Arthur had thought sure his mother had known them all.

"Christmas sprites, Mr. Dodd," the man replied, leaning in secretively and whispering. All around them the soft, voluminous breaths of the organ twirled as the candle flames bowed in time with the sombre carols. "They make magic for us, Arthur. Moon magic—they straighten the handlebars on a boy's bicycle while he sleeps, and make the Christmas pudding perfect every year, and heal a young girl's puppy before it dies, and bring loved ones back to visit—"

"Loved ones?" Arthur whispered back, his voice cracking.

"Yes, Arthur. The Willowfolk are everything you can't explain. They live in the willow trees, in plain sight of those who stop to look. And their magic is strongest tonight—their moondust is fresh and thickest. Look, Arthur," the man smiled, pointing to the window. Arthur looked out and saw the sharp sparkles of snow beyond drifting down again. "Is that snow, Arthur?" the man whispered dramatically. "Or *Christmas* snow?"

"Moondust..." Arthur said softly. He turned to the man with a wide, understanding smile, but he was no longer seated beside him. The man now stood in the center of a raised platform at the front of the church. Behind him, a small orchestra tuned up in the candlelit moonlight, and Arthur saw that the man now held a conductor's baton. A woman touched Arthur's left arm, startling him, and urged him to follow her to the front. Helix yapped once excitedly, urging Arthur to follow the woman, so he dropped his dog's leash and did as they requested. She led him out a door to the right of the orchestra, and he followed her along a corridor which led behind the altar. They re-emerged on the other side of the church, in the wings beside the orchestra.

Standing at the entrance, stage left, Arthur had a slight panic attack: The only open seat on the stage was that of Regilia Smith—clearly his performance earlier had been duly noted and he had finally been forced into retirement. This was just an extremely odd and cruel way of informing him of the fact, especially since the walk had made him feel more alive than he had in years. Even his back had stopped aching, and his knees had ceased popping as he moved his weight.

"My seat—" Arthur began, turning to the woman with a plaintive stare.

"Your seat is waiting, Mr. Dodd." It was the man—the conductor—who answered quietly, now beside him again, waiting for him to make his entrance. The warm-ups were apparently over and Arthur could hear the slow rumble of the audience as the conductor bided his time until he could return to the stage. Arthur just looked at him with mild shock.

"Your seat—there," the conductor said, pointing with his baton. "First violin."

"*First* violin?" Arthur stammered, his voice quivering with nerves.

"You've earned it, I'd say. Wouldn't you?"

"I ... But ... I—"

"Mr. Dodd, our audience is waiting." The conductor gave him a friendly nudge and Arthur stepped forward to catch his balance, his toe breaking the circle of light on the stage—too far for him to turn back now. He followed his first step with another and another and soon realized the applause was for him: Arthur Bates Dodd, first violin. When he finally assumed his seat (after a light bow), he heard, but did not see, the audience take their own seats—they had been on their feet for him.

"My dog is sitting in the first row," Arthur whispered to the second violin, his mind feeling fuzzy. "Do you suppose she'll be all right?"

"Quite sure, sir," the violinist replied congenially, smoothing out the music on his stand to feign attention to something other than frivolous conversation. "I'm sorry," he then added, as an afterthought. "I thought your dog had passed just last night?"

"She did," Arthur agreed without hesitation, the sudden clarity serving only to further cloud his thoughts. He turned to his own music and lifted his violin.

"Then I imagine she will certainly be waiting there for you, sir," the second violin explained, glancing at Arthur out the corner of his eye and smiling. "In the front row, as you said."

Arthur nodded, his thoughts cut off by the sound of more applause as the conductor walked onto the stage. Arthur stood nervously to receive him and the two men offered each other a slight bow as they shook hands. Arthur caught a glimpse of his own sleeve as he did so—at his own gray morning tuxedo that looked as crisp and new as the freshly falling snow. He didn't stop to wonder how he had become so dressed because when he glanced over the conductor's shoulder he saw the tiny blobs of faces floating in the darkness, hands moving beneath them in blurred prayers of applause.

"You must be quite good," Arthur whispered to the conductor. The man smiled knowingly, then turned and assumed the podium. Arthur took his seat and raised his violin again, aware only peripherally that his back was straight and rigid and his attention completely focused.

* * *

Throughout the oratorio, Arthur Bates Dodd worked his violin like a woodcutter, his back arched into every note, his bald pate shimmering beneath a sheen of sweat, his white shirt wrunkled underneath his tuxedo's strained seams. Every sound, every measure, came to him as if it were the last, each note dripping from the one before, forming a chain that stretched to encircle the church and its congregation. His playing enlivened the orchestra, each member inspired to ply their strings or caress their reeds to keep up with the fervency of the first violin.

But Arthur Dodd was oblivious to any of it. He simply played, watching his cues and bleeding his violin for every ripe, untouched sound he could muster. The strings quivered beneath his nimble fingers like his strings had never quivered before. Arthur slowly became aware of the heat under the lights, and that the exertion was causing him to sweat more and more; he was also dimly aware of the orchestra fading around him. First the horns and percussion distorted like heat shimmers and faded from view, into the sound of their instruments. Next faded the cellists and violins, and the reed instruments, and even the chorus, yet Arthur could still hear them all, leaving the energy of their playing in the air around him, though they had faded away.

The conductor caught Arthur's eye and winked, then he, too, faded, along with the enrapt audience behind him. But even the sight of an empty church couldn't break Arthur's concentration. None of it mattered in the movement of the music—the full notes like waves carried him aloft and Arthur Dodd quite forgot where he was or that he sat alone in a ruined church, snow falling in clumps from the rafters around him.

Then, slowly, the sounds of the other instruments faded, like echoes reaching the summit of a valley and escaping into the aether. Arthur could still hear his own violin, its sound now far above that of the others, its pure strings vibrating in unison with the universe, not creating sound so much as giving voice to the beauty of a winter's night.

Finally, he pulled the last glimmering note from his violin, its music evaporating into the air, bouncing softly from the sodden rafters and crumbling pews before escaping from the roofless building forever. Arthur Dodd sat in the first violin's seat and slumped his back. A dog barked three times and he heard the soft clatter of its claws as it trotted across the wooden floor toward him.

"Hey, girl," he said absently, dropping his hand to her. Then Arthur Dodd slumped forward and fell from his seat, the shadow of his music stand like a weight across his back.

Outside, the moon moved on and glistened somewhere else.

27

These ghosts that shimmer across my eyes may only be cataracts, but they may also be something else. My mom called them the fuzzy edges of reality, but then my mom was always thinking about things like that—about reality, and the edges of it. Nine, 18, 27—that's how Mom said reality is divided. When we turn 27, we change—that's what Mom said it meant. I was nine when she died. She was 27.

"Val, what do you want to do tonight?"

That's Maggie, my girlfriend. She calls me Val, just like everyone else, but my mom named me Value. Value Kraymer. She told me it was so I would never forget that I had value. These are the memories she left me—names and numbers that would make me question her sanity if I didn't know now how right she was.

"It's your birthday," Maggie said, coming out of the bathroom as she clipped in an earring. "We should do something special."

"It's no big deal," I lied, because this was the big one and I knew it. Maggie set her face in a smile that told me she was pretending to understand but was really just humoring me.

"Okay, then." She bends over the bed and kisses me on the forehead. "You just stay home and play your video games. I suppose you don't magically change your ways just because you're 27."

She doesn't see me wince.

After she's left for work I sit and stare at the wall for an hour, watching the shapes and forms that could just be my genetically bad eyes.

Or they could be those other things, the things Mom told me about when we turn 27. The things she said would come to wish me happy birthday.

* * *

I lie in bed waiting for the footsteps to stop. I can hear them downstairs, pacing, or marching, or—more likely—searching. It's not the neighborhood kids, I know that. Ten years ago, it would have been, but Maggie has a good job and I moved in to her house, out in the suburbs, finally away from what my dad called White Hell (the city planners called it White Hall). Back in White Hell, boundaries were only dimly recognized things that just clarified whose stuff you could take, to make sure you weren't stealing from yourself.

After an hour or so, the footsteps stop. There's no door slamming, no whoops of success out in the front yard as they run off.

"They don't leave, they just stop for a while," Mom told me that night, when she turned 27. "Do you hear them?"

I shook my head "no," my eyes wide with childish innocence and awe.

"Of course you don't," she agreed, hugging me tightly. "But you will, Value."

"Who are they?" As a child, when your parents tell you something, no matter how crazy it seems, you believe them, especially when it's your mother—the one soft, kind heart in all of White Hell, always ready to wipe away the tears and bandage the scrapes.

"It's the Wraich," she says quietly. I only ever heard her say the word that once. I never asked her to repeat it and I never forgot it. It has a certain sound to it—perhaps in the way Mom had said it, her eyes gazing off into nothing, distant and calculating, trying to figure out where she went wrong—that sticks with you.

"They're here to help," she finally said, wiping away the handful of tears that had oozed down her cheeks. She tried to smile and looked at me, kneeling before me, her eyes level with mine. In the half light of her curtained bedroom her eyes looked yellow.

I remember recoiling from her, but she pulled me in and hugged me tighter.

* * *

Maggie gets home early, her usual smiles and laughter, telling me stories about things from her day that would upset most folks—but Maggie, she just laughs at them. Her friends call her "light and airy," usually in the same breath they call me "dark and brooding" when they think I'm not listening.

"He's an artist," she always defends me. "It comes with the territory. Besides, when you get to know him... He's just as light and airy as me."

What they're really saying, beneath the surface, is that I'm some tattooed street survivor from White Hell and they're afraid I'm going to hurt her, which only proves that they have no idea.

"Did you have fun on your day off?" she asks, tossing her keys and purse on the kitchen table as I walk in. I try to sound chipper.

"Sure—I just played games all day."

"Which one?" she checks with honest curiosity. "The alien one in space or that other one, the futuristic one with the totalitarian cops?"

"Actually, I just did the puzzle one. I didn't feel like..."

I trail off. I'm afraid if I tell her I didn't feel like anything violent she'd asked why, and then I'd have to tell her: Because I've heard the Wraich all day, first downstairs when I was in bed, then down in the basement when I was sitting on the couch, and my gut told me to stay away from blood imagery.

She meets my eyes anyway as I trail off, asking me without words to finish the thought, and she recoils a little when she sees me.

"Val—Jesus!—are you feeling okay?"

"Yeah. Fine." I try to play it off and look away from her.

"Your eyes look kind of yellow, Val."

"I'm okay."

"That could be your liver, Vally," she soothes, rubbing my arm and trying to look into my eyes again. Finally I let let her. Her light and airy face is streaked with a real dark concern. "You should go to the doctor."

"I don't have health insurance."

"I can pay for it, Val—it's got to be jaundice, which is a sign of liver fail—"

"It's not jaundice," I say with the biggest smile I can muster. "I think it's my allergies."

She mulls this over and finally lets go of my arm, trying to return my smile. She's a paralegal, not a doctor, but I know the excuse won't put her off for long. Allergies clear up, but I know my eyes won't. Mom's never did, not even the last time I looked in to them.

It's my first gift from the Wraich, and these are gifts you can't give back. That's what Mom said, and I believe her.

"Do you want to go to Archie's? Get a burger?" she asks with uncertainty.

I smile widely again and it seems to put her at ease. "You know I do. Can I get one of the birthday hats, too?"

She giggles and it makes me feel good to hear that sound. "Sure, Vally—it's your birthday. You can do what you want."

* * *

On a whim I order a steak instead of a burger. And maybe because it's my birthday, or maybe it's because I've been listening the

190

soft drumming of footsteps downstairs all day, I send it back to the kitchen for being too well done.

"Really?" Maggie checks. "I mean, I know you like 'em rare, but that was bloody as hell already."

I just smile. Her eyes linger on mine and I read the worry in hers. Beyond her a man is sitting in a booth alone, a brimmed hat pulled down so all I can see is one thin wedge of silvery jawline. At first I think it's his beard, gray and reflecting in the garish light of Archie's, but then I realize I can see bone and skin and that the wedge of his jaw jutting out beneath that brim is silvery white skin, not hair.

"Vally? Are you listening?"

I look back at her and she smiles at me.

"That guy back there has weird skin," I say, leaning in conspiratorially. She shakes her head and twists her lips into a wry grin.

"Just go the doctor tomorrow, okay? What time do you have to be at work?"

I shrug. Work doesn't exactly make me punch a clock: The only people paying for my artwork these days are the freaks and wannabes who need something etched into their skin forever. Apparently I've earned quite a reputation for creating the most realistic dragon tattoos—as if that makes any sense. Everybody knows dragons aren't real.

"I'll go in late," I agree, to appease her. Now that I'm out of the house I feel a creeping annoyance coming in: What if it is jaundice? Liver failure? What if that was Mom's problem?

She smiles and pats my hand. "I'll call them first thing. It'll all be taken care of."

"Maybe we should get married first?" I quip.

"What?" she snaps hopefully. I nod.

"Well, I mean, if it is liver failure and we get married *after* the diagnosis, they'll deny me coverage."

She shakes her head slowly and sits back, smirking. "That's not exactly the proposal I'd hoped for, Value Kraymer."

"Sorry, love." I really am, too. "Say, can liver disease make you crazy?"

"What do you mean?"

For no reason, the man with the silvery jaw occurs to me again and I look over Maggie's shoulder at him, but he's gone. I look around, but don't see him anywhere, though those shadows I've been chasing out the corner of my eye for the last week are there again, dancing along like shapeless schoolchildren running home. I meet Maggie's eyes. She looks politely concerned because she knows my question is sincere.

"Can cataracts make your eyes yellow?"

Now she's starting to look concerned; confused.

"No, honey, those form on the lens, which is *inside* your eye. Just go see the doctor tomorrow, okay?" She laughs through her nose and grins at me again. "And despite the fact that I would marry you, I don't think health insurance is a good enough reason to do it. You'll have to come up with a better reason than that."

"You're the only thing keeping me sane, Maggie," I blurt. Her smile falters, but she catches it and puts on a brave face. She thinks she knows what this is all about, and maybe she's right.

"This is really about your mom, isn't it?" she whispers sympathetically. "I mean, she was 27, wasn't she, when...?"

"I don't think Mom had liver disease."

"Okay. But I don't think it has to be hereditary."

"But she did have yellow eyes," I finish. Maggie looks startled. I nod. "I remember. It happened when she turned 27."

Maggie looks guilty, but purposeful. "Maybe this isn't the place to discuss this. Look, let's not bother waiting for the food—"

"No, I *want* that steak, Mags. I'm okay. We can talk about it at home. Maybe it was liver disease. Maybe it makes you crazy."

I offer her a weak smile, but she's not convinced. At that moment she knows as well as I do that the doctor isn't going to find a thing wrong with me, except a yellow discoloration in my eyes.

"You're *not* crazy," she says emphatically in a low breath, her eyes darting to the sides to catch any eavesdroppers. "It can't just *come on* like that."

"All artists are crazy," I counter, offering her my most winning grin. She melts a little and sits back straight in her chair shaking her head. "Haven't you heard?"

"You're lots of things, Val, but crazy isn't one of them."

"What did you get me for my birthday, Mags?"

"I'm wearing it," she mouths so softly I barely hear her.

When we get home, we don't end up talking about my mother.

* * *

The nights are the worst. That's when the footsteps get loud, though Maggie sleeps through the whole thing. Had I been my mom, I'd have gone down the hall to my nine-year-old son for comfort.

Dad wasn't home that night. He was working second shift—that's what Mom always called it. She said that meant he was either at the factory or at the bar, making money or spending it, but whatever the case, he wouldn't be home before two. I think she saw it coming—or heard it—and she tried to come clean that night. I saw it in her yellow eyes, and it frightened me more than I'd ever been frightened before.

Until I turned 27 myself. Until I heard the Wraich on the stairs, skittering up and down; rattling my doorknob.

At first I try to ignore them, but I can't. The sounds call to me like a flashing blue light on the wall, and I have to go see what the fuss is; see who called the cops.

"Do you see them?" Mom whispered that night, when she told me about her numbers and her age. "Just on the fuzzy edges of reality, like they're only halfway here?"

The doorknob rattles again, breaking the memory. My heart pounds somewhere through my whole body: My chest, my feet, my hands, my fingers—it feels like my heart is everywhere at once. My throat clicks and I glance at the glass of water on my beside table in the moonlight. Maggie stirs, but doesn't wake.

"Drink more water," I mumble to myself. That's what the doctor said, just as I'd known, just as Maggie had feared: There's nothing wrong with me.

"An imbalance of some kind," he put it kindly. "You need to go on a strict diet and drink more water—see if we can clear it up."

It's a flimsy prescription, and he knew it. He had no idea what's happening to me.

But I think Mom knew.

"Value!"

A sharp whisper from the other side of the door. It's the tone of voice Mom used when I was doing something she thought was dangerous. I start to cry and try to wake Maggie for comfort, but she won't budge. I set my hand gently above her left breast to feel her breathing, to feel her heartbeat. She still has both.

"Value!"

No, I realize, it's the tone Mom used that night. Instead of knocking on my door or just coming in, she stood at doorway and called to me in a whisper. She wanted me in the hallway. She wanted me to see if I could hear them or see them. She took me back to her room with her and she tried to explain.

"Who are they?"

"It's the Wraich. They're here to help."

There's a dull thud against the door and I realize I've sat up and swung my legs off the bed, ready to open the door and let her in. Instead I regain my senses and whisk silently over to the door, resting my fingertips ever so slightly on its surface.

"What do you want?" I whisper.

"Don't fight the rage, Value," the voice whispers back. It sends a long chill over my body until my arms bristle with freezing straight hairs and pinpricks of fear. I rest my forehead against the cold door, trying to remember what else Mom said to me that night 18 years ago.

"You're not helping," I reply tightly.

"Yes we are, Value."

I reach slowly for the doorknob, watching my hand move toward it as if watching a movie of someone else. I was scared then, hearing Mom talk about it and seeing her yellow eyes for the first time, and I'm scared now, living it, and in that moment I realize that these memories—buried so long in the repressed recesses of my soul—are mine, not hers. I was afraid that night so I assumed she was afraid, too.

My hand closes on the doorknob. The cold metal seems to bend under the pressure as I squeeze it. There's another memory trying to creep out, but this one hurts. This is one I don't want to think about, not at all, but it comes anyway: Mom wasn't afraid. She wanted to share her excitement with me.

"Reality is divided by birthdays, Value," she said as she hugged me that night. "Nine, 18, and 27. When we turn 27, we change. And when we change, they come to wish you happy birthday."

The door catch snicks as I turn the knob. I hear the feet outside jostling with anticipation, waiting for me to swing it open.

How long after her birthday had that been? Not long, because she was dead a week a later—

"No!" I admonish them. The footfalls vanish and Maggie gasps awake in bed.

"Value!" she cries, shocked to see me standing with my head against the door. "Val, baby, what is it?"

She stands up and walks over to me, touching my back tentatively, afraid to wake me.

"I'm not sleepwalking," I say quietly. "I had a nightmare."

She holds me as I cry, not asking any questions or offering me any hollow sympathetic sentiments. She knows better. She knows about the nightmares that I've long since stopped trying to describe. I just can't tell her yet that this time I was awake during the dream.

"It's my mom," I finally offer, pulling away from her. In the moonlight she can't see the color in my eyes. She puts her hands on my cheeks and smiles, all light and airy.

"I know, Vally."

"She died a week after her birthday."

I see her fighting back tears of empathy. She has such a big heart—so much compassion and joy. It's what attracted me to her in the first place. I know it cuts her up to think about any child, especially me, losing his mother, and I don't want to do that to her.

"I think I want to visit my dad," I say softly. She snuffles in a big breath and wipes her eyes, shaking her head.

"Why, Vally? Why now, after eighteen years?"

She knows it's not a good idea, and she's right. But at the same time, she knows exactly why I have to see him.

I tell her my reason anyway: "I have to know why he killed my mother."

* * *

I've been wearing sunglasses all the time for two days now. This is day three and at least I can finally answer the question of who those people are who wear sunglasses all time: People like me.

People with something to hide. The yellow eyes freaked me out, but as I pull on motorcycle gloves, I know it's not over.

"You painted your nails black again!" Maggie said this morning. She looked surprised, but happy, like she thought it showed I was my old self again.

"Yeah," I agreed with a shrug. "Just trying to freak my dad out."

She laughed nervously. What I can't tell her yet is that I hadn't painted my nails at all. Last night, they turned black. Solid black. And they thickened, too—this morning when I tried to trim them with the clippers, it was like trying to trim a bone. I think they changed when I heard the Wraich at my bedroom door.

"They bring you gifts," Mom said, as if they were Santa Claus. I should have known then there was something up: She never told me what the gifts were or how they brought them.

"Do you really think you should go and see your dad?" Maggie asked again before she left for work. She sort of cocked her head and looked at me in the way she does when she's trying to be really serious. A smile flickered across her lips. God, she looked so beautiful. I just moved over and kissed her, a good kiss, a long kiss, the kind of kiss she had to break off.

"I have to go to work," she reminded me, running her finger across my lips and down my chin. "We'll finish this when I get home."

"Be careful, Mags," I said, like always.

"You, too," she quipped back with a tinge of seriousness again. "Do you still want me to dig up his case file?"

"Yeah," I replied. "I have a feeling he's not going to tell me the truth."

She nodded slowly and left. Now I sit here, in front of the jail, covering up the nails I told her I painted to piss off my dad.

Truth is, I don't know what I'm hoping to find out from him. He's either going to be overjoyed to see me and want to spend all the time catching up, or he's not even going to talk to me. Or he'll lie. He'll proclaim his innocence, beg me for help. He'll play the father card, even though it was his brother who raised me and my mother who gave me values.

Inside the jail, the cops checking me are polite enough, but I can tell they're surprised to see me.

"He kept telling us he had a kid," one of them says—an old guy who's probably been there with him the whole 18 years. "We figured it was just more of his B.S.—no offense."

"None taken," I agree. "Does he lie a lot?"

"You'll see, kid," he says. "He should be excited, at least. The only visitor he's had in years is some priest from his parish."

"Yeah?" My surprise is genuine. I never knew Dad to go to church, and I can't imagine why a priest would give a crap about some guy who killed his wife and orphaned his only son almost two decades ago.

"Through here," the cop says as he nods, opening the door to the visitor's room. "Last window on the end there."

It strikes how much I *don't* look like my father, assuming I sit down at the right spot. He looks old, like a man who's sick of fighting the same battles over and over but knows there's no other way. I don't see any prison tattoos, which I take as a good sign. His hair is graying and he's losing it, but what's there is slicked back. It could be hair gel, it could be sweat—I can't say for sure. He looks a lot older than he is and I feel my heart turn for just a second: This is him, the guy who gave me my first and only runner sled; the guy who gave me rides on his back, when he was home, and played me his old records; the guy who took it all away again that night he sent me to Uncle Joey's, so he and Mom could go out to see a movie.

I don't want to make the first move. He eyes me cautiously then stubs out his cigarette and snatches up the phone. I unhook mine and put it to my ear.

"Take off the glasses, kid," he says smoothly. My heart turns again: I recognize that voice. He probably doesn't even know how many times I was awake when he got home. I always knew he'd come in and check on me, and I looked forward to it. Most days, it was the only time I saw him. He'd come in and stand looking at me for a few seconds, then that same smooth voice would say, "Love ya, kid. Maybe I'll see ya tomorrow."

"I can't, Dad," I lie. "I went to the doctor today—he put those drops in. They hurt."

I can't tell if he knows I'm lying, but he doesn't pressure me.

"So you finally came to see me, huh?" he wonders. I feel my lip quivering. Seeing and hearing him reminds me strongly of Mom, and I badly want to see her again, but I can't. In the reflection of the glass between us I see a shape flit past—one of the fuzzy edges of reality—and I hear someone whispering. I manage to ignore it.

"I'm not here for you," I reply evenly.

"No?"

"No." I suck in a breath and hold it, trying to regain my nerves. I hadn't expected so many good memories of him. Maybe deep down I knew they were there. Maybe that's why I stayed away. Certainly that's why Maggie told me not to come, not after all these years. The last time I saw him or heard his voice I was nine—a boy who didn't understand the whys and wherefores of a world that seems, at times, mostly bad.

"I just want to hear you say it," I finish.

"Say what, kid? Sorry? You want me to tell ya I love ya?"

I shake my head and suck in another deep breath, blowing it out like smoke from a cigarette.

"I just want to know why you killed her."

"No one ever told you about it?"

I shake my head again. It's getting easier, probably because he doesn't deny it. I know if he had, I might have believed him.

"I know you killed her. Uncle Joey told me that much."

"Damn—*Joey*? He never visited me once. He still alive?"

"He had a heart attack last year."

He does the math in his head and narrows his eyes, "At 52? Joey died at 52?"

I nod once.

"Was he good to you?" he checks.

"He was fine, I guess. He fed me, clothed me, and he didn't beat me, so compared to a lot of the other kids, I had it real good."

"I never beat you," he offers.

"Yeah," I agree before he can go any further. "You were a banner dad. Father of the fucking year."

"Hey—watch your language."

I snuff a single laugh through my nose and shake my head in disbelief.

"Seriously," he says. "Take off the glasses, just for a second—I want to see you again, kid." He stops for a second, weighing his words, then finally adds, "I missed ya."

"Shoulda thought of that before you killed Mom," I reply, ignoring his request. "Just tell me why you did it, so I can go home."

"You married? Got a girlfriend?"

I shake my head. Another lie.

"You're a good lookin' man," he says, shocked. "You need to find yourself a good woman."

"Like Mom?"

"Look, I'm not sure what you want," he admits. "I loved your mother, I really did. And you, too."

"That why you went out drinking so much?"

"Is that what she said?" He looks genuinely hurt, and I know he's going to have a lot to think about in his cot tonight. "No, kid—I was working. I was always working so we could get outta White Hell—swear to God."

I don't respond. Hearing him call it "White Hell" makes my heart turn again. I'm starting to feel a bit queasy. I think back to all those nights when I waited for him to come in and check on me and it occurs to me that I don't ever remember the smell of beer or smoke on him. At least, not the smoke like you get from a bar. Maybe he's telling the truth, but the old cop's words are still fresh in my ears.

"Maybe so," I allow, sitting back and crossing my arms as best I can while holding the phone up to my ear. "Look, are you going to tell me why you did it or not?"

"Why the sudden interest?"

"I've been thinking about it a lot lately. I think the stress is affecting me badly."

It's the first truthful thing I've said. I've begun to think that the voices and the shapes and the Wraich are nothing more than me trying to go back to that night with my mother, to feel her hugging me again. So I have to believe the imbalance Maggie's doctor talked about is all in my head, and if that's true, then maybe I just need to put this last nail in Mom's coffin and finally let her go.

"I see," he says, calculating again. "You must be 27."

"Yup."

He considers this profoundly, biting his lip and rubbing his nose and scratching his stubbly cheeks. Finally he sighs and looks me right in the eyes—well, in the sunglasses, anyway.

"Look, it'll sound crazy," he begins. "That's what they've been telling me for years, anyway."

"Try me."

He shrugs and states it simply, as if he has no other option than to finally come clean: "She was a demon."

"*What*?" I sit forward, inches from the glass and his simple told-you-so visage. "You *are* a liar!"

"She turned," he tries to explain, and there are actually tears welling in his eyes. "I loved her, kid, I really did, but she turned. I couldn't let her hurt anyone else—"

"Anyone *else*?" I shriek. The cop standing guard moves over a few steps toward me. "*You* killed *her*, you crazy fucking *bat*!"

He shakes his head, crying for real now. "You remember little Joey Martin? You remember how he got mauled by those dogs?" He doesn't wait for me to answer; he knows I know what he's talking about. "Those weren't dogs, kid. I saw it all. That was your mother—"

"Fuck you!" I scream, standing up and slamming down the phone. He's stood up, too, so he can push his face right up against the small circle of holes they cut in the glass. I know why they installed the phones now—even that close, his voice is muffled, but it's clear enough: "You saw it in her eyes, too!" he yells. "I know you did! You told me! You told me about that night! I didn't want her to hurt you, kid! I was trying to protect you! And me! And *every*one!"

I've stopped listening. The cop is standing behind me, putting a calming hand on my shoulder, urging me to leave. I'm dimly aware that two other cops have joined him, as well as a couple of cops on my dad's side of the glass.

I don't remember telling him anything, and I don't want to. I don't want to think how scared I must have seemed, and I don't want to think about a man trying to protect his son from a woman who has *turned*, as he put it. Instead, I try to prove him wrong. I rip off my sunglasses and stick my face up to the glass, an inch between our noses, slamming my hands against the window to make a point.

"You mean *this*, Dad? Is *this* what you saw in her eyes?"

He recoils so powerfully he knocks one of the cops off balance, the chair he was sitting on skittering across the six-foot wide room and slamming into the wall. In a second both cops are on him, subduing him.

"Sir?" the cop behind me says. "I really think you should leave now."

I slip the glasses back on and straighten up.

"Yeah. I think you're right."

The older cop comes into the room, shaking his head dismally.

"I told you," he says, clicking his tongue. "I was afraid he'd start with that demon crap again—don't let him get to you, son."

I try to remain calm, but I'm shaking pretty badly. The old cop nods and winks to the other cops and takes me by the elbow, taking me back into the other room so he can sign me out.

"We've tried to have him committed," he says as I sign the paperwork with a quivering hand that's too weak to fully grip the pen.

"But the experts tell us he's not crazy." He chuckles amiably and offers his assessment: "If that ain't crazy, though, I don't know what is!"

"Yeah," is all I can think to say. "Thanks." My voice sounds strange, even to me. Deeper, like a low-purring engine.

"Hey, I mean no offense—"

"You said there was a priest who visits him?" I interrupt. I can't tell if he's happy to change the subject or upset that he didn't get to finish his apology.

"Right—yeah. Father Jacobs, down at the Assumption in White Hall. It's over—"

"I know it," I reply. "Thanks."

"I'm sorry, kid," he says, looking honestly hurt and regretful. "I wish it woulda been a better visit."

"It wasn't bad," I offer. "But I don't know if I'll be back."

* * *

I sit in my car for a good 15 minutes, waiting for the shakes to die down. Dad really got to me. I can feel this *rage* in me that seems so purposeful and indirect, all at once. I want to rip off my father's head, but I know that any head will do. It was all I could muster to get back behind the wheel of my car without doing something dumb to one of the guards

Eventually I pull out my phone and call Maggie at work.

"Val? What is it?" she answers. I can tell by her tone that she really doesn't have the time to chat, which is why I never call her at work, and she knows that I know that, so my call concerns her. "Did you see your dad?"

"Yeah," I manage to breath. It sounds like a growl, coming out of my throat low and guttural.

"Are you okay? You sound... You don't sound good."

"I fell like crap, Mags," I sputter in a hoarse whisper. "He made me feel like crap."

"Jesus, Val, I *told* you not to go."

"It's not that," I blurt. The growl is gone from my voice now and I take a deep breath. Just imagining her there, taking the time to talk to me, makes me feel better. I close my yellow eyes and rest my head back against the headrest, sighing heavily.

"What happened, Val?" she asks, her voice so sweet, so full of genuine concern. If she was busy before, she suddenly doesn't care.

"I just found out... he told me... I think what's happening to me happened to my mom."

"What do you mean? What's *hap*pening to you?"

"The eyes and the..." I trail off, remembering that I didn't tell her about the nails yet. She waits a second for me to finish, then prods me.

"The...?"

"The nails, Mags. I didn't paint my nails black."

"What? What does that mean? You mean they *turned* black?"

"Yeah."

"That can't be good, Val. God, you have to go to a hospital. I'm coming home—"

"No, Maggie, really—I feel fine."

"*Fine?*" She sounds scared; terrified for my well being. Ironically, I feel better again. My hands have stopped shaking, my voice sounds normal.

"Yeah. I know it sounds crazy. I'll try and explain tonight. I just have to go and see some priest that always visits my dad, see what he knows."

"A *priest?*" she stresses, trying to keep her voice down. "No, Val, really—just go home. I'll meet you there."

"I shouldn't have called you at work," I admit.

"No, no—I'm glad you did. Meet me at home?" Her voice has softened now. She's trying to sweet talk me, and it usually works.

"After I see this priest."

She sighs heavily. She can't deny that I sound better now. She also understands that I drove to the jail and talked to my dad, and none of the cops between my car and him (and back) saw anything wrong with me.

"It just seems weird, Val," she finally decides. "I mean, if I woke up with yellow eyes and black nails—"

"I think the priest will explain that," I say for no good reason, but it sounds right.

"That just makes it weirder," she says dryly. Good—the fear and panic has left her voice. We're both back to normal now

"He's over at the Assumption in White Hall."

"Did your dad go to church?" she wonders.

"No. That's why I want to see this priest. He said my mom was a demon, that's why he killed her."

She ponders this for a few moments then sighs like a good mother.

"Okay, Val, maybe you're right. Maybe this is all about, you know, the stress, with your birthday and your, you know..."

"I know, Maggie. Don't worry."

"But then go *straight* home," she admonishes. "I'll try and leave early. Okay?"

"Okay. And thanks."

I pause, mulling it over. Finally I shrug, then add for her benefit: "You always make me feel better.

"Take care, Val, okay? I love you, you know that?"

"I love you, too, Mags."

I hang up the phone and glance up the street through the windshield. There's a man in a black coat and hat standing at the corner. I swear he's looking at me, but that's not what catches my eye. What makes me stare is his skin—how it reflects the sunlight like brushed chrome. How it stretches into shadow around his grin.

"It's that guy from the restaurant," I mumble to myself and dig the key into the ignition, starting my car and jerking it into gear almost before it's ready. It dies from the strain, so I dig the key again and wait to make sure it's caught. The man turns the corner and disappears behind the massive wall of the jail.

By the time I get there he's gone—or well hidden. I don't have time to figure him out, though, so I keep going, back toward my old stomping grounds.

* * *

The Church of the Assumption isn't easy to miss. It stands like a stubborn relic between two highrises, determined to puff up its chest even though the other buildings are each at least ten floors taller than the church's tallest steeple.

I park across the street—it's not hard to find street parking in White Hall—and jog over to it, hoping no one from the old neighborhood recognizes me. I haven't been back for almost ten years—I finished high school because my uncle talked me into it, but I wasn't going to stick around when I didn't have to.

I stop at the top of the stairs to the door and look both ways. Ten years, and everything seems to still be in the same static state of disrepair: No better, no worse, just endless urban decay. Only the graffiti has changed. I see someone walking down the sidewalk toward me and it breaks the spell of memories. I push the door open and step into the church.

It's cool and seems a lot bigger inside than it looked from the street, but I suppose that's just the illusion of the wide open floor plan. In 18 years moping around White Hell, this is the first time I've ever set foot in the neighborhood church, and I have to believe my dad has never set foot in here, despite how it would appear.

Because something this beautiful he would have shared with me, I realize, then throw the thought away. I'm here to find out what the bastard told this priest about my mother, not to get all soft and fall asleep on the memory train.

I step into the congregation hall and a breath catches in my throat. I whip around, sure that someone is behind me, meaning to do me harm, but there's no one there. It occurs to me that the Wraich won't be able to come in here after me, and I wonder why such a thought would even occur to me. The stink of incense is giving me a headache. I stumble a step, back into the foyer, and the world comes swimming back. Maybe Maggie was right. Maybe I should have gone straight home.

"I thought I heard someone come in," a man's voice says softly in a kind tone. "Can I help you, son?"

"I'm looking for Father Jacobs," I mumble, turning to look at the guy. He's older—maybe 65, almost 70—but he looks like he could still bounce any thugs who tried to bust up a service.

"Well that's me," he replies happily, smiling a wide smile. He seems genuinely pleased. "Who sent you?"

"The jail." My tone is clipped; I can hear in my own ears that it doesn't sound like me. I feel my heart racing and the blood pounding in my head. For no reason, I imagine what it would be like to grab this guy's head and pull—

"Oh. Did you just get out, then?"

"No," I growl. "I was visiting my dad. You've been visiting him, too, and I want to know why."

His smile falters a bit and his eyes waver from the main door to the congregation hall. He's weighing his odds; planning his escape. I imagine I'm not the first pissed off relative to look him up.

He chuckles amiably. "Well, I do a lot of work out at the jail," he admits. "Especially if it's someone... well, someone from the neighborhood. Did you or your dad grow up in White Hall?"

I nod. My throat seems to be constricting and my hands are quivering again.

"Who's your dad, then, son?" He either won't step toward me or he doesn't want to, but the look on his face says he's registered that something's going on with me. "Are you okay?"

"Larry Kraymer," I blurt. My head is spinning now; dark circles are blossoming and shrinking around me like flowers of darkness.

"Kraymer?" he says, and now *his* tone is clipped. "Then you must be Value? Value Kraymer?"

"Yes," I manage to force through my constricting throat. He moves a step to the side, into the congregation hall, and crosses himself. His face has paled and his eyes are wide. He looks shocked and confused, and I just want to see if my nails could cut into his flesh, maybe along the collar of his priestly shirt...

As I step toward him he says something in Latin and holds up his right hand, his fingers bent oddly, as if blessing me. But the words hurt—that's all I can think. Each one is like a punch to my gut, and a wide nausea starts to overcome me. He's still saying something in Latin and when I look at him the color has come back to his face. Suddenly the sight of him repulses me. I have never seen anyone so ugly, so malformed, so frightening in all my life: His stick-like arms and quivering jowls bobbing under wisps of white hair, a fire in his eyes full of malice and discontent.

I have to get away from him—every fiber of my being tells me so. I have to get away from him before he lunges at me and rips me limb from limb.

My heart pounding, I slam back through the main doors and into the street, sprinting over to my car. I dry heave as I dig my keys out of my pocket, but I don't throw up.

"Baker!" I realize he's yelling. As I open the car door and slide behind the wheel I glance back and see him standing at the top of the steps, his hands cupped around his lips. "Alistair Baker!" he shouts. "You need to find Alistair Baker!"

The black blossoms have faded and the nausea is gone, but my hands are still shaking.

"God, I hope Maggie's home," I whisper to no one as I slip the car into drive and leave White Hall behind.
Again.

* * *

Maggie's sitting at the kitchen table when I get home, her face drawn and her eyes on the verge of tears. As soon as she sees me she jumps up and rushes over, throwing her arms around me and giving me a hug with a tiny kiss on the cheek.

"I was worried," she whispers, then adds incidentally. "You look awful."

"I'm tired," I admit. "I've had a long day."

She leads me over to the kitchen table and urges me to sit. My eyes linger on her hair, her shoulders, her back, as she gets me a coffee cup. She catches me looking when she turns around and smiles shyly, pulling a stray bang back over her ear

"Why are you looking at me like that?" she asks because she wants to hear me say it out loud. She knows what I'm thinking.

"You're beautiful," I breath. She tries to suppress a grin and turns back to the counter, pouring me a cup of coffee.

"Look, do you want to hear about... you know?" she asks the coffee cup, then turns back to me and brings the coffee with her to the kitchen table, setting the cup in front of me before she sits down.

"Yeah, I do."

She sucks in a deep breath and lets out a sigh.

"Why?"

"I have a suspicion," I explain. She nods once.

"Well, okay... It's true that he always claimed your mother was a demon, and I think he really believes it. The only reason he hasn't been institutionalized is because of that priest from White Hall."

I nod. It's making sense so far.

"He turned himself in—he never denied killing her—and you know the rest."

This time I shake my head. "I don't know how he did it. Did you look that up, too?"

"Val, you can't really want to—"

"It's important."

She sucks in another long breath and lets out the sigh. "He burned her body—that's why your house burned down. He killed her in the basement, then he burned her body."

She meets my eyes and I can tell she doesn't understand why I'm grinning. "What else? He cut her head off, didn't he?"

"Yes," she gasps. She looks shocked, like I shouldn't have known. "Did he tell you? Is that why–?"

"He didn't tell me," I cut in. "That's just what you do to a demon to stop it from rising again: You cut off its head and burn the body."

She still looks confused, so I change the subject. "What about Joey Martin?"

She shakes her head stiltedly, trying to keep up with the sudden change of conversation, then takes a big sip of her coffee. "He was mauled by your neighbor's dogs. The dogs were put down and everything, though your neighbor denied it—"

"Joey Martin used to pick on me," I intone slowly. "Mom knew it. She was always telling me to stand up to him, but I couldn't. The day he died he'd come over to pick on me because he thought it'd make him look tough in front of my neighbor, Susie Watkins. Everybody liked Susie, but Susie liked me, and when Joey found out, he ramped up his efforts to beat me down."

I pause long enough to sip my coffee. She's listening to every word, fearing the punchline, her hands clasped under her chin.

"He called us both out, then he marched right up on to Susie's porch and started kissing at her and groping her, trying to put his hand up her skirt and under her shirt."

"Christ," she whispers. "How old were you?"

"He was 12, I guess. She was ten and I was nine. I knew I had to go over there and stop him, so I did. Only he punched me until I passed out. When I came to, my mother was carrying me back into the house. I remember thinking her eyes looked especially yellow in the sunlight, and her skin seemed almost metallic."

"You were pretty badly beaten, I'd say," Maggie manages to fit in. I shrug.

"Susie told me later he didn't even touch her after that—he just beat me up, then left. Later he wound up mauled in her front yard, and everyone blamed her dogs."

"You say that like it's not true," Maggie offers, reaching out and touching my hand.

I look her right in the eyes: "Dad didn't think it was the dogs. Dad told me it was my mom."

"What?" She's stunned, and she should be. "Are you kidding me? Your dad thinks your *mom* mauled a kid? I looked it up, Val—there's no way a human did that."

I nod slowly. "I know, Mags. But Dad was right: Mom wasn't human."

"*What?*"

"She was a demon, Maggie—and so am I."

* * *

Maggie didn't take too well to my theory. She said it was guilt at having finally visited my dad. It was natural, she said—I was siding with him because he was all I had left, but I really missed my mom.

I wasn't so sure any more, but I didn't tell her that.

That night the Wraich came back. I heard them whispering before I heard them moving this time, and the breathy little wisps of sound made me cold with fear. I knew now what Mom had meant: They were there to help me along in my transformation. The gifts they brought were different aspects of my new self: Yellow eyes, black claws for nails, and that night, thicker teeth and sharpened canines, like a dog's.

The difference between me and Mom is that I don't want the gifts. I stood in the darkened living room and cursed at the shapes as they swirled around me, denying the whispered, gleeful claims of how they had me. Finally, I turned my back on them and went back upstairs. They followed me in a hurry, feeling me pulling away, but I ignored them as they tugged at my boxers and pinched at the hairs on my arms and legs. One thing I'd figured out is that they couldn't stand to be near Maggie. If she was in the room, they'd only come up to the doorway and push their ghastly white faces into the opening, their glowing eyes wide with fear and a certain sense of betrayal.

"Don't fight the rage," they kept repeating.

In the morning I begged Maggie not to leave me. I got down on my knees and held her hand and stared at her through tear-blurred yellow eyes, my voice deeper and my lips looking slightly swollen over my larger teeth. She couldn't deny it any more, not really, and she looked at me like I was a dog she knew she should be afraid of.

"They stay away when I'm with you," I begged. "I need you, Mags, more than you'll ever know."

"Is this another idea you had for a proposal?" she asks after what seemed like a lifetime of silence. I look up into her eyes and she's smiling through her tears.

"No," I answer truthfully.

She pulls me back to my feet and hugs me. "We'll get through this, Val," she promises.

"My mom wanted this," I try to explain. "But I don't."

"I know."

"Hey," I state simply. "At least it's not kidney failure."

She chuckles and cries at the same time. "I'm glad you still have your sense of humor."

"I love you, Maggie."

She pulls away and holds my face in her hands—Christ, how difficult it must have been for her to look into my eyes then, knowing how impossible and true my dad's claims were, and how my parents' relationship had ended.

"I love you, too, Value Kraymer," she replies and kisses me firmly on the lips.

I make sure not to open them, not even when I smile as she leaves for work.

* * *

The worst part about this whole thing has been how it continually forces the past back upon me. White Hell stinks in my memory not because my Uncle Joey didn't do the very best he could to make it good for me, but because I spent my whole life there not letting any emotions come out. I knew what would happen if they did: I knew I'd miss my dad, despite everything, and I feared I'd find out something about my mom I'd rather not know.

Like how she didn't get a few days at the tanning booth for her birthday at all: Her skin changed, just like the rest of her. Just like her eyes and her nails and what was behind the puffy lips she said looked odd because dad had hit her.

The last thing you want to learn is that your mother lied to you. That your mother took you in her arms in her room and told you joyfully about things you couldn't see that were bringing her gifts, but that she left out large patches of fabric that would have made the quilt whole.

The night she told me she didn't think she could fight the rage. The night before I skipped school so I could meet dad on his way to the bus stop and tell him everything.

The tears come unbidden now. I pound on my steering wheel and try to and make it go away.

"No! *No*! God damn it! *No*!"

It's all unraveling. I can feel it flittering away like a sheaf of loose paper in the wind, and the fear returns, the essence of that night that has been buried under 18 years of hatred for my father: That I was always more afraid of my mother than of him.

"Value?" a voice asks kindly near my ear.

"Go *away*!" I scream at them, the damn Wraich, now out in broad daylight, prowling around my car.

"Value," the voice demands. "Mind the rage, Value. Think of Maggie."

It seems an odd thing for the Wraich to say. Usually I can feel them trying to stir me up... but the voice. It has the same cadence as the whispers and the same forceful attitude. I look over slowly and see him there, standing on the sidewalk several feet from my car: The man with the silvery skin, smiling at me, his eyes hidden behind yellowed sunglasses.

"Good morning, Value," he says in the same smooth tone. "I believe you've come to see me?"

I feel the anger begin to burn again: A low visceral sensation that can only be quenched with blood. I clench my teeth and actually growl.

"Maggie," is all he says, quietly. I take a deep breath and picture her as she left for work, the expression on her face pleading with me that it wouldn't be the last time she saw me.

"If the priest told you to find this Alistair Baker, go and find him," was the last advice she'd given me, though I could tell she didn't want me out and about again. "Maybe he can help."

"Father Jacobs said you'd be by," the man on the sidewalk says in the same smiling tone. He bends over just enough to catch a glimpse of my eyes before I turn away. "I'm Alistair Baker."

"Then who are the Wraich?" I growl. It sounds like a test question, like I'm trying to trip him up, but it's really the only thing I want to know: Who are they and how can I keep them away.

"Well, that's an odd question," he replies thoughtfully with a sigh, then answers slowly, "We are the Wraich, Value. You and me and your mother..."

"Fuck you," I mumble, but I don't really mean it, and he knows it.

"Half demon, half human, " he states simply in response. "The Wraich."

I sit and let this soak in for several minutes, and he does nothing to interrupt me. He doesn't move, he doesn't lean down to look at me, he doesn't tap his foot or jiggle the coins in his pocket, he just waits.

With the patience of a saint, I remember my dad always saying in the echoes of some faraway memory.

"Then who's been doing this to me?" I finally ask. "Who's been running around in my house and driving me *nuts*? Mom said *that* was the Wraich."

"No, no," he soothes. "Those are full demons, Value, trying to take away your humanity. Your mother was confused."

"Did you know her?"

"I'm afraid I didn't. I knew *of* her."

"What did you know?"

He doesn't answer immediately and eventually bends down a bit again so he can look into the car at me. "Look, would you like to go inside my office? We can speak more freely there."

I think about it for a few seconds then forcefully snatch the keys from the ignition and get out of the car. Now that I'm standing, walking toward him, I see that he's a touch shorter than me—*the height is in his hat*. That was another one Dad always used to say. I shake my head to clear the thought and arrive beside him on the sidewalk. He sticks out a gloved hand.

"It's nice you meet, Value Kraymer."

I extend my own gloved hand and we shake. "Likewise."

He leads me into his office—through one of the many nondescript doors in the row of offices along the street—and once the door is closed behind us, he slips off the hat, sunglasses, and gloves. In the half light poking around the drawn heavy curtains his skin is still shimmering slightly, like brushed chrome or that plastic they use when they want something to look like brushed chrome. He looks over at me and I see that his eyes, too, are yellow.

"Do we all have yellow eyes?" I wonder. He motions for me to sit on a leather sofa situated on the other side of a coffee table from his desk. The office is very well decorated, with rich red carpeting and beautifully crafted woodwork filigrees all along the walls and ceiling. The walls on either side are nothing more than giant book-cases holding row after row of books, many of which look older and more valuable than the office building itself.

"All of the Wraich do, yes," he replies, removing his jacket and slinging it over the back of his desk chair. I expect him to sit at the desk, but he doesn't. He moves over and sits on the couch beside me, crossing his legs and considering me with rapt curiosity. "That's why you need to buy some yellowed glasses—it cancels the color so people can't tell what your eyes look like. Besides, they're easier to see through indoors."

"So how did you know of my mother?" I wonder, not willing to let the thread of our former conversation break so easily.

"She was somewhat famous," he admits wistfully. "She ran away from home when she was eighteen. Said she was going to be human. She ended up here, in White Hall, pregnant almost the day she arrived. Your father married her and I was sent to keep an eye on things."

"She *knew*?" I demand. "She knew her whole life what she was?"

"Most of us do," he agreed.

"So why didn't anyone tell *me*?"

He considers this for a moment, twisting his lips and nibbling at his inner cheek. "I might have handled that badly," he finally decides. "She should have told you when you were nine. I assumed she did, but in hindsight, I think she truly believed you wouldn't turn, so she didn't see the point."

"She told me the Wraich were bringing her gifts," I said slowly.

"She tried to tell me, the week she turned."

I lapse into silence and he lets me. Mom knew what would happen and she couldn't fight it. She had me before she turned because she was hoping the demon seed wouldn't be there yet, and she named me Value so I'd never forget I had worth—*human* worth. Before she

217

embraced it, she fought it, not in any big ways, but in the subtle ways that make deep impressions. I've never even seen a picture of her parents.

"Why didn't it work?" I ask him. He squints at me, waiting for me to finish my thought. "If she was only half demon, wouldn't I only be a quarter demon?"

He chuckles apologetically. "Humanity is a recessive gene," he explains. "A *very* recessive gene—just one drop of demon is enough to make a Wraich. The demon never gets more diluted than that, no matter how much you try to breed it out."

I wonder if she realized that, too. If something I said or did, or the way I looked at her, clued her in to the fact that I was never quite normal. I wonder if that's why she tried to tell me, and why she tried to make it seem so great. She was covering for herself, trying to convince me of the promise and wonder in something she herself had tried so hard to get rid of. In that way, I suppose, I was her final failure: She'd run away for nothing because she'd still turned and she'd still passed it on to me.

I feel tears welling in my eyes and wipe them away. For some reason the thought of this man seeing me cry is too much to bear. I turn away from him as I speak.

"Is that why she did that to Joey Martin? Sure, he was a jerk, but I can't say he deserved it."

He chuckles again, but this time he sounds happy. I look back at him and he's smiling proudly.

"That's your humanity talking," he says. "And that's what the full demons want to take away, leaving only your... other side. A side more easily swayed to the inhuman urges, such as revenge and jealousy and anger."

"The rage," I whisper.

"It's a good job you have Maggie," he states unequivocally.

I shoot him a look and snap, "Why?"

"She brings out your human side, Value. I saw how you changed—calmed—just at the mention of her name. Demons feed off hate; humans feed off love."

I snicker condescendingly. "You sound like you're making a wedding toast, Mr. Baker."

"Alistair," he corrects me, chuckling at himself. "And I suppose I do. But it's true, Value—your mother knew it."

"But my mom had my dad..." I start, my brow furrowing in confusion. "He loved her."

"He did," he agrees. "But I don't think *she* loved your father as much as *he* loved *her.*"

I let it sink in for a few moments, eying him warily as it does. I don't like how this week has rewritten my past and redefined my future, all emanating from a single woman who was murdered 18 years ago. A woman who, in my eyes, could do no wrong but had great wrong done to her, by the man I had also thought could do no wrong and never meant anyone harm.

"So what now?" I wonder, trying to deflect the conversation.

Alistair Baker sucks in a deep breath and leans in to me, locking my gaze with his eyes. I can't look away.

"Value, you can hide your eyes behind yellow glasses and never show your teeth when you smile. You can wear black gloves and use a belt sander to file your nails every night. You can make up a rare skin condition to explain why it looks so strange—"

I raise my eyebrows, and he continues.

"Oh yes, Value, your skin will change tonight. But the one thing you can never hide—the one thing that makes the transformation complete—is the rage."

I think about how much I wanted to punch my father senseless back at the jail, and even the cops who had nothing to do with it; how I'd wanted to rip the arms off Father Jacobs, and even Alistair Baker when he was standing watching me. He nods slowly at me.

"Yes, Value—eventually it will get the better of you if you don't stop it."

"Did you... stop it?"

He nods slowly again and smiles with a twinge of pride.

"How?"

"I had a theory. I thought that if a demon can be bound to a human—which it can be—then perhaps I could bind the demon side of a Wraich to the human side. That way, the human would control the demon and, in theory, prevent the rage."

"So you've done this?"

"Once or twice," he admits, his pride deflating somewhat. "It's very hard to get there in time. We Wraich are very drawn to our demonic side, Value, and we're very untrusting."

"My mother...?"

He shakes his head apologetically. "I did try, but she wanted nothing to do with me. She thought it was a trick; that I wanted to do to her what the demons haunting her did instead. It's a very complex ritual, and it hurts. And the pain brings the rage..."

"So who did you do it to? Where are they?"

He smiles again and opens his arms wide.

"*You*?" I gasp in disbelief. "But how did you do it to your*self*?"

"I didn't," he grins. "Father Jacobs performed the ritual."

"*What*? The *priest*?"

He shrugs.

"But he kicked me out of his church!"

"You are unbound, Value. But you are also different. You've been fighting the rage all by yourself—your humanity is strong. Value, would you like to be number three?"

"It's not *my* humanity that's good," I mumble thoughtfully, staring out the window. "I have to get back to Maggie—she'll be worried."

I stand and Alistair Baker grabs my arm, his face long and pleading. "*Value*? Please!"

I pull my arm free. "I need to talk to Maggie first."

* * *

Maggie listens to the whole story, her hand clasping mine the entire time. She looks strangely complacent, considering everything she suddenly has to accept and rethink. Humans are amazingly resilient when they have to be. I feel bad for her. This whole week it's all been about me and she's been suffering just as much.

"So that's it?" she finally whispers. "You're done *changing* now?"

She looks at my hand and arm. True to Alistair's word, my skin changed overnight. It's impossible now to tell if patches of my skin darkened while the rest remained light, or if my skin just lightened in patches to be without pigmentation. Alistair was overjoyed—apparently piebald is a rare turning.

"There's still the rage," I tell Maggie. "Although the *full* demons didn't even show up last night. I think they know it's no use, not with you here."

"What's no use?"

"Trying to make me lose my humanity. Trying to make me give in to the rage."

"How could *I* stop a demon?" she whispers, tears welling in her eyes at the very thought of invisible forces being held at bay by her, even though she can't see them and doesn't know how she affects them.

"Because I love you, Maggie," I reply with a wry grin. "*You* are my humanity."

She sighs and touches my cheek with her other hand.

"I know this is tough for you, Mags—impossible even. But I'm serious. You really do make me human, Maggie. And Alistair Baker has this theory—"

She bristles at the name—I can tell she doesn't entirely trust him, which is ironic, all things considered.

"Can you think of anyone more qualified?" I wonder.

She shakes her head and rolls her eyes with acceptance. "Okay, so he has a theory...?"

"He has this theory that if you bind a Wraich to its human side, the transformation will never be complete, because once a demon is bound to a human, it has to do the human's bidding. It becomes a demon possessed by a human."

"So he wants to do this to you?" she asks suspiciously.

"Yes, and I want him to. But Maggie, I don't know if my humanity is strong enough—"

"You could *die*?" she spits, shaking her head emphatically.

"No, no, no," I assure her. "I just think you're a better person than me, Maggie. I want to be bound to *you*. To be sure that if nothing else, I can never harm you."

She mulls this over, but I can see a grin flitting across her lips already. Finally her eyes narrow and she can no longer suppress the smile.

"Value Kraymer—is this another attempt at a marriage proposal?"

"I think it is, Maggie," I reply.

She barely shakes her head, as if she knows better but doesn't care.

"Then yes, Value. Of *course* I agree."

Unknown North

The following excerpt is the first nine chapters of Unknown North, *the debut novel by David Powers, available from Graveworm Press in December 2011.*

1. Four More Stars in a Starry Sky

No one really paid any attention to the stars that appeared one morning, where no stars previously had been. Which is to say, the mystics and stargazers noticed and found it odd, even disturbing, and they created web pages and spent hours dialing into radio talkshows, searching for an explanation. Dr. Angelo Moore finally emerged, three days after the first appearance of the stars, and told the public that there was nothing to worry about. That if any "new" stars had suddenly appeared, he or one of his colleagues would certainly have noticed, and none of them saw anything amiss. That was exactly what the media wanted to hear, and that's exactly what was fed to the public, and—it turns out—that was exactly what the public wanted to hear, so they could go to work and to the mall and to soccer practice and to sleep without having to consider that their world was no longer what it used to be.

Three days after Dr. Moore's assessment, the stars—which had hung bright as planets in an arc around the left side of the moon, no matter where the moon was in the sky—disappeared as suddenly as they had arrived. The kids continued to play soccer, moms continued to sprint through malls and fast-food drive-thrus, and dads went dutifully to work. Perfect America was still intact, its shiny surface freshly buffed and polished with a new coat of whitewash. But the scientists who knew—the ones whose names never appeared in the papers and whose voices never spouted facts on talk radio—toiled far below the blinding white surface of reality, scouring thousands of images captured by telescopes and satellites in the days before, during, and after what became known as the Star Event. And they, like the mystics, were unnerved. Because the one thing Dr. Moore had got absolutely correct was that the stars were not asteroids heading for an Earth impact.

No, they weren't that at all.

2. A Spider in a Wheel

Bransen really didn't like the looks of the bar, yet he had no choice but to enter. His was the only four-wheeled vehicle in the lot, and he veritably tip-toed past the lineup of hogs and choppers lest his footfalls topple them like dominoes. A couple of bikers had just arrived and glanced at him suspiciously as walked toward the doors. He'd opted to fit in as little as possible, going on the assumption that a nervous man in a golf shirt and khakis would pose no threat as either interloper or poser and thus would be left alone. Besides, his careful swoop of brownish-blond hair, stubbled chin, and beaming smile looked best with grown-up frat-boy garb; anything else would've been immediately suspect and would undoubtedly have drawn more attention to him than he wanted.

The bouncer at the door—paid, no doubt, in beer—raised his eyebrows in mild surprise as Bransen approached and asked (with an air of genuine concern), "Are you looking for someone in there?"

The unasked follow-up to which was, *Because if you aren't, why not head to the wine bar down the street?*

"Yes," Bransen said, his voice strong. Nervous as he was, the outward sign of such something he had long ago learned to quell. Nerves looked bad when you were applying for loans to fund a private scientific research facility that steadfastly refused government money and was weighted with a name like the Private International Space Administration (a.k.a., PISA). "I'm looking for Mouse."

The bouncer's eyebrows raised a bit higher, then he nodded. "He'll be at the bar, most likely doodling on a napkin." He opened the door for Bransen and ushered him in. Bransen didn't see it, but he was sure a silent signal had been given to the bartender to *watch this guy.* The barkeep shouted, "What'll ya have?" before he'd even taken three steps into the place.

Fortunately, most of the bikers were huddled around the pool tables or loitering on the dance floor. The haze of smoke was like walking through a forest fire, but at least there was no music blaring, for the moment. All the noise was mumbling voices punctuated with loud laughs and swearing. Bottles clinked into trashcans and the low rumble of glasses moving from table to lips and back seemed like distant thunder in the clouds of cigarette smoke. Bransen headed for the only guy at the bar who seemed hunched over and possibly doodling. The barkeep paced him and and met him at the bar, so Bransen ordered a beer ("anything that's wet") and glanced at the the man to his right. He was large from a diet of hamburgers and beer, and his hands and face had the grime of engine repair on them. His beard was long and unkempt, but, like his lengthy hair, not hanging in dirty clumps. In the dim lighting, Bransen couldn't tell if he was a dark blond or a graying brunette.

"You Mouse?" he asked. The man—who was indeed doodling on a napkin—stopped what he was doing and straightened up before looking at him. He met Bransen's eyes and nodded once.

"My name's Bransen. I run PISA. I have only two questions for you." The barkeep plopped a beer in front of Bransen and looked suspiciously at Mouse. Mouse shook his head almost imperceptibly: No, he wasn't being bothered.

"Go ahead," Mouse replied.

"What were you figuring out just now?" Mouse looked at his napkin and chuckled, then held it up for Bransen. There was a rather artfully rendered doodle of a spider in the center of a wagon wheel.

"I was thinking how much better off a spider in a wheel would be if it used the spokes to reinforce its web. Could probably catch grasshoppers. Thing is, spiders are too small to see the big picture, and they make the same old weak web between the spokes."

Bransen smiled widely. This was indeed his man. The mythical biker named Mouse. The man who could fix—and improve upon—any motorcycle on the road. The man who should hold the patent for the next generation of Tesla power coil, if not for the fact that the patent office thought him crazy.

"Then my other question is simply this," Bransen said softly. He glanced around just to make sure no one would hear him. "Would you like to go to Mars?"

3. The Not Knowing

Henry Jacobs adjusted the focus on his Bransen Labs Deep X Telescope ("bigger, better, cheaper") and tried in vain to relocate the four stars of the Star Event. He'd got the telescope last year for his tenth birthday, and was only dimly aware that his mother had forgone replacing the dishwasher in order to afford it. In fact, she was even now at the kitchen sink, washing the dishes by hand.

"Henry!" she called. "The silverware's ready to be dried!" Henry swung the telescope wildly until the temporary blindness of the moon filtered through the lens. He recoiled a tad at the strength of the illumination, then swung the telescope back to the left. He was definitely aiming at the right spot in the sky. He stood up straight, hands on hips, and sighed heavily. The four stars were gone and he, for one, did not believe Dr. Angelo Moore's excuse that anyone who had seen four anomalous stars didn't know what they were looking at, because Henry knew damn well what he'd been looking at.

"Henry!" his mother called again.

"Coming..." he grudgingly replied, deep in thought as he wandered into the kitchen and picked up the dish towel. His mother smiled at him and wiped some splashed bubbles off her cheek with her shoulder.

"It'll only take a minute."

"I know, Ma. It's okay," he answered, sighing again.

"Still can't find those stars, eh?" Henry nodded, his young brow furrowing under his rail-straight, jet-black hair that absolutely refused to part any other way but to the right. His eyes were bright, and even when he was down in the dumps they belied the optimism he always let win out in the end. His mother chuckled lightly. "Well, Sophie will be here soon. Maybe she can help."

"Yeah..." Henry agreed with a sigh. Sophie was the ten-year-old daughter of his mother's employer, and though Henry didn't fully understand the camaraderie two single, working moms had, he knew that his mom looked forward to "no work Friday nights" and he did all he could to make it easy on them. His grand act of compromise had, however, turned into a real friendship with Sophie—though he didn't want to let on too much that he'd been counting the days all week to show her the stars through his telescope. And now they were gone.

"What do you think they were?" his mom asked. Henry shrugged.

"I can't find anything like it in any of my books. It was like they'd gone into orbit around the moon, then just froze. Then vanished. And that Dr. Moore's an idiot..."

"Well now, he probably just doesn't understand either, and he doesn't want to scare people."

"Are *you* scared, Mom?"

She smiled and stripped off her kitchen gloves, placing them behind the faucet and taking the towel from Henry so she could wipe up the splashed water. "No. But then I do the paperwork for a freelance microbiologist. I know there's a rational explanation, Henry, they just haven't found it yet."

Henry grunted dismally then marched back to his telescope. Dr. Angelo Moore might be satisfied pretending something he didn't understand would just go away, but Henry was not.

4. The Quintessence of Light

Dr. Howard Fobell had been asked to work on the Star Event because of his views that natural light might actually be conscious. It was an odd take, to be sure—and one that would never reach as close to the surface as even the scholarly mainstream science journals—but here, in the shadows where science still asked the left-field questions, Dr. Fobell was highly respected. In his model, the Sun was more like a massive dandelion, with light like seed pods constantly streaming from the surface on the solar wind. And UFOs, by his estimation, may indeed be nothing more than balls of light—albeit balls of light with intelligence.

"The Star Event is definitely consciously controlled," Dr. Fobell told the smattering of shadow scientists in the well-lit room around him. Were it not for the lab coats, one might have assumed the meeting—replete with paperwork on the table and bar graphs on the overhead—to be some conference of a board of directors. "The stars appear to have positioned themselves before turning on, as it were, and then maintained their relative positions, using our moon as a guide, before they again turned off."

"Why our moon?" an innocuous young man asked.

"Quite simply, Dr. Brown, they wanted to be seen." The thought set up quite a loud murmur among the eight or so other men and women in the room, and Dr. Fobell had to clear his throat twice before continuing. "Think of it like a child hiding behind a hedge who wants to be chased. The child will peek out—even step into full view—until Mommy or Daddy sees him. Then he runs away, and Mommy and Daddy follow."

"All right, Howard, I'll buy it," the woman at the head of the table said. "Then where are they leading us?"

Dr. Fobell smiled privately to himself then scanned the faces in the room, all turned to him expectantly.

"What none of us noticed—or, rather, ignored because we knew what it was—is that there were actually *five* stars in the Star Event: four anomalous stars and one perfectly normal planet. While keeping their basic arc the same, and compensating for the movement of the moon and the planet, they managed to hide in plain sight what I think was their destination. We all thought they were frozen in the space above the moon, but we need to consider perspective. The lights were nowhere near the moon. The Star Event was all about that fifth star—the *planet*. The lights, I believe, were heading for Mars."

5. A Ladder With Nine Rungs

Bransen knew this would be the hardest sell, but he didn't know it would be so difficult simply to gain an audience. His "simple hike" through the woods had elicited ripped jeans, the loss of his left shoe, and a thorn-born scratch on his left breast. Still and all, when he finally reached the clearing and saw the homespun cabin of Dr. Carlos Resua (anachronistically wired with solar panels, a 21st-century windmill, and three satellite dishes), his mood instantly lifted.

"Dr. Resua?" he called out, hoping to high hell he'd pronounced his name correctly. There was nothing like a bad first impression. Hearing no reply, he walked up to the hut and climbed the nine-rung ladder to the deck that surrounded the hut. The stilts the hut was on, Bransen realized with a twinge of vertigo, were necessary to correct for quite a slope to the land. He stood in front of the door and looked up, the roofline of the cabin looking like the peaks of a crown from this angle, and took in a deep breath until the nausea passed.

"Dr. Resua?" he said again, in a normal voice, then knocked firmly on the door. He glanced to his left and right in search of a doorbell and saw instead a piece of heavy paper flapping in the breeze. It was a handwritten note that said, in a tidy script, "Back in a second, Mr. Bransen. Please go in, if you want."

Bransen looked all around at the woods but saw no signs of life. No one except Bransen's assistant knew he was coming here—and Dr. Carlos Resua, apparently. The idea made Bransen grin gleefully: his research had been right on the mark. But rather than impose on Dr. Resua's hospitality, Bransen decided to sit on one of the chairs on the deck and wait for him there, bathed in the dappled light of the sun.

6. The Hollow Oak

"Let's go to the oak," a voice said, jarring Bransen back to wakefulness. He opened his eyes and shielded them from the bright sunlight. The man standing over him moved so that he was shading him, and Bransen looked into the clean-shaven face and curiously wild eyes of Dr. Carlos Resua.

"Dr. Resua?" he asked rhetorically, jumping to his feet and extending his hand.

"Please call me Carlos, Mr. Bransen," the doctor replied as they shook hands. "You made it here faster than most people. Glad I left a note."

"Yeah," Bransen said thoughtfully, glancing at the piece of paper. "About that..."

Carlos grinned knowingly and tapped his right temple with his index finger. "That's why you're here, is it not, Mr. Bransen?"

"Please... Everyone just calls me Bransen."

"*Bran*sen?" Carlos chuckled at a joke only he understood, then turned and indicated the woods indiscriminately. "We should go to the oak for a drink. You must be parched."

"Yes..." Bransen agreed, following him back down the ladder.

"That stream there?" Carlos explained, indicating a thin ribbon of water gurgling behind the house. "The spring is just up the slope, right at the base of an old, hollow oak. I thought it made the area a good place to settle down."

"I'll say," Bransen gasped, puffing up the hill behind his host. "It's beautiful."

Carlos smiled but didn't reply and the two walked in silence to the oak, which was obvious among the other deciduous trees for a girth that belied great age. There were still leaves fresh and green on almost every branch, but the inside was hollowed out with a gap in the bark just about big enough for a grown man to squeeze through. As they approached, Bransen saw a small gurgling flow of water, like a stream from a broken drinking fountain, that looked to be emerging right out of the tree. As they rounded on it, however, he saw that the spring was actually a few feet away from it.

"I imagine the oak's roots released the water," Carlos said as he sat on a mossy rock, indicating Bransen to do the same. Bransen sat down across from him and smiled. "Oaks have a way of divining. So what can I do for you, Bransen?" Carlos asked.

"How did you know I was coming?" Bransen replied, using the question as an excuse to catch his breath. He motioned to the water and Carlos assured him it was clean, so Bransen leaned over the stream and drank from his hands. The water was sweet and crisp.

"Every morning I meditate and remote view that little parking area I built. Luckily, I caught you getting out of your car and I recognized you. I assume you want me to remote view the Star Event? Tell you what it was?"

Bransen chuckled and sat back down on the rock, drawing himself up with sincerity. "Close, Carlos. I need to go to Mars and I need your technical skills—as well as your remote viewing—for the trip."

Carlos sat silently for a moment, then started to laugh. "Now *that* I didn't see coming."

7. Def Con 4

Howard Fobell couldn't be entirely sure he wasn't under arrest. The room was stark and furnished only with a plain table and two chairs, there was a tape recorder on the table, and the overhead lighting was dim and flickering. It also didn't help that behind him paced Admiral Thomas and sitting across from him was General Rauchbach. Both men were cordial enough, but Dr. Fobell still had the willies.

"So you don't believe the Star Event was made up of crafts piloted by intelligent creatures?" the General asked again. "But were themselves intelligent balls of light?"

"Honestly, I don't know," Dr. Fobell admitted. He pushed up his thick, round glasses and rubbed his rusty beard with a pudgy hand. He was not grossly overweight, but he knew he could stand to lose a few pounds. Still, he couldn't focus enough on his appearance to comb his haystack of twirled dark red hair in the morning, so focusing enough to exercise probably wasn't going to happen either. "As I said, based on our observations and photographs, there is nothing to indicate a structure to the lights. Given my own theories of terrestrial UFOs, this leads me to conclude that light may be all there is to the Star Event."

"But *intelligent* light," Admiral Thomas pointed out. "*Conscious* light. Light that gets up in the morning, brushes its teeth, and gets itself a bowl of cereal. Light that is alive and cognizant, correct?"

"In a manner of speaking, though I think its form of intelli—"

"That's what I don't get," the Admiral cut in. "I don't get how light can think."

Howard sighed heavily and asked what he thought was an obvious question: "Admiral Thomas, have you read my papers on the subject?" He heard the Admiral stop pacing behind him and could tell by the General's eyes that he was moving over to the table. Admiral Thomas leaned in close to Howard's right ear and whispered with amusement, "I was hoping you could give us the Cliff's Notes version, Dr. Fobell." The General snickered and winked at Howard.

"We don't read more than we have to," he tried to explain. "And honestly, your work is a bit outside our purview, I'm afraid."

"All we need to know, for now, is one thing," the Admiral added, scooting around and perching on the table so he could look at Howard. "We need to know if the Star Event is dangerous. Frankly, I don't really care if a ball of light has a brain or if My Favorite Martian is real—I just want to know what I need to do about it. You see intelligence... We see the unknown. We see a *threat*. Do you see?"

"Yes," Howard replied, lowering his eyes. "And I'm afraid, gentlemen, that I can't really say." He looked up and held each man's gaze for a second, then continued. "I am certain that whatever they were, they wanted to be seen and they wanted us to follow them. Logically, then, I would say they are not coming here and thus would not appear to be any threat."

"But what happens if we follow them?" General Rauchbach asked kindly. "Is this an interstellar ambush?" Howard sat silent, his mouth slightly open, and shook his head slowly. His lack of words spoke volumes to the two men.

8. Bransen's First Dream

Bransen stayed as a guest of Carlos Resua that night, after a long afternoon of hiking and talking. In hindsight, he was sure Carlos would've gone to Mars without all the talking and hiking, but Bransen didn't regret the time spent with the computer programming mystic.

"There are a few people in the military who will have to be told," Carlos said, when he finally (officially) agreed to go. "But other than that, I have no ties. Does it bother you that the military will know of this expedition?"

Bransen had laughed. "I would seriously doubt the military's ability to defend the country if they *didn't* know, after the press I intend to drum up." They'd both laughed at that, albeit suspiciously. Bransen knew no more than Carlos as to how the press—or military— would receive a manned expedition to Mars made up of the crew Bransen was assembling.

That night, Bransen had a dream. A deep, lucid dream—the first such dream he could ever recall having. A dream in which everything was ethereal, but entirely in his control. A dream in which he found himself in a woodland glen, sunlight sparkling in a light mist.

"What is it?" he asked a woman hunched over something at the edge of the glen.

"I'd say a mushroom," she replied, turning to him as he approached. "Except that we're on Mars."

Bransen awoke with a start, the dream as fresh as a memory, with only one thought in his head: Dr. Luci von Embers, microbiologist. He scrawled down the name on the pad of paper Carlos had left with him ("Just in case you dream"), then lay back down, wide-eyed, unable to sleep for a driving sense of urgency, awe, and wonder.

9. Wooing Luci

"I just don't understand why you'd want *me* to go to Mars," Luci said for the umpteenth time. Bransen couldn't really answer ("Because of a dream I had" didn't seem too compelling), but had hoped that dinner on him in the city's finest restaurant would earn him a few points. Perhaps it had—she'd stayed for dessert, after all.

"I need a microbiologist," he replied again. "Surely you don't mean you can't understand why I need that?"

"I can understand that, Mr. Bransen," she agreed, smiling demurely and sipping her coffee. She had the refined appearance of someone who could afford to look however she wanted. At the moment, the dark but soft makeup and black bobbed hair gave her the air of a 1920s starlet, her eyes bright behind black eyeliner and shining above the subdued red of her lips. "But everyone else you've outlined for the trip so far has no ties. Yes, I'm a freelance worker, too, but I have a daughter. Can't you find some young, single, hotshot grad student to go?"

"Is it the trip itself or leaving your daughter that's bothering you?"

Luci froze, cake-encumbered fork midway to her mouth, and slowly lowered her arm. Truth be told, Luci had always fantasized about being on a manned mission to another planet—it was the sort of feather in her cap that would earn her renown on its face, but also offer unimaginable potential for microbial discoveries. Of course, this was all before she'd had Sophie. Everything changed when you had someone more important than yourself to worry about.

"Both, I guess," she mumbled. "Leaving my daughter is one thing, but possibly leaving her forever is something else entirely."

Bransen nodded compassionately. In fairness, he had made it very clear to each of those he'd asked that there was the possibility they'd never see Earth again. Not that he thought it at all likely, but he had to admit to the danger.

"What if she came with you?" Bransen replied simply. "This isn't going to be some government-run space program in tin cans controlled by punchcard computers—this is going to be a *Bransen Labs* Cadillac. You won't even know we're in space, unless you look out the window."

"What about school?" she asked suspiciously, willing to accept Bransen's promise at face value for the time being.

"We can take her textbooks for the year with us. The crew *is* quite smart," he added with a smirk. Luci laughed with something like relief and finished her last two bites of cake, washing it down with the last of her coffee.

"Well, I'll have to ask her, Mr. Bransen. If she doesn't want to go, *I* don't want to go."

"And if she does?" Bransen asked with a grin.

Luci paused, then replied, "Then I guess we'll *both* go."

To be continued...

Look for *Unknown North* by David Powers, coming in December 2011 from Graveworm Press.

graveworm.com

For more short fiction from David Powers, visit **graveworm.com**.